THE GLASS SLIPPER

THE GLASS SLIPPER

Marion Athorne

Also by Marion Athorne – Merlyn's Legacy Trilogy

  Book 1:   Wizard's Woe
  Book 2:   Merlyn's Heir
  Book 3:   Arthur's Ark

© Marion Athorne

Published by Green Dragon Books
www.greendragonpublications.com

ISBN 978-0-9565563-1-8

Cover illustration by Catriona O'Neil

Prepared and printed by:

York Publishing Services Ltd
64 Hallfield Road
Layerthorpe
York YO31 7ZQ
Tel: 01904 431213

ACKNOWLEDGEMENTS

I would like to acknowledge my indebtedness to the WRNS and everthing I learnt in the Service, as well as pay tribute to my father, Osbert Norman-Walter who helped me so much with his constructive viewpoint while he was alive; to Editor Jo Murray for her interest and support, and to my family for theirs, and now to the expert and professional help of the York Publishing Services team; Clare Brayshaw, Cathi Poole and Paula Charles. Finally, and not least, my thanks to artist Catriona O'Neil for her enthusiastic execution of a great cover illustration.

ABOUT THE AUTHOR

Born Marion Elizabeth Walter in 1928, in Sydenham, London, she spent her childhood during the war with her sister, father and stepmother living in and around London and on the south coast. As a head strong young woman, she ran away from home at 16 and enrolled in the WRAF at 17. At age 21, she joined the WRNS, and served at RNAS Eglington's shore establishment in Northern Ireland, '*HMS Gannet*' before being drafted to HMS *Falcon* (HALFAR) on Malta, where she met and married her husband Tom Athorne, who was serving with the RAF on the island.

On their return to the UK, they lived first in Yorkshire and then Kent where they brought up three children before retiring to Shrewsbury for twenty very happy years.

When Tom died shortly after their 54th Anniversary, Marion went to live with their eldest daughter and her husband in Sutton Coldfield. Since then she has published the first two books by her father and herself of a romantic fantasy *Merlyn's Legacy*.

CONTENTS

CHAPTER ONE

Uncle Fox Oboe

'Control to X-Ray Charlie. Are you receiving me? Over.'

Silence.

Jennifer Howard sighed. She was seated with three other wrens at a lino covered work surface, each facing small individual blackboards propped against the wall. On Jenny's were the call signs of three aircraft. She glanced up at the control tower's clock above the rhomboid windows overlooking the runways: 11:51. She took in the sweeping contours of County Derry's landscape, mottled with sun-chased shadows of clouds and devoid of aircraft, before looking away to record the time in her logbook. Her other two aircraft had been three and five minutes ahead of the twenty allowed – unlike X-Ray Charlie; now fifteen minutes behind. She knew he could be low-flying behind a range of mountains, or working on a correction to his flight plan, perhaps even cursing her irksome interruption while he was trying to work. However, she had to allow him a fair margin before alerting the attention of the Controller, a chief petty officer sitting at the console on a raised platform behind her.

She turned over the now full page, dating the next: 26 September 1954, before writing in the new call sign she had just been given for a flight en route from a distant airbase to Derry Down.

Logging her words as she asked the pilot his position and estimated time of arrival, again noting the time, she heard his immediate but faint response abruptly over-ridden by a stronger transmission:

'*X-Ray Charlie to Control. Reporting Uncle Fox Oboe approaching airfield from north west. Estimated height two hundred, speed one thousand. Over.*'

Jenny blinked at the interpretation: *Unidentified Flying Object...! S*carcely believing her ears, but answering automatically: 'Control to X-Ray Charlie. Wait. Out.' She twisted in her seat.

'Chief, X-Ray Charlie is reporting an Uncle Fox Oboe,' she informed the Controller, before turning back to log her exchange with the pilot.

The Chief rose at once, gazing intently out at the horizon and surrounding blue sky.

He jerked his head back to her. 'You've got it wrong,' he said, reaching for the earphones connecting her position to his. 'Tell him to "say again".'

Jenny obeyed while the Chief called to the other personnel, who were craning their necks, searching the skies.

'Anyone see anything?'

'Seagull landing on Runway Two,' offered a leading hand with a grin.

'*X-Ray Charlie to Control,*' came the pilot's reply to Jenny's request. '*Uncle Fox Oboe now directly over airfield. Estimated height now one eight zero, speed eight hundred. Following. Over.*'

'He's bloody seeing things,' said the Chief, staring out at an entirely empty sky. As he spoke, X-Ray Charlie's Firefly came into view, engines roaring, in a low dive over the tower before streaking down the airfield and banking in a steep climb in the direction of the Irish border and Donegal.

Several things then happened at once.

'…*lost the beggar!*' came X-Ray Charlie's voice, followed immediately by: '*Wait … no, I've …*'

Jenny's eyes flew back to the clock, but was distracted instead by a silver shape flashing to the other side of the Lough where it vanished in a sudden bright wink of light – and her headset went dead. Then everyone was speaking at once, informing the Controller of radio failure.

Jenny stammered out the message from X-Ray Charlie, but the Chief was already hand-ringing his landline, barking 'Emergency generators' at the leading hand, who dived for the door just as everyone's headphones crackled to life again.

One and all rushed to account for any aircraft still on their frequencies, but Jenny was unable to raise X-Ray Charlie.

'I need radio silence,' roared the Chief and, as everyone hushed, he raised a station alert for the missing Firefly. A 'flap' was on.

As suddenly as he had disappeared from Jenny's frequency, however, the pilot's voice was again sounding in her headset – but this time sounding distinctly bored and quite normal:

'*X-Ray Charlie to Control. Do you read me? Over.*'

Turning to wave quickly at the Chief, she answered, 'Control to X-Ray Charlie. Loud and clear …' She caught the Chief signalling her as he grabbed his own transmitter '… report your position. Over.'

'*Over airstrip,*' answered the pilot, ending somewhat curtly, '… *and over to Channel Able. Out.*'

The Chief looked apoplectic with rage.

Emergency procedure relaxed, and her mind in turmoil, Jenny tried to concentrate on raising the distant aircraft again for his position and estimated time of arrival.

Unable to make contact, she turned back to the Chief to find him shouting on his landline.

'… Of course he did,' he said vehemently. 'The man's a complete idiot … What? No, not a bloody sign. … "Over the airfield," he told us. … Well, we were all looking.' He slammed down the receiver muttering, 'Crazy pilot chasing shadows and hasn't the guts to own up to it.'

'But there was something, Chief,' Jenny said quickly. 'I saw it! A long silvery thing – over there.' She pointed north west, and the Chief glared at her.

'Now don't you start,' he said belligerently. 'There wasn't a damn thing. Even the pilot's refusing to admit he ever said there was. Not that it'll do him any good now.'

He ran a finger down her logbook notes. 'Yes, we've got him all right. There'll be an enquiry about this … which is bad enough without *you* making it worse with nonsense about seeing things no one else did! Show imagination like that and we'll all be shut in the loony bin.'

'But the radio failure, Chief?' she said, convinced that what she'd seen had been no hallucination.

'So what?' he snapped. 'Power cut – they happen.'

Jenny gave up. Whatever X-Ray Charlie thought he had to gain by denying his initial report, she had no idea. She tried calling her remaining craft again, vaguely conscious of the Chief behind her groaning in answer to news he'd just received over the intercom from the direction finding hut.

'That's all I need,' he grumbled. He picked up the land phone. 'Ambulance and stretcher party to the d/f hut at O'Donohan's Farm at the double,' he ordered. 'Wren Price has collapsed with severe abdominal pain.' He looked over at Jenny as he put the down the receiver. 'And you, Wren Howard, can take her place in d/f for the rest of the week.' He made it sound as if it was what she deserved for causing him grief, but Jenny was happy at the prospect. Working in the isolation of the direction-finding hut out in the fields always held a sense of adventure. The Chief's bad temper, though, made her hesitant to report that she was unable to raise the still incoming aircraft.

'Flying still on for tonight then, Chiefie?' asked one of the wrens beside her.

'I wouldn't make any dates if I was you,' was his dour reply as the door opened and the relief watch trooped in.

Jenny handed over her position, telling her relief that the one remaining aircraft on her board had still not responded, while her mind raced ahead with new plans for that afternoon. She did not have to wait for transport back to camp. HMS *Arctic Tern* – also known as Royal Naval Air Station Derry Down – was a scattered shore establishment, so most people requisitioned a bicycle as soon they arrived, and Jenny had been no exception. She had also made more than duty use of hers on excursions into the surrounding countryside, which offered plenty of places to explore.

As she collected her bike from its rack at the foot of the control tower, she shot a look in the direction where the silvery object had disappeared and wondered at her chances of finding its crash site – if there was anything to find. She had memorised the figures on its diminishing height and speed, and she estimated a trajectory to its approximate fall as being just over the Irish border, about six miles away. She decided dinner could be scrapped and, after a quick change of clothes from her uniform into slacks and sweater, she could be on her way by half-past the hour. She reckoned she could be back in time for night duty by allowing two and a half hours cycling there and back, including ferry time across the lough, plus an hour searching. She wanted to prove to herself, if to no one else, that what she had seen that morning had been no optical illusion.

Entering her nissan-hut, she noticed a set of dusty footprints on the black composition floor they had all polished to a sheet of inky glass the previous evening. These marked the Quarters' Duty Wren's distribution of mail from bed to bed and three white envelopes lay on her blue and white counterpane.

In all the excitement she had quite forgotten it was her twenty-first birthday.

She slung her hat and shoulder bag on the bed, and pushed all thoughts of unidentified flying objects out of her mind. The first envelope, with a Sussex postmark, was a card from her uncle, a widowed professor who had become her guardian when her parents had died. It held a letter and a cheque for fifteen pounds – an extraordinary sum considering her pay was little more than twelve shillings and sixpence a week. Promising herself she would spend it on something special but sensible, she put it back in the envelope along with the letter for later reading. The next was an ornate card from her uncle's housekeeper and her one-time nanny, Peggsy, while the third was a short letter from a friend with news that he'd been posted to Northern Ireland and would be looking her up. This made her smile – Paul Ronan was fun.

She put the cards and letters away in her locker as an explosion of noisy arrivals made her glance down the room for the girl she would be on watch with that evening.

Bea Meecher was among those already upsetting their neat bed spaces as they sprawled across them, spreading their belongings in all directions. There was a great deal of clanging too as forks, spoons, knives and enamel mugs were taken from lockers for lunch. In the hubbub of squeals over mail, and the laughter and confusion of half a dozen shouted conversations going on at the same time, Jenny had to raise her voice to make herself heard even from the foot of Bea's bed.

Tall, dark and slimly built, Bea was something of a rough diamond, but a good friend.

'Appendicitis!' she was exclaiming to another girl. 'Must have been in agony all morning and never breathed a word. Just how dumb can you get!' She yanked off the heavy seaman's boots they had to wear on the farm and finally noticed Jenny. 'So what was happening your end?' she asked. 'We had a power cut and missed the fun.'

Jenny told her about the UFO.

'Go on!' said Bea. 'You saw the thing?'

'But the pilot's denying now that he said or saw anything.'

'The hell he does,' Bea snorted. '*I* heard him.'

Jenny was relieved. 'Of course, I was forgetting. So it won't be just his word against mine.'

'Oh, come on, kiddo,' Bea said. 'Wakey, wakey! You weren't the only one listening, remember? That is, of course,' she added, 'If radar were on their toes. And no one's telling Bea Meecher she's hearing things in her old age. Wonder which of our bright little boys it was?'

As if on cue, the hut's three radar wrens walked in swinging their hats by their chinstraps and discussing the pilot in loud cultured accents. It turned out the culprit was a Lieutenant Perry Edward Nance – or Pen as one of them called him with the familiarity of a close friendship.

'A crumb from the upper crust, if ever we had,' Bea said with a grimace at the three girls, known as the 'Debs', their nickname for any girl born into privileged society where a young woman was presented or 'came out', as a debutant with her first social engagement.

'Have you ever come across him, Bea?' asked Jenny.

'If you mean, has he ever come across *me*,' said Bea, mocking the Oxford accent that carried down from up the room, 'the answer's in the negative. Do I look like a Deb?' She shrugged. 'Well, come on, kiddo, let's get fed.'

Jenny made her excuses, saying she had to get over the border and back before tea. This implied she was going shopping because many things were cheaper in the Republic – especially cigarettes and canned food.

*

What with pot-holed cart tracks, a disused airfield and waiting for the ferry – no more than a rowing boat – to take her and her bike across Lough Foyle, Jenny felt she had made good progress to be near the general area of her search only an hour later.

The magnitude of the task began to dawn when she hid her bike in the undergrowth and looked about her, perplexed.

Where on earth should she even begin? She had only the vaguest idea of what she was looking for – and to be even a half mile out in reckoning would render the whole expedition fruitless.

The warble of a skylark above her, and the whisper of wind in the grass made her suddenly feel vulnerable. 'You need your bally head examining,' she told herself crossly. But she wasn't going to admit defeat, not now she was there. Using a small compass brooch, she set to work.

About an hour later she sank down on the trunk of a fallen tree, staring hopelessly around her. The whole idea had been completely crazy – like searching for a needle in a haystack. There wasn't a clue anywhere.

She squinted up at the sun, and that's when she saw it: a cleanly severed tree trunk twenty feet above the ground. She had been searching at ground level, when she should have been looking up! She stood slowly and gazed up at the other trees, which looked as if they had been reaped from above by a giant scythe.

Her heart pounding, she clambered along the line of felled wreckage. Ignoring a rip in the leg of her slacks and the twigs tearing her sweater, she came to the edge of a large circle of black and white that looked like ash, but somehow different. Across this lay the last tree, neatly cut at its base. Oddly, it showed no sign of burning or blast effect.

She was vindicated! Only a flying object, travelling at incredible speed could have caused such havoc. Now let someone tell her she had imagined it!

Tense with excitement she examined the area more closely, impressing on her mind every detail she could see.

Why, oh why didn't I bring my camera! She chided herself. Then wondered whom she should tell about the find. She was in the Irish Republic, so if anyone should to be informed it was the Eire authorities – and she felt no obligation to them. It was their land; they could look for it for themselves. Reporting it to the British authorities, though, could cause trouble. A British team of scientific and military boffins could hardly carry out an assessment, which they would want to be secret, without being spotted – although that wouldn't be *her* worry, either. No, she decided, her duty was to report the find to her superiors and leave it to them to take whatever action they wanted.

Conscience and allegiance squared, she was turning to leave when a sparkle of light caught the corner of her eye. It had come from under the tree lying across the 'ashes'. She walked gingerly over for a closer look, but had to move her head again to catch the same angle of sunlight before spotting it once more. Reaching under the trunk, she pulled out a piece of dirty, oddly shaped glass. Wiping it clean with the edge of her sweater, she realised she was holding a small, perfectly formed and exquisitely beautiful crystal shoe, about twelve centimetres long. Angling it this way and that in the sun's rays, she played with the light that caused the slightly faceted cuts and setting of tiny diamonds to sparkle with scintillating pricks of light. Then, turning it over, saw the sole marked with lines of small straight cuts which she recognised, with something of a jolt, she had often seen on her uncle's desk: an Oghamic script common to the ancient Celtic peoples of the British Isles. Whether this was in Gaelic, Welsh or Erse, she had no idea – although the latter appeared more likely, seeing where she had found it.

She decided it must have either come from a hollow in the tree when it fell, or been uncovered by the explosion. But what dreams it seeded, catching her imagination in a web of fantasy: a fairy shoe! There were legends and stories in Ireland, especially Donegal, of the 'faerie people' said to '*dwell in the hills, in the hollow hills … when they laugh and are glad, and are terrible …*'.The few words she could remember she sang softly under her breath, thinking how she would copy the marks on the shoe and send them to her uncle for translation ...

The sound of a twig snapping startled her out of her reverie.

Feeling suddenly afraid and defenceless, Jenny took to her heels, her precious find clutched tightly in her hand as she ran without stopping until she reached the edge of the woods and the safety of her bike. Fear lending speed to her flight, it was not long before she reached the ferry and had put the river between her and whatever it was that had snapped the twig in the woods. Her legs were still shaky when she got back to camp not knowing what the time was, or how late she might be.

CHAPTER TWO

Lt Nance speaking

It wasn't until she had stacked her bike that she put the little glass shoe in her pocket, having ridden with it in her hand for fear she might lose it. It was as well she did for, on opening the door to her hut, she was immediately aware of a scuffle of movement caused by three girls darting back to their bed spaces where they assumed such a contrived look of nonchalant innocence, her eyes flew to her own bed.

Jenny was immensely proud of her uniform, her hat being its crowning glory. Where most girls would reduce theirs to a shapeless droop as soon as they could in order to look like long-serving personnel, Jenny's always stood out for its brand-new 'sprog' appearance, with its top as flat as a pancake. Had it not been September, when they were still wearing their white caps, it was unlikely the idea would have occurred to anyone, but there, in solitary splendour in the centre of her bed, lay her pride and joy, its white surface neatly decorated with twenty-one cake candles.

The tension she had been feeling promptly dissolved in both tears and laughter at the sight, but the girls were horrified at her bedraggled appearance and greeted her with a chorus of concern.

Wiping her eyes on her sleeve and trying to calm herself, Jenny managed to persuade them she was okay.

'I came off my bike and got caught in some bushes,' she told them, not untruthfully.

'Well, it looks as if you could do with a jolly good bath,' remarked one of them, producing a small brightly wrapped package which she held out, saying, 'Many happy returns, Jen. You're a good sport!' The other two echoed the sentiment as they also gave her little gifts, and Jenny was left exclaiming her thanks over civvy stockings, perfume and a speedometer for her bike.

'That's to keep tabs on you,' said one of them, laughing. 'We'll keep a log of your mileage and see if you really do spend all that time haring round the countryside instead of snogging on the quiet with some secret 'pash' in the long grass!'

'She could always up-end the bike and turn the pedals by hand,' one of them joked.

'I'd call that an impedimenta, not a speedometer,' said Bea from where she was curled up on her bed writing a letter. 'Hasn't anyone here discovered that you need *all* your wits and *two* free hands to fend off an amorous matelot?'

Jenny suddenly remembered Bea had asked to bring her back fifty cigarettes. She apologised sheepishly. '… I totally forgot.'

'Don't worry about it, kiddo. I've enough for tonight and can get them myself tomorrow. How did you get on with the rest of your shopping?'

For a moment Jenny was totally lost for an answer, then stammered, 'I didn't get that either … coming off the bike and all that, you know … getting so dirty. Thought I'd better call it a day and get back to clean up.' She felt her cheeks flame with the untruth.

'Okay, kiddo,' said Bea mildly. 'Only wondered.' She returned to the letter she was writing, apparently reassured, although Jenny suspected Bea knew she had lied.

Jenny sat on her own bed, wondering where she could hide the shoe. She dared not take it out of her pocket while anyone's attention was still on her – it was bound to bring immediate enquiry. Anything really valuable was supposed to be handed in to be kept in the admin office safe, otherwise things were kept in their lockers or drawers, secure in the knowledge that they were as safe in their bed space as anywhere. She rose abruptly, scooping up her wash bag and towel, a pair of navy blue bell-bottoms and a blue and white square-necked seaman's shirt.

'I'm off to shower and change,' she told Bea. 'See you in the mess?'

'Okay.' Bea said. 'I'll pick up rations.'

When Jenny returned with the shoe stowed in her wash bag, the tannoy was sounding a piped whistle before warning 'First dog-watchmen to tea' It meant any further action was going to have to wait until morning.

Although discipline was not as strict for wrens as it was for ratings, a higher standard was expected from them and duty was sacrosanct. It was small wonder then that Jenny should put that first, and leave her personal dilemma until later. She couldn't help thinking about it though.

She knew she was already viewed by her superiors as imaginative; an attitude which Chiefie had again impressed on her earlier and which was likely to prove a snag in itself. The first thing she would be asked – if she insisted on pressing the matter to higher channels – had she reported what she had seen immediately upon sighting it that morning? And she had: to Chiefie. And that would put him on the spot – something for which he would probably never forgive her.

Then again, supposing she was believed, and an investigation of some sort made, would it help X-Ray Charlie – Lieutenant Nance, as she now knew him to be? He must be in trouble enough as it was. Wouldn't it complicate matters still further if it was then discovered that his 'UFO' really existed? Surely it would be wiser to say nothing at all, and save herself and everyone else a lot of worry.

After a good deal of soul searching, she came to a decision. She would contact Nance himself in the morning and leave it to him to decide the correct course of action. An unorthodox solution, but it gave her immediate peace of mind, even if it did cause her heart to flutter.

She had had only his voice to go on, but imagination, well served by what she had seen of young officers at a distance – or gathered about them from the Debs in particular – made it impossible for her to think of them as ordinary men. They lived in another world too remote to have any reality in hers. So what could be more romantic than a shy dream about contacting this handsome – which went without saying – young pilot whom she had never seen nor met, but for whom she had been his only line of communication during the morning's little drama?

'*Get anything on that aircraft, d/f?*' came the Controller's voice over the intercom.

'Bearing zero-three-zero reciprocal, sir,' Jenny replied promptly, swinging the heavy wheel round to the opposite degree for any further transmission, while Bea logged the exchange. When it came, Jenny was ready, depressing the heavy plate on top of the wheel hard down, to report.

'One-six-zero, true bearing, sir.' She received a brief thanks in return and nothing more was heard on the subject.

Yet how near she had come to missing it, she reflected.

She had automatically alerted to the bearing in the first place because it was faint, and therefore likely to be called for, and pursued with extra diligence because the pilot's voice had so reminded her of Nance.

Bea handed her a cup of tea, and Jenny apologised for her absentmindedness.

'Who cares so long as he's worth it.'

Bea's observation, so shrewdly near the mark, made Jenny's face go pink with an involuntary blush and wish it hadn't. 'It's nothing like that,' she said defensively. 'I was just miles away —'

'With or without speedometer?' Bea said teasingly, before adding; 'Don't worry, kiddo. Auntie Bea is *not* being inquisitive. Time enough for that when you start howling your eyes out. By the by, how about a drink tomorrow evening: my treat for your birthday, seeing as how I couldn't get you anything today.'

Jenny seldom drank, but Bea's offer was touching. 'That's nice of you, Bea. Just a *very* quick one, then? I had planned on going to the music circle tomorrow night; they're doing *Aida*.'

'Well, tomorrow's Friday, and we're on twelve to sixteen hundred hours watch. I'd like to call in and see how Jean is. So if we go straight to sick bay from here, we'll be back in quarters by five-thirty with time to change, have tea and be down to the NAAFI by seven. That'll give you plenty of time to make it to the music circle by eight, won't it?

And Jenny nodded, never dreaming for a moment that it would be anything different from what Bea had proposed.

Thoroughly tired when they came off night watch, Jenny slept soundly until the following morning brought back the recollection she was going to telephone the pilot.

In five minutes she was up, washed and dressed. It was gone nine and she had missed breakfast, but the YMCA situated a hundred yards up the road, would be open at ten and could be relied on to supply tea and sandwiches on tick to their regular customers; something the NAAFI never did. This way she could save her few remaining coppers to ring the officers' mess from the coin-box in the wrens' quarters, rather than risk a possible eavesdropper on an internal line through the switchboard.

She waited apprehensively at the end of the phone while someone went in search of the man she had asked for. Now that she was committed, her mind was racing through what she was going to say and, more importantly, exactly how she ought to say it. She must be clear and concise, and impress Lieutenant Nance from the first with the importance of what she had found …

'Hello?'

The brisk tone suggested that the speaker had not a lot of time to spare for callers who refused to give their name. It sounded so unlike the one she had heard over the air traffic intercom that her breathless query for confirmation of his identity seemed a bad start.

'Lieutenant Nance speaking.' The cultured accent added nothing but panic to her state of mind, and she was mortified to hear herself gabbling, so fearful she was that he might cut her off before she had a chance to explain.

'Wren Howard, sir. I was on Channel Baker yesterday when you reported that flying saucer. I've found it! I mean, I haven't actually found it … the place where I think it came down … a woods just over the border in Donegal. I cycled out to find it yesterday afternoon. And it's there, it really is! A kind of burned-out circle you can't mistake … and all the trees—'

'Wren Howard,' she was interrupted, 'I don't know what kind of game you're playing, but I can assure you that I have neither the time nor inclination to listen to such drivel. For your own sake, I strongly advise you to credit a little more intelligence than you yourself appear to possess to those who will be conducting an enquiry into what was said or not said in the first place over this business—'

She cut him short. Like a slap in the face, his patronising air of superiority transformed her incoherency into sharp clear words of fury. 'Lieutenant Nance! I heard your transmission, I saw the thing itself. I subsequently followed its trajectory and found indisputable evidence of its destruction—'

'But—'

'I am neither a liar given to invention, nor a deluded fool sticking my neck out over a phantom. I phoned to tell you because I imagined – mistakenly it appears – that you would be relieved by my corroboration of your original report. However, if you prefer to abide under a cloud of suspected mental aberration, then you're welcome to it. And much joy might it give you because I'm certainly not going to deny the plain evidence of my own ears and eyes.'

With which, and shaking like a leaf, she slammed down the receiver and burst into tears.

CHAPTER THREE

How are the mighty fallen in battle

Back in the hut, Jenny threw herself on her bed. What an utter idiot she had been, allowing her imagination to run away with her like that. It was pathetic! She hated Nance with all the vehemence she could muster.

Ten minutes later, when she sat up, determined to put a stop to the nonsense, the Quarters' Staff Leading Wren put her head in at the door to inform her there was someone waiting to see her at the gate.

Surprised, she wondered who it could be, then remembered Paul Ronan's note of the previous day saying he would be looking her up. Bless his heart! Wasn't he just the right person to arrive now?

Hurriedly, she did what could to fix her red and swollen face with cold water, and went to meet him.

An old blue jalopy standing in the lane made her eyes widen with delight that Paul had somehow managed to acquire a car. Things were even getting better. Then her steps slowed as she realised that the fair-haired young man in the grey flannels and navy-blue blazer getting out of it was neither Paul nor anyone else she knew, even if he was obviously expecting her.

He stood watching her approach, and then asked, 'Wren Howard?'

The way he spoke identified him as an officer. Jenny gave an apprehensive nod, jumping to the conclusion that this must be some friend of Lieutenant Nance who had volunteered, in an unofficial capacity, to deal with her.

Yet the steady grey eyes held nothing of disapprobation. On the contrary, his rather good-looking features broke into a friendly smile as he introduced himself.

'I'm Perry Nance. Look here, I'm most frightfully sorry I upset you, but you weren't very clear on the phone at first, were you? If you had only explained the facts in the first instance, I'd have got the gist right away instead of the entirely wrong impression.'

Jenny said nothing.

'Anyway,' he carried on, 'now that's cleared up, perhaps you'd care to show me where this place is, so that I can investigate it for myself and make a report. Is it far off the beaten track?'

If he thought that this was a sufficient apology for his behaviour, then he could think again. She tilted her head and gave him a look that was both frosty and hostile. This seemed to irritate Nance and his manner changed abruptly.

'For God's sake, what's upsetting you now?' he said.

'Nothing at all, sir,' she answered stiffly. 'If you want to see the place, I can show you.'

'I'll wait 'til you change,' he said.

For a moment she wondered what he meant, then realised she was still in her uniform. With a sinking heart she realised she only had the slacks and sweater she had worn the day before, and had had no time to clean or to mend.

A few minutes later she climbed into his car in the torn and dirty clothes, wrapping her arms around herself self-consciously, and feeling obliged to excuse their state.

'I hardly expected you to change into evening dress for gallivanting around the countryside,' the pilot responded, turning to survey the road behind with one hand on the steering wheel, and the other across the back of her seat in order to reverse in the narrow lane. 'What time you do you have to be back?'

'Eleven-fifteen hours, sir.'

'Cutting it fine if we've far to go,' he said with a glance at his watch, swiftly turning the car and putting his foot down to shoot smoothly ahead. 'One hour, three-quarters to be precise.'

Jenny did not see how they could possibly do it in the time, but left it to the pilot to work out. She gave him rough directions then settled into a silence, in which he seemed content to leave her. Had it not been for the company, she would have enjoyed the ride, which was a longer way round over the bridge at Londonderry than the direct route she had been able to take with the bike over the lough.

Once over the river and up to a point roughly opposite their station on the other side of the lough, Nance asked her to direct him until he parked the car on the verge of the field she had visited the day before.

Wordlessly, she led the way across to the woods. His whistle of surprise at the extraordinary sight was gratifying. She watched while he prowled like a hound on a scent, making a cautious survey of the swathe of trees before approaching the apparently burned circle with its single fallen tree. After a careful look round it, he bent down on his haunches for a closer examination, then took out a matchbox from one pocket, emptied its contents into another and gingerly scooped a little of the calcined dust into the box. He was about to rise when she saw him stiffen. Pointing at the impressions left by her shoes in the ash the previous day, he asked, 'Those your tracks?'

Taken by surprise, Jenny admitted they were.

'Didn't it occur to you that evidence like this should be disturbed as little as possible?'

She didn't say anything, lost for words.

'What did you find under the tree?'

'Why should I have found anything under it?' she countered defensively.

'It doesn't need a red Indian to read the signs,' he said. 'So come on, out with it.'

'A crystal slipper, sir,' she said, finding it almost impossible not to laugh at the expression on his face. She had to admit it sounded outrageous, even to her own ears. She stared at him with a defiant expression.

'A *what*?'

'A crystal slipper, sir.'

'Sure you wouldn't like to settle for something else?' he warned, rising to his feet. 'If you're hiding something …'

'I'm telling you,' she protested, 'it's got nothing to do with the UFO. It was obviously either hidden in the tree at the time it fell, or got uncovered by the explosion—'

'I'll be the judge of that,' he said. 'Where is it now?'

'In my wash bag at camp, sir,' she confessed reluctantly.

He stared at her a moment in silence. Then, 'Right,' he said. 'You can hand it over to me when I drop you off there. This all goes in an immediate report to the Captain, including your so-called "crystal slipper".'

Jenny took a deep breath. 'No, sir. I found it – it's mine.'

'You will do as you're told, Wren Howard,' he said. 'You will turn it in or find yourself charged with disobeying an order, to say the least. If it is what you say it is – although I doubt it – it'll be treasure trove and therefore Crown Property.'

'I beg pardon, sir,' argued Jenny, somewhat surprised by her own temerity, 'but aren't you forgetting we're the other side of the border, now – in the Irish Republic?'

He swore softly, then took her arm.

'Out,' he ordered, and practically pushed her along at a half trot, branches whipping her face.

At the edge of the field he stopped and swung her round to face him. 'Now look,' he said, 'I appreciate that you think you know what your find is, but you could easily be mistaken. Practically all non-inflammable materials are distorted under the influence of excessive heat. You say what you found was a crystal slipper. All right, that might well be what it looks like to you, but it almost certainly wouldn't to a scientist. A scientist would recognise the piece for what it is: a chance distortion of an artefact destroyed in the burn-up. Have you never seen the odd shape that glass can take when subjected to heat?'

'Yes, I have,' she said defiantly. 'I've seen them in the ashes of the stove at home, and they go all grey and twisted – and dirty. And this isn't. It's bright, clean and clear—'

'So what?' he said. 'It might be a type of mineral which takes on that appearance—'

'With two lines of Oghamic characters cut into the sole?'

'Og-what?'

'Oghamic, sir. It's a form of writing the ancient Celts used.'

'Never stop learning, do I?' he muttered. 'You have *got* to hand this thing over. Don't you see it's the most vital clue that's come to hand so far?'

Jenny stared at him. 'What? That the Americans or Russians are printing their technical instructions in Oghamic script? I'm sorry, sir, but I can't help laughing.'

'Everything points to the craft destructing before it actually touched the ground. What's more, *you* disturbed the dust getting it out from under the tree, meaning the thing had already been pressed into the earth by the falling trunk. So you *will* hand it over for examination by the proper authorities without further argument.'

'I don't know where it came from,' said Jenny, 'but I do know it has nothing to do with the flying saucer, and I am *not* giving it up. They can clap me in the brig for all I care.'

He regarded her thoughtfully, then said slowly: 'Look, I don't usually bargain with ratings, but I'll buy you anything you care to name – within reason of course – in exchange for this "shoe". What do you say?'

Jenny raised an eyebrow but said nothing.

'I probably need my head examining for saying that because I'm damn sure the authorities will get it from you somehow. But it'll take time, and they'll make mincemeat of you in the process. So this is your easy way out. Come on. There must be something you'd like?'

She shook her head and to her annoyance felt her eyes slowly welling with tears.

'Now what's the matter?' he asked. 'Here …' He fumbled in his pocket and produced a handkerchief. 'Come on, dry your eyes and tell me what's wrong.'

'You don't understand, sir,' she said, sniffing into the handkerchief.

Nance put an arm round her shoulder. 'What is it that's so difficult to understand?' he asked. 'From what you say, this "shoe" appears to be quite beautiful? Well, I can easily buy you something just as nice –'

'No, no, NO!' she cried, pulling herself away from him. 'I've told you what the shoe means to me,' she said, 'but you simply ignore that. Once and for all, I'll never, *ever* give it up … not if all the Lords of the Admiralty ordered it – nor,' she ended witheringly: 'for anything *you* could give me.'

'I'm sorry,' he said awkwardly. It was clear he was getting the message at last and felt embarrassed. 'I'd no idea it meant that much to you.' He hesitated, then said: 'Could you forgive me?'

Jenny saw his contrition was genuine. 'I shouldn't have been so silly,' she said quickly. 'And I'm sorry I spoke to you as I did; I shouldn't have done that. But you do understand now, sir, why I must keep the shoe?'

He shook his head. 'The 'why' remains beyond me, but I suppose you'll keep it anyway. I'll still have to mention it in my report, though, you understand?' His voice was softer, and Jenny nodded, smiling through her tears now that she had at last got through to the man behind the officer.

Suddenly, Nance put out his hand and gently turned her face to his.

'I'm going to kiss you,' he said. 'Any objection?'

She stared back at him, shock sending her mute.

'Oh, come on, there's no need to look so scared,' he laughed softly and then pressed his lips firmly on hers.

Jenny froze. On the one hand she distrusted his intentions simply because he was male and they were alone miles from anywhere, yet on the other longed to respond with all the ardour of wishing her dream was true after all. Vividly conscious of the stillness about them, the fresh smell of his face against hers and the roughness of his sleeve where it touched her neck, she became aware of his annoyance at her lack of response.

'You know, you could be a nice girl if you'd only relax and let yourself be one.'

Jenny could have wept afresh, but before she could think of anything to say back at him, he had turned away– only to trip over a strand of rusty barbed wire which sent him sprawling into a bed of nettles from where he gazed up at her his face red with humiliation.

Horrified, Jenny fell to her knees beside him, helping to free his sock and trouser leg from the wire barbs.

Suddenly Nance laughed out loud causing Jenny to look at him in bewilderement.

'How the mighty are fallen in battle,' he said by way of explanation.

She saw what he meant and laughed shyly, before rushing to his defence. 'You mustn't say that, sir.'

'You don't let up, do you?' he said, smiling. 'That's the second time you've told me off.'

The intimacy confused her and she quickly lowered her gaze to his foot, her heart quickening.

'Your sock's got blood on it,' she said. 'I think we'd better roll it down or it'll stick.' But as she started to roll the sock down, he winced.

'Hell! Don't say I've gone and sprained the bally thing?'

It was clear, though, from how quickly the ankle was swelling that he had. 'Try and find a stick,' he said looking around them. 'Look, there's a possible.' He pointed to a branchlet lying a short distance away. 'Let's hope it's strong enough.'

She fetched it and, as he struggled to his feet, she found herself grabbed involuntarily for more support. She instinctively put an arm around him.

'How am I to get you back to camp?' she said despairingly. 'I can't drive.'

'Get *me* back to camp?' Nance sounded as if he was about to laugh as he cautiously tried more weight on his ankle but winced instead. '*You're* the one I have to worry about,' he said.

'But if you can't walk …'

'Hopefully, I can still drive. It's the left foot. If I can work the clutch sufficiently, we'll be okay. At least I can hop, can't I?'

'Well, I can help there,' she said, pulling his arm more firmly around her shoulder.

His arm tightened a fraction and Jenny felt an unexpected surge of happiness at its unspoken indication of appreciation for her help.

CHAPTER FOUR

Bird watcher

They didn't speak until they reached the car. Nance carefully tested his foot against the clutch, a gave her a thumbs-up sign.

'Thank goodness for that,' Jenny breathed, with a sigh of relief as he glanced at his watch.

'It's eleven-thirty,' he said.

'Heavens!' Jenny was panic stricken. 'I'm late!'

'Don't worry. I don't imagine you'd have been on duty too long before you're hauled in to see the CO.'

He glanced at her expression of dismay.

'Oh, he won't bite *you*,' he said. 'It's me who's in the cart in that quarter.'

Jenny guessed his meaning, 'Do you really and truly not remember seeing the object?' she asked.

He shook his head and lapsed into silence. But Jenny wanted to sound out a theory that had been forming at the back of her mind.

'Sir …?' she said tentatively.

'Mm?' His thoughts were evidently far away and his eye remained on the road. 'And the name's Perry – or Pen – whichever you prefer. Yours is Jennifer, isn't it?'

'How did you know?'

'Simple enough. When I asked at the gate for you, they wanted to know *which* Howard. I knew if you worked in the control tower that you'd be Signals and they said, "Oh, that'll be Jennifer".'

'Well, I've been thinking … Pen, this UFO; I'm sure it was the cause of the power failure.'

'What power failure?'

She gave him the details, including her sighting of what she had seen of the object's destruction.

'Did you report it?'

'Yes, but Chiefie wouldn't believe me. I don't blame him. Everyone in the control tower was on the look out, and couldn't see a thing, and the Chief was getting as mad as a hatter. I'm wondering though if there might be any connection between what you said you saw and then your amnesia …? If radio transmissions can be jammed, why not the human mind?' she asked. 'The brain sends out electrical waves …'

He laughed. 'You do think 'em up, don't you?'

'But don't you think it's a possibility?'

'I think one needs to know what one's talking about,' he answered.

It was a put-down that made Jenny flush and she fell silent.

*

Nance shot a glance at her, noting the mutinous set to her mouth. *Poor girl*, he thought, and supposed he was being rather rough on her but in his view it was necessary to keep the female imagination under control. She was also beginning to pose a problem. On the one hand he felt drawn by a certain sweetness and lack of sophistication; on the other, there was that infernal inferiority complex she would have to snap out of if she was to be seen associating with him … *Here, hang on!* he thought. Did he intend to go that far? Granted, he had come to the conclusion that having defied him in respect of the 'shoe', she could equally well defy the Captain; and there was a certain appeal in the prospect of succeeding where he knew his CO was likely to fail. But the girl had wren written all over her, and all the time she was in the Service, he would have to be careful how and where he was seen with her. To her credit, her accent was good, and she could possibly be tutored in the finer essentials of his social class. But what a task! He could already see the fur flying. Was the 'shoe' really worth all that effort? No, he was a fool. He had neither the time nor the temperament to do it, so he ought to leave well alone. Then again, he never could resist a challenge …

Knowing his CO as he did, Nance considered it an almost foregone conclusion that Captain Mansett would want to make an investigation. It was one thing, however, to have a damned good idea that one's Commanding Officer would have no compunction in carrying out such a nefarious activity; quite another for a junior officer to tacitly infer it by keeping a rating off duty to lead him to the site. On the other hand, with Jenny well adrift by now, he would have to carry the can for that so he might just as well take her straight to the Captain. It would draw far less attention to any operation Mansett might wish to undertake, than having to call her off duty. There was, of course, the possibility that he might decide against any investigation, but Nance mentally shrugged it aside. He might as well be hung for a sheep as a lamb. He was already suspended from duty pending a medical report with the promise of an enquiry to follow, which could well result in his dismissal from the service – or ground him for the rest of his career – so what difference would it make?

The rest of the journey passed in silence, until they reached the barracks and Jenny immediately questioned why

Nance was turning into the road to the officers' married quarters.

'What are we doing here?' she asked.

'We're more likely to find the Captain at home – presuming he's there for lunch – rather than in his office. If he *is* still in his office, I'll ask his wife to phone him.'

He pulled up in the road outside the house in time to see the Captain letting himself in the front door.

'Sir!' Nance's hail and grimace of pain as he struggled out of the car and limped with the stick towards his CO caused the tall, grey-haired officer to pause enquiringly and walk over. Nance straightened to attention with a salute and began his report in quick low sentences.

'It appears there was something after all, sir. Wren Howard, here, was on duty at the time yesterday, saw the explosion and found the site of the incident this morning. I have seen it and am satisfied …'

Mansett's attitude was immediately alert. Shooting a glance in Jenny's direction, he took Nance's arm and manoeuvred the young man out of earshot.

*

Jenny watched as the pair in low voiced conversation, before the Captain turned and strode into his house.

Jenny could see Nance visibly relax, before he too turned and hobbled back to the car. He said nothing however until he had turned the vehicle round and was on the road to the village.

'Everything's under control,' he said. 'The Captain's going to carry out a personal investigation and you're going with him. In order to avoid comment, I'm to drop you off outside the village at the corner of Knotts Lane where you're to wait until he arrives. And when he does, remember it will be *Mr* Mansett and *Miss* Howard, okay?'

Jenny was puzzled. 'Why?'

'The Captain can hardly go over the border in uniform,' he said. 'Anymore than you can. No one must guess who either of you are.'

'Yes, of course,' she agreed. 'But what about you, sir … Pen?'

'My orders are to get the jolly old ankle attended to as soon as possible.' It appeared to occur to him that they would both be missing out on lunch. He glanced aside at her. 'Look, it'll be an hour or more before the CO turns up and I'm hungry. I know a small guesthouse not far from where I have to drop you off. We could get something to eat there.' Jenny agreed at once; she was hungry since she had missed breakfast and even a snack at the YMCA after being so upset. Then she remembered the state she was in.

'But I can't go like this,' she said. 'I'm filthy.'

'Don't worry. The hostess is a good soul. I'm sure she can help.'

The proprietor did, taking Jenny into her huge kitchen and supplying her with hot water, soap and a towel; even a needle and thread to patch up the tear in her trouser leg.

Neither of them spoke much during a meal of sausage, egg and chips, and mugs of hot tea. Jenny was hungry and had too much to think about before committing thoughts to words. She was grateful Nance had the money on him to pay for the food. It made her feel a good deal better and ready to face the afternoon.

Drawing to a stop at the rendezvous a few minutes later, Nance pointed out a log she could sit on while she waited, but made no move to release the door catch.

'I thought I was to wait here alone?' she said.

'There's time yet.' He fished out some cigarettes and offered her one. 'Ever been dinghy sailing?'

'No thanks, I don't smoke. No, I've never been dinghy sailing, but I'd like to.'

'I could take you tomorrow,' he said casually, 'if you'd care to come?'

Her eyes lit up with delight, then she remember his foot. 'But your ankle …'

'Oh hang the bally thing!' He lit a cigarette, snapping the lighter shut. 'If I can drive a car, then I'm damn sure I can handle a tiller. I'll pick you up after lunch tomorrow. Are you off duty?'

'The whole day,' she assured him.

'Excellent.' He leaned forward to open an ashtray in the dashboard and tapped his cigarette ash into it. 'We'll round it off by going onto 'Derry afterwards for a quiet drink at The Shaun Hotel,' he said. 'Actually, forget that, we'll make it dinner instead of a drink. How's that? We'll need to return to camp first to change …' he broke off, seeing Jenny's look of dismay. 'Ah, I was forgetting. You said you have no other civvies.'

Jenny shook her head. 'It's nothing, nothing at all. It sounds lovely – and thank you very much.' She felt certain there was sure to be someone who would lend her a dress.

*

Nance eyed Jenny speculatively, guessing at once what she intended to do, and did not like it. He wanted to see her in something that fitted his idea of how she should look. But how? He had either to go completely back on the arrangement, and have them turn up in the bar in their sailing togs, or buy something suitable for her himself. Desirable as that might be, it was also an extremely delicate proposition. He decided to take the plunge.

'Amendment number two. I'll be round for you some time tomorrow morning.'

'Why?' she asked. 'Where are we going?

'That's my business,' he told her, glancing at his watch. 'Anyway, I must be off. The Old Man will get the wrong idea if he finds us nattering cheek by jowl.' He grinned as leaned across and opened the door for her. 'Ten-ish tomorrow morning then?'

*

All Jenny had ever seen of the Station CO was a passing glimpse when he inspected the monthly station parade: a truly distant figure that she was afraid and nervous she might not even recognise in civilian clothing.

She need not have worried. When a black saloon drew up and the driver, in deerstalker hat, tweeds and plus fours, leaned over and opened the nearside door, there was no mistaking the strong features of Captain Mansett.

'Miss Howard?' he asked with a smile, making it plain that rank and authority were indeed suspended.

'Yes, s … Mr Mansett,' she replied.

Getting in, she recognised the familiar features of Chief Petty Officer Browning, also in a civilian suit, seated in the back with a large black photographic case. He nodded to her with a straight face, and said nothing. She would learn later that he knew least of the three of them what this odd rendezvous was in aid of. That at lightening notice he had been ordered to get changed and present himself in ten minutes with photographic equipment and to keep his mouth shut, and that he was still getting his breath back, and still keeping his mouth shut.

'I'm not awfully familiar with the other side of the border, Miss Howard,' Mansett confessed as they started off. 'I'll have to ask you to direct me as soon as we're through Londonderry.'

Mansett was friendly and there was no protocol. Jenny was soon at ease and responded readily to his questions about her original sighting and ensuing search. She privately wondered if he would say anything about the shoe, but the Captain remained silent on the subject.

When they arrived at the field beside the woods, he pulled up, turned off the engine, then looked round at the CPO.

'We're going for a walk in those woods over there, Browning. I don't need to inform you that we are now in foreign territory with the intention of making what amounts to an entirely unauthorised military reconnaissance; that is why we are all in civvies and using surnames only.'

'Yes, Mr Mansett.'

'Mansett will be sufficient, Browning, with the exception of Miss Howard, of course. It's just possible there may be other people about and it would be deucedly awkward if they learnt our real identities. For the record,' he went on, 'we are mere acquaintances. Point one: I am a retired forestry official. Point two: Miss Howard has informed me that she has seen an unusual formation in some of the trees over there … or rather, a curious phenomenon which suggests that the forestry experts of Eire have discovered a revolutionary method of deforestation. Point three: by interesting coincidence, I happened on you, Browning, and, upon learning that you are a professional photographer, persuaded you to accompany us in the event that her contention should turn out to be as worthy of preservation as I hope. Now, if we all bear this relationship in mind, I'm sure we shan't go far wrong. As an actor,' he concluded, 'I'm probably as lousy as you, Browning – I can't speak for Miss Howard, of course – but I'll do my best to get into the part, so it's up to you to do the same.'

To give him his due, Captain Mansett certainly seemed intent on making the best he could of what might prove to be a delicate job, and even appeared to be enjoying the faint air of cloak-and-dagger it suggested.

He played the part as they walked through the woods, holding forth on the variety and quality of the trees in relation to the soil and climate, until Jenny pointed out the first fallen tree she had come across. The two men came to a halt and stared at the downward sweep of devastation.

'Shoot from here, Browning,' Mansett said crisply. The CPO waved the others out of the way and started snapping.

The Captain stuck to his playacting as they clambered over trunks and foliage.

'Got to hand it to these Eire experts, they certainly don't do things by halves. What do you think, Browning?'

They arrived at the central circle of calcined earth, and his voice carried clearly through the glade. A figure rose from the side of the felled tree. He looked destitute in an old raincoat over a tatterdemalion suit, but in one hand was what looked like quite an expensive camera, and in the other a brown paper bag. He stared at them through a pair of thick-rimmed glasses from under an old hat.

'Hello, don't tell me I'm not the only pebble on the beach, after all!' he said.

If the sight took Mansett back at all, he gave no indication of it. 'Apparently not,' he drawled. 'We were taking a stroll through here and came upon this, ah, unusual trail of devastation.'

'That's just what attracted me, too,' said the man, putting the paper bag in his pocket and looping the strap of his camera around his neck. 'Astonishing, isn't it?' He stuck out a hand. 'I'm Johnson. Who are you; if that's not a rude question?'

'It is, actually.' Mansett ignored the outstretched hand. 'I fail to see what business it is of yours.'

Johnson shrugged, seemingly unperturbed by Mansett's rudeness, then looked at the camera and case that Browning was carrying. 'Looks to me as if you're professionals,' he said. 'If you are, then it's very much my business. Look,' and Jenny was amazed to see his whole attitude change, his tone becoming a wheedling plea as he came towards them, 'I'm an amateur photographer – I do it for bird watching, actually – but I know a scoop when I see one and a scoop to me spells lolly in any language. Have you taken any photographs?'

'I really don't see—'

'Meaning you have,' Johnson interrupted. 'Well, I was here first …'

'So what if you were?' Mansett said. 'I still fail to see—'

'Oh, come off it. Type like you can't be deaf, dumb *and* blind! You know as well as I do what caused all this: it was a flying saucer. If it was a 'plane, it would've been smashed to smithereens and there'd be debris scattered all over the place, *and* sent the woods up in flames. How do you account for that?'

'I can't, but I'll try to when I've seen it,' said Mansett pushing past him and gazing into the circle. 'So you've decided the thing burned itself out just here after crashing, is that it?

'Well, didn't it?'

'How should I know?' asked the Captain. 'I'm only a forestry man.'

'Oh yeah?' Johnson challenged with a suddenly cunning expression. 'Look mate, I know you're English, all three of you are – same as me – but you don't really expect me to fall for a story like yours? Be your age!' he dug Mansett in the ribs. 'Ask yourself, what would a middle aged bloke like you be doing walking this little bit of crumpet around a woods ...' he paused with a significant leer, 'accompanied by a professional photographer — ?'

'Are you inviting me to break your jaw?' snapped Mansett with an aggressive stare.

'Yep!'

The man stuck his chin out invitingly but the Captain, in spite of obvious temptation, resisted it.

The gad-fly went on: 'Suppose we cut the chat and get down to brass tacks?' Johnson moved to stand in the middle of them. 'I'm not a rich man and I can't afford anything like as expensive as your pal's camera, there. But I do know that what I've already got in my modest Leica is good enough to earn me six month's rent.' He paused, appraising Mansett through narrowed eyes. 'I don't believe you're a forestry type ... You're a serving officer – no names, no pack drill, eh? You got wind of this and you're conducting an illegal investigation in foreign territory in the cause of patriotic fervour. Well, that's okay by me; so far as I'm concerned you do what you bloody well like and I won't breathe a whisper. But me, well, what I'll have to tell – and show – will have the world rocking on its heels by tomorrow morning.'

He turned away and walked off.

'Mr Johnson,' Mansett called after him. Johnson stopped and looked back. 'Have you considered the consequences of what you are doing? If, as you believe, this *is* damage caused by a flying machine from outer space, then that burned ash you have in your pocket could well be radioactive. The very air around us could be infected with organisms capable of destroying half the world's inhabitants ...'

'Oh my God!' Johnson stood still, apparently transfixed with terror, and nervously wiped his hands on his trousers.

'I hadn't thought of that.' Then abruptly, he tugged the bag out of his raincoat pocket and hurled it towards the one person least expecting it – Jenny – and turned and ran. But Mansett was quick. He pushed the girl to the ground and the bag sailed over their heads, splitting and spilling its contents as it hit a tree behind them.

'Sorry,' he said, helping her up. 'Didn't hurt you, I hope?'

'No, I'm fine.' She stood up, dusting herself down.

Mansett stared in the direction taken by the fleeing bird watcher. They could still hear the sounds of his departure as he crashed though the undergrowth. 'There are few people in this world who have ever incited me so cruelly to murder, but there goes one.'

'Shall I go after him, sir?' asked Browning, putting down his equipment.

'No, leave him. Get as wide a shot of this area as you can, Browning. You're the technician in charge here. And don't forget the tree,' he said, pointing. 'It must have fallen seconds after the thing disintegrated, yet there isn't a shrivelled leaf anywhere. Get a close-up of that, will you?'

*

Mansett was silent on the return journey back, until he brought the car to a halt at a deserted spot not far from their base and turned to the CPO.

'Keep this under your hat, Chief, and don't forget it,' he said. 'Everything – and I mean everything – that you've seen, heard and done comes under the Official Secrets Act. Understood?'

Browning, attempted a weak smile. 'Knew I shouldn't have dabbled in photography, sir.'

Mansett switched his gaze to Jenny. 'I know I don't have to remind *you*, Wren Howard. You have shown yourself only too conscious of the fact. But there is one point you should bear in mind. If the press does get hold of that fellow's story – and we ought to be prepared for the possibility – certain people might remember you saying that you spotted it in the first place, so be prepared and don't go rushing out for a paper first thing in the morning if you don't usually do so. As to where you've been this afternoon, well, everyone thinks you were excused duty by your WRNS Chief Officer on compassionate grounds. Of course she knows nothing more than anyone else, but acted on my authority, and you have every right to remain silent concerning whatever 'personal news' it was that's she's supposed to have given you. You and I know there was no interview, but no one else will know that, so you can act up to it and be assured of her tacit support.'

He looked at them both. 'In spite of my previous remarks, we shall all have to go through the decontamination procedure as a routine precaution. I'll go first … let me see, it's now fifteen thirty hours … give me, say, half an hour and time to get clear. I'll inform the officer in charge that you will be following, and to keep wraps on it. Good luck!'

CHAPTER FIVE

Yankee Doodle

It was seven that evening before Jenny was free to return to quarters. Although everything had been laid on in sick bay for the decontamination procedure, and she and the CPO had only to follow one another through the same routine as had been given the Captain, it was all under wraps and had meant a large amount of waiting around. They'd had to surrender everything they were wearing and wait for someone to collect a change of clothing from their respective quarters. They were assured their civvies would be returned as soon as possible. The CPO had sincerely hoped so. In conversation with Jenny about the afternoon, he told her it was his one and only good outfit and it had better look as good when he got it back. Jenny wasn't so dismayed on being deprived of hers. They would at least be clean for sailing on Saturday – assuming she got them back in time.

Hanging about also increased her worry. The Captain had said no one had to know why the Chief Officer WRNS had kept her off duty all afternoon. True enough, but the Captain didn't know what it was like to live in a roomful of girls who would think it odd if she gave no hint of what was so amiss that it needed the Chief Officer to deal with it personally. They might even take offence at her not confiding in them. So, if the news she was supposed to have received was so important, or so bad, she was going to have to act up to it in some way or other.

She was still pondering the question when she ran into Bea on the way out, and her heart sank. Bea was the one person who was going to be the most difficult to fool.

However, Bea refrained from questioning her. Outwardly cheerful, she said, 'Good-oh! Just in time for that drink I promised you.'

It was still early enough for the NAAFI to be empty, which pleased Jenny. The NAAFI wasn't her favourite place to be seen in. She preferred the YMCA – only the latter sold no alcohol.

Opting for a shandy, Jenny sat at a corner table where Bea joined her a moment later with their drinks.

'Sorry, Jen,' Bea put the shandy in front of her. 'I can hardly wish you many happy returns, now. It wouldn't be right.'

Jenny blinked. 'Why ever not?'

'Well, after what's happened … it isn't one you'll want to remember, is it?'

'It was all right by me,' Jenny said, confused.

'Well, of course, you being you, you would put a brave face on it,' Bea fiddled with the drink mat. 'But you know me, Jen, I speak as I find, and right now, I find you're in trouble. It's no use keeping things bottled up; it only makes them worse, and while there's nobody here but us chickens … well, look on me as a mother hen.'

'Bea … would you mind telling me just what kind of trouble you think I'm in?'

'Okay, you're pregnant, aren't you?'

For a moment Jenny was too taken aback to speak, and when she did her voice was an incredulous squeak.

'Pregnant! Me? Oh, Bea, how could you?'

'Bloody easily! You don't turn up for duty, and then I'm told you've been to see Old Mother O'Riley. The next

I know, you've been to see the MO – with CPO Browning! Well, what with the state you came in yesterday afternoon, and crying yourself silly this morning, I thought at first it was a case of rape, only it didn't quite add up sending you to see the MO without a WRNS officer in tow. So there are the facts, and don't sit there asking me "how could I?" *I'm* not making them up.'

'You're still jumping to conclusions, though, aren't you?' complained Jenny.

Bea shrugged. 'Okay, so put me straight. I'm all ears.'

'I can't,' said Jenny. 'It's not my story to tell, and it's nothing at all like you think it is, so I'd be grateful if you just didn't say any more about it.'

Bea looked at her thoughtfully, making Jenny squirm under her gaze. 'Sorry I jumped the wrong gun,' she said at last, fishing lighter and cigarettes from her bag and offering them to her. Jenny shook her head. Bea lit one herself. 'Official secret, I suppose?'

Jenny nodded, glad that Bea might now understand and stop questioning her. She was wrong.

'Of course, the trouble with the Official Secrets Act is that it fails with use,' said Bea. 'Rather like throwing mud at a brick wall. What hits, sticks. And in this case, my chick, it looks like you're plastered.'

Jenny kept quiet. Bea probed harder. 'I suppose you were in sickbay having your eyes and ears tested for the enquiry?' she suggested. 'Vital evidence for or against our lieutenant's state of mind yesterday, that would be it, wouldn't it?'

Jenny did not like the remark but seized on it. 'Something like that.'

Bea's eyebrows rose. 'Really? And I suppose CPO Browning was there to photograph the results for the record?'

Jenny lost her temper. 'Oh, shut up, Bea. You're deliberately provoking me into talking, and I've already told you, I can't. I would have thought *you* would have understood, you said —'

'Keep your voice down,' Bea's low warning cut her short as she cast a significant look at the bar on which two American Navy men were now leaning and looking curiously in their direction.

Jenny was surprised. 'Where do you think they've come from?' she asked.

'There's an American sub in the lough,' Bea said. 'And if those two come over here, bags I the tall, dark and handsome one.'

It was obvious which one she meant; a broad shouldered man with an angular face and a crew cut of black hair. He gave his slim, sandy-haired companion a nudge in the ribs when he saw the girls' glances. Jenny could well believe Bea was serious and was apprehensive. Bea might not be bothered about her reputation, but Jenny most certainly was about her own.

'If they do, I'm off,' she said.

'Then you'd better look slippy,' Bea said. 'They're on their way.'

'Hi there,' came a deep voice from behind Jenny, making her jump. It was the large navy man, glass in hand. 'Mind if we join you two? It's kinda lonely in here. He gestured the bar behind. 'Name's Abe – Abe J O'Riley. And this here,' he pulled his slighter built friend forward, 'is Don Rossini – just call him Rosy.'

Bea smiled sweetly at the pair of them.

'Hi Abe ... Rosy. Take a pew.' She gestured the vacant chairs beside them.

Abe slid his large frame onto a seat next to Bea, and glanced up at his more hesitant pal still standing. 'Come on, bud, squat someplace,' he said. 'You're making the girls nervous.'

Don pulled out a chair by Jenny, smiled at her somewhat self-consciously, and nodded her empty glass.

'What are you drinking?' he asked in a soft drawl.

'Oh, no, thank you,' she answered quickly. 'I'm not stopping.' To her embarrassment, his face flamed with colour.

'Gee, ma'am, I'm sorry,' he said. 'We sure meant no offence.'

'But I'm not offended,' she protested in surprise. It's just that I have to leave in a minute, and it seems wrong to accept a drink that I shan't have time to enjoy.' There were times when Jenny surprised herself that she could be tactful. Don's face brightened immediately, but he didn't get chance to reply.

'What's your poison?' Abe was asking Jenny, having already ascertained what Bea was drinking.

'No, thank—'

'Thank you,' Bea cut in firmly. 'She'll have a whisky mac, same as me.'

'Bea!' Jenny hissed, but she was ignored; Abe was already making for the bar.

'I see you're both from this station, ma'am,' Don said, directing his comment at Bea as Jenny's eyes were staring resolutely down at her hands. 'We're from the USS *Chimera*.' He indicated his shoulder flash.

Thoroughly uncomfortable with the situation, Jenny made no effort to listen to what was being said. She wondered if she could get up and leave, only shrank from the thought of Bea's likely reaction, and the attention it would inevitably rivet upon herself. There was also the complication of the navy men themselves. From what she had heard, Americans were very difficult to get rid of and it seemed quite on the cards that one might insist on accompanying her if she went – and then what? She concluded it might be better to stay with Bea than be separated under those circumstances.

She eyed the American next to her surreptitiously, reflecting on the oddity of his having fair hair and blue eyes with such an Italian sounding name: Don Rossini. Having it shortened to 'Rosy' seemed an attendant misfortune. Thinking about it, the name could be Spanish … or Mexican even, come to that, although that still didn't account for his colouring. Abe's return with the drinks broke her reverie.

'What's a guy got to do to get introduced around here, anyway?' he said.

Despite his brashness, or maybe because of it, Jenny found herself beginning to think he couldn't be so bad after all. He was really just like some great friendly bear taking it for granted that others found him as welcome as he did them, and couldn't understand any objection.

Where Abe was the life and soul of the party, however, his companion was quiet, looking around the room. Sipping her drink, Jenny wondered if he might be feeling pushed out, and ventured to ask where his home was.

He turned to her at once. 'Phoenix, Arizona, ma'am,' he said. 'But I was born in Scotland, near Inverary in Argyllshire.

In an odd way she felt cheated, and said, almost accusingly, 'So you're not really American, then?'

'Sure I'm American. My dad died during the war, and ma remarried. My step-pa's an ex-GI – Guiseppe Rossini. He's a great guy. He took ma and me back to the States with him after the war, and ma and me, we became American citizens.'

Jenny went pink. 'I'm sorry, I didn't mean to be rude.'

'Nothing to apologise for, ma'am,' he assured her. 'I'm proud of my origins, and proud of being American.' Then, with a nod to their surrounds, 'You come here often?'

She shook her head, and explained the intended short celebration.

'Well then, ma'am, I sure am glad to wish you a happy birthday, too.'

He really was the politest serviceman Jenny had ever met, and his attentiveness was extremely flattering. 'It's very unusual to see any Americans on camp,' she said. 'I know your ship is in the lough. But I would have thought you'd want to be in Londonderry when you come ashore?'

'Sure do,' he agreed. 'But Abe and me, we were given an assignment to deliver here. We don't have to be back before midnight, so we just dropped in here as we passed.'

Jenny felt a slight twinge of alarm at this. If these two were free until midnight she did not see how they were going to break away from them unless they did it soon.

She gathered her hat and looked across at Bea, who looked up in surprise when Jenny got to her feet and reminded her of her promise. Don stood up with her.

'Well, you go ahead, kid,' said Bea. 'Don't worry about me.'

'But, Bea …' Jenny began imploringly. Don was already speaking to Abe, telling him not to wait for him and he'd see him back on board later. Then to Bea, 'Night to you, ma'am.' And stepped aside to allow Jenny to precede him before following.

*

Bea had a belated prick of conscience. She had no delusions about Americans, only whereas she considered she knew how to deal with them, she also knew Jenny could well find herself in a situation she couldn't handle.

She interrupted Abe's flow. 'Come on, big boy. We're off to the music circle. I promised the kid I'd go, and I don't trust that pal of yours alone with her. So move it.'

'Gee,' he protested. 'You don't mean that?'

'I never say anything I don't mean ... especially to big strong men. So, if you're coming, you're welcome, and if not, well, you can do your own thing.'

'Aw, you got it all wrong about Rosy. The guy's on the level. He ain't like me; he's different. He's a Six-Sided Testamentor or something. He don't believe in women —'

'Then I *am* worried!' said Bea, and made for the door.

Bea and Abe caught Don and Jenny up just before the Wrennery, and they all continued up the hill together past the YMCA to the Education hut. There was nothing to stop the girls inviting the Americans in to attend the meeting, although they were almost too late.

Trooping in just as the Wren Petty Officer in charge was about to make her introductory speech to the first record, they slid as quietly as they could onto chairs at the back of the room. A few heads turned to look at the latecomers – and Jenny found herself looking straight at Nance. He had an armchair in the front row next to a brother officer who was keeping him company.

His glance of surprise changed to one of contempt at the sight of the Americans, making Jenny wish the floor would open up and swallow her. It was obvious that nice girls and US Navy men did not go together in his book.

She bit her lips, trying to hide her feelings and concentrate on what was being said. But it was a losing battle. All she really wanted was to be back in her hut in her bed space.

*

Her tension could hardly have escaped Don's notice. From the moment she had first looked at him, he had fallen for her and now, in his state of intense awareness of everything about her, it bothered him to see her unhappy.

He reached for her hand.

'What's wrong?' he whispered, concerned.

She pulled her hand back as if scalded.

He was shocked to see her eyes brimming with tears. Shaking her head, she mumbled, 'Excuse me, please.' and was gone before he quite realised what had happened. He caught up with her outside, trailed by Bea and Abe.

'What's going on?' asked Abe

Jenny couldn't explain, Bea was exasperated, and no one wanted to return to the music circle.

Abe gave up. 'See you back on board, Rossini,' he said. 'Come on, baby, you and me's gonna get better acquainted.' And taking Bea by the arm went off back the way down towards the NAAFI.

But Don had his own suspicions of what was wrong with Jenny and, as they walked at a slow pace allowing the other two to get well clear, he said, 'I guess you must be real serious minded to take things to heart so.'

Jenny stopped. 'What do you mean?'

'Well,' he began slowly, 'couldn't help noticing the looks we were getting back there from those guys in front. I mean, it's real kind of you to feel concerned for me, but you shouldn't have let it upset you. We're used to it. Your guys don't like us Americans taking their girls out. It's only jealousy. You should have heard the things they were calling my ma back in Inverary when she and Zip – that's my pa – were courtin'.'

'I'm sorry some people have to be like that,' Jenny said.

Don grinned. 'So were they, ma'am. I couldn't teach the older folks manners, but I sure saw to it that the younger ones grew up a mite more respectful.'

Jenny smiled. 'I'm glad about that,' she said quietly.

'Sure you don't want to go back?' he enquired, 'You don't have to worry on account of me.'

'I'd rather not. I'm not as brave as you.'

'Well, ma'am, you don't have to be while I'm around to protect you,' he said quietly as they started walking again.

Her smile encouraged Don to take the plunge. 'I sure would appreciate it if you could see your way to coming out with me tomorrow evening.'

'Oh, I'm sorry, but I have a date for tomorrow.'

Don was crestfallen. 'I was kinda hoping I could see you again.'

'I don't see why not; I shall be off all day Sunday.'

'You really mean that? You really would come out with me? And the boyfriend? Won't he be mad?'

Jenny smiled. 'We don't have that kind of an understanding. I'm quite free to go out with whomever I please.'

CHAPTER SIX

Kittens and tenterhooks

Daylight was almost gone when Jenny and Don reached the Wrennery gates after their slow walk down the hill. There was nothing to be seen of Bea or Abe, but a motorcyclist was laboriously pushing his bike into the circle of lamplight where he leant it against the fence. He looked extremely hot and uncomfortable with leathers done up to his neck, while the red perspiring face under his helmet was marked with a deep scratch.

Slumping against the bike, he pulled off the helmet, and took out a large red and white spotted handkerchief to mop his forehead and neck, wincing slightly where he touched the line of glistening red.

'What's the trouble?' Don asked him.

'Think it's the clutch, old man. Could hardly even push her.' His middle-English accent set him somewhere among the station's personnel.

Jenny was concerned. 'Have you had an accident?' she asked as Don bent to look at the engine. Still getting his breath, the young man gave her a smile and jerked a thumb down at his jacket.

'Not really. Been doing a Sir Galahad on a kitten,' he said, and went on to tell how he had found the animal crawling out of the village duck pond with a tin can tied to its tail. 'Thrown in by some louts – they ran off. Seems to have survived though – landed in shallow water.' He showed a well clawed hand. 'And this is what you get for thanks.' He eyed Jenny hopefully. 'Suppose you wouldn't happen to know of a good home for a water-logged moggy, would you?'

She shook her head. 'We aren't allowed to keep animals in the mess,' she began, but then remembered that it didn't apply to offices. 'But there is a place I *could* try. I'll go and ask.'

With Don still deep in the intricacies of the engine, Jenny went to the gatehouse.

'Hi Jen,' said one of the two wrens on duty. Did you get your phone call?'

'No, what phone call?'

'About twenty minutes ago. Some woman said she had to get hold of you. We saw you walking up towards the YM, so we gave her its number. She didn't leave a name, just that it was important she should get you as soon as possible.'

The only female voice she could think of was Peggsy, but it wasn't like Peggsy to use telephones. That meant it could be anyone, and after the day's events this one sounded ominous.

Remembering why she was there, she told them about the kitten. Their response was immediate and unanimous: Jenny must bring it in at once.

When Jenny told the young man with the bike the news he looked immensely relieved, and retrieved a now sleepy looking white and ginger kitten from the depths of his jacket.

'Well he's certainly been christened,' he said with a grin. 'You could even call him "Drippy".'

By the time Jenny had delivered the kitten to the gatehouse and got back to the two men, Don had fixed the engine, which started to life with a splutter.

Its owner held out a grateful hand to the American. 'Thanks, pal. Anytime you need a hand, the name is Hamble, Norman Duncan Hamble. You'll find me in the officers' mess here, for my sins.'

'Rossini.' Don shook the proffered hand after wiping the oil off of his own.

They were interrupted by a shout from the gatehouse window. 'Jen, it's that woman on the line again. Hurry!'

'I'll wait here for you,' said Don, pre-empting any intention she might have had of using it as a way of saying goodbye. Jenny rushed to the gatehouse.

'*Good evening, Miss Howard,*' said her caller, and for a moment Jenny's fear evaporated. The voice sounded distinctly American, which was somehow reassuring. Apprehension returned in force however as the voice went on. '*You won't know me, Miss Howard. My name's Mary Little. I'm on a research project: an investigation into flying saucers. I've just read an account of your sighting in the evening press tonight. I'm so thrilled, I just had to contact you as soon as I could. Do you think you could be so kind as to give me just a little of your time to tell me all about it? If you're too busy, though, I'll settle for just a short questionnaire we keep for contactees? All strictly confidential, I do assure you, Miss Howard. No one would ever publish anything from such a record without your permission in writing. But the data is essential to our work. We just want to collect all possible facts on this most fascinating phenomenon of our time ...*'

Jenny's mind worked furiously. The bird watcher must have been even craftier than they had supposed to have identified her so quickly. Then she remembered his dig at the CO: 'You're a serving officer ...' *What an awful man!* she thought with a shiver. *Truly horrible!*

'I'm sorry, Miss Little,' she said stiffly as soon as she could get a word in. 'But I cannot possibly help you. As a member of Her Majesty's Services, I am unable to talk to anyone without permission from my Commanding Officer.'

'*Of course, we do find a lot of people naturally shy of publicity,*' the woman sympathised. '*I can quite understand your shock if you had no idea you were quoted —*'

Quoted! 'But I never said a thing,' Jenny protested. 'I'm sorry, Miss Little, but I cannot possibly speak to you a moment longer —'

'*Not even about what you found on the site?*'

Jenny gasped, remembering the sharp crack of sound that had sent her flying from her original visit. She forgot all about the legality of her position, and fierce defence of the shoe when she refused to hand it over to Nance. She could not even find the words to tell the woman straight out that it was none of her business. All she could think of was this woman being in league with the bird watcher. They knew who she was and, even if they might not know what she had found, were obviously after it.

She licked her dry lips and asked in a barely audible whisper, 'What do you want?'

'Only *to talk to you. Is there anywhere you know that we can meet in private?*'

'No,' answered Jenny at once. 'I don't.'

'*Then I suggest I have a word with your Commanding Officer,*' said the woman sweetly. '*I'm sure he could arrange something when he hears of your little find.*'

Jenny's panic turned into confusion. How could this woman possibly know of the Captain's ignorance? Could she be someone Nance had put on her trail?

'Who are you?' she asked.

'*I could be your very good friend … if it turns out that you're on the same side as I am. Now are you going to meet me quietly, or do I have to do it the hard way and tell your CO that you picked something up from the site?*'

Jenny's mind was in a whirl. *Blackmail!* There was a lot more to her caller than she'd initially suspected.

'I shall be in Derry, tomorrow – Saturday,' she said at last. 'Can you wait until then? I could meet you at The Shaun Hotel … about seven in the evening.'

'Good girl. We'll discuss things then, okay? Oh, and take good care of that little find of yours … I wouldn't talk to any stranger I might meet, no matter how innocuous they appear. The one who is after you is a very dangerous man. All right?'

Bewildered, Jenny agreed. *It's anything but all right, though*, she thought miserably as she walked back to the gate where Don awaited her reappearance.

'Hi there. That guy was telling me what the transport is like around here. I told him I'd have liked to show you over the sub on Sunday, and he said how difficult it was getting to Londonderry, especially on a Sunday. He said he'd willingly give you a lift.'

Jenny thought of the warning she had just been given. Come to think of it, both men were complete strangers, and both of them appeared completely innocuous. But Don couldn't be the one she had been warned against, she decided. He was too patently open and above board wanting to please her. But the other one? Why should he be so interested in offering her a lift? On the other hand, wasn't it natural if Don had done him a service? And it wasn't as if she *wouldn't* like to see a submarine – and an American one at that. Making her mind up that she was being silly to object, she agreed. They needed a place to rendezvous, though. At the moment, the *Chimera* was still in the lough and Don didn't know which berth she'd be in until it docked the following evening.

'I'm still new to 'Derry, but would a hotel called The Shaun be all right? We could meet in the foyer?' Jenny said.

'Yeah, sure, that sounds great.'

'And if you're in the lough tomorrow, I'll look out for you,' she told him. 'I shall be dinghy sailing.'

Bea appeared with Abe in tow.

'Time we were in, my chick,' Bea said briskly with a veiled look that signalled she wanted Jenny's compliance without argument.

Abe's disgruntled 'Aw, Bea, baby' made Jenny smile a little. It was quite something to guess that the redoubtable Bea had met her match that evening and wanted rescuing.

'Phew,' breathed Bea when she and Jenny were safely inside the gates and waving off their new friends. 'Thanks, Jen, you're a real pal. A clinch with Abe's like an all-in wrestling match without the referee. Hope I didn't spoil it too much for you.'

'Don's nice,' she said evasively.

Bea nodded. 'So you're seeing him again – good-oh. Aren't you glad now that I made the intros?'

Jenny quelled a surge of exasperation into one of mild protest. 'It's not my way of going on, Bea.'

'I know that, dumbbell. Why else would Aunty Bea need to take a hand? You'd have never done it for yourself.'

CHAPTER SEVEN

I spy, you spy

Jenny's feeling that there was a lot more to Mary Little than flying saucer investigation was correct. Mary was an extremely clever woman. She had to be. To the Americans she was someone they had planted in the Russian secret service, and to the Russians an agent they had succeeded in infiltrating into the British Ministry of Intelligence.

Leaving aside the question of which government actually held her allegiance, it was MI5 who had hurriedly despatched her to Northern Ireland.

Speed being of the essence, Mansett had worked fast. His report, categorised and labelled top secret and urgent had been encoded, telexed, decoded and digested on reaching its appropriate addressee by five-thirty that evening. In that quarter it was taken that the Russians – or the Americans – had lost an experiment and Mary was on the first available aircraft from the nearest service airfield to land at RNAS Derry Down by seven-thirty that evening. Her assignment: to nail the missile's origin and to supply, if possible, the place for a curious piece of jigsaw with a bird watcher on it.

She could have made herself known to Mansett as soon as she arrived, it being his airfield, but her immediate instructions were to keep an appointment in Londonderry at The Shaun Hotel, where a reservation had also been made for her to stay.

When she found just who it was waiting for her in the lounge, it was evident that the stops were out on both sides of the Atlantic.

Gene 'Legion' Gauss was one of the most brilliant agents she had ever had the fortune – or misfortune depending on circumstance – to come across. Geologist, botanist, mineralogist and psychologist, he was also a consummate actor; effacing himself so completely in whatever role he was playing, it had been said of him that his name was Legion and it had stuck. That evening, it was a faded nondescript looking remnant of humanity that identified itself as her contact in the guise she had been told to look for. She recognised him with the slightest of shivers. She neither liked nor trusted the man. She knew Gauss could probably say he felt the same way about her. She knew he had an immense respect for her, even if of the kind that the male tarantula is seen to hold for the female of the species. One admired the lady tremendously, took care to hold her powerless while in contact, and kept an avenue of escape for a quick getaway.

There was none of this caution apparent in his manner, however, unless it be noted that he did prefer keeping to his own brand of cigarettes, and both played their exchange of information strictly tit for tat.

They had the place to themselves, so he gave her his description of the site of the incident. She then gave him what she thought fit of Mansett's report.

He listened to the account of the bird watcher without even the ghost of a smile, and Mary had to remain guessing. The role of the bird watcher could have, and just as easily not have been Gene. And looking at him at that moment, she found it difficult to credit even the legendary ability of 'Legion' with the kind of histrionic performance described by Mansett.

In turn, Gene offered his own finding of at least one, possibly two, visits to the site prior to Mansett's and his own. Having got there himself ahead of the Captain, he said he had been able to photograph two separate sets of shoe prints in the ash deposit and, in particular, a disturbance that meant something had been removed.

From what Mary told him, one set of prints were obviously those of the young woman who had originally found the site. So what, he asked Mary, had the girl found of takeaway value?

Mary categorically denied that there had been any such find mentioned in the report. 'Perhaps the second pair of prints?' she suggested, 'Or the bird watcher?'

'They were male,' he conceded. 'So possible. How about the pilot?'

At that point, Mary decided a telephone call to WRNS quarters at Derry Down was next in priority. She said nothing of it to Gene, though, merely excusing herself for a moment before disappearing into the foyer.

When told that Jennifer Howard had gone 'ashore', Mary played extreme disappointment, saying she had some very important news for Wren Howard. Had anyone any idea where she might be? The on-duty wren told her she had just seen Jenny and another girl in the company of two US Navy men going up the lane towards the YMCA. She gave Mary the phone number.

However, on replacing the receiver, Mary made no attempt to try the number she had been given, but paused in reflection. If the 'flying object' was American, then what she had just heard would be a most artless way of returning whatever 'it' was the girl had found to its country of origin. But where did that leave Gene? Could it be that the right-hand of US Naval Intelligence was ignorant of what the left-hand was doing? She hardly thought so. If, on the other hand, the thing was Russian, then the girl and the Americans were all suspect …

'If I were you,' she told Gene on her return to the still empty lounge, 'I'd run a spot top security check on whatever naval base I had around here … it could be in for one helluva leak.'

'Thanks.' he said. 'And who did you call?'

'WRNS quarters in Derry Down,' she said. There was no need for her to be more explicit. Her call could have concerned only one person, of whom they not only already had their suspicions, but now appeared to be in contact with the only US Navy personnel in the area: namely those of the highly secret and experimental USS *Chimera*.

Mary retrieved her gloves and handbag. 'You find the man,' she told him. 'I'll look after the girl.'

*

Gene made a gesture that she was welcome to the girl, although in reality she was anything but … only that was his secret. He had no real explanation just then for the UFO itself, but he did know that the missile that had caused its annihilation was American.

He had been let in on Project Jump at a deeper level than had been thought either wise or necessary at the start, but the agent had to be given some idea of what to look for and why.

The two civilians who were mainly responsible for the project – a Harvard University scientist and a ballistics expert on loan to the Office of Naval Research, and on board the USS *Chimera* – had explained the discovery of a material with incredible properties. It had been found capable of absorbing immense quantities of electrical energy at enormously high potential, without discharging it to whatever else was in the vicinity, and then at a particular level to displace itself from point A to point B in the blink of an eye.

Its uses were still experimental and somewhat limited by the adverse effects it had been found to have on anyone in the proximity of its final state. As these ranged from momentary amnesia to more severe physiological disturbances, it was confined for the present to unmanned experiments such as Project Jump. This had been set up to explore the pros and cons of delivering a missile, which could be neither seen nor tracked in flight, to a target where it would arrive before anyone could stop it … except that in this instance it seemed something *had* intervened. An object had appeared out of nowhere travelling at great speed to meet their projectile at the moment it had also appeared, resulting in a head-on collision. Gene's most fervent hope was that the cause had not been Russian.

He was shown the radar plot with two blips appearing simultaneously three miles apart on perfectly matched reciprocal courses and the cine-assessment film shot at the same time that had recorded their meeting and merging in a mass of incandescence, resulting in the complete disintegration at ground level – the site of which Gene had seen for himself.

He was chary, however, of trusting what he had seen on the film. The whole thing teased him with a similarity to something he could not quite pin down in memory, but he would have been quite happy to swear that, so far as the hardware was concerned, no more than their own missile was involved. It was what had caused the split that troubled him.

Mary's information came like the offering of a new piece of jigsaw that might yet make sense out of opposing nonsense. The wren was now vital. Whatever she had found could be the very key he was looking for.

At that time, however, it was more than imperative that he followed the lead he had been given back to the *Chimera* and to rest easy that it would be as difficult for Mary to abduct the girl at that time of night as it would be for himself. Unless, of course, Mary had simply set him to chase his own tail.

It was a chance he had to take, and would still have taken even if he had known Mary would be far nearer success after her second telephone call that evening than he was to be for quite some time himself.

CHAPTER EIGHT

Togs and talk

Normally as soon as Jenny's head touched the pillow she was asleep, but that night her mind churned with questions. One of the girls had a copy of the evening paper, but there was nothing in it concerning the flying saucer or herself. This was even more disquieting than if there had been. Who was this 'Mary Little' who knew so much about her that she could threaten her with lies and with the Captain? And who was the man she had been warned against?

It was worrying and uncomfortable, and it wasn't as if there was anyone she could turn to. She had picked up a crystal shoe which had nothing to do with the flying saucer, and brought all this upon herself.

When she eventually got to sleep, she had a nightmare of being chased through the woods by the bird watcher. She could not see him, but knew he could see her because the shoe she was carrying was as bright as an electric light bulb that she could neither turn off nor hide. Then she tripped and fell, and the bird watcher caught her, only it wasn't a man at all but a faceless woman who kept whispering something to her that she could not hear, although she knew it was terribly important that she should hear and understand what the woman was saying.

After such a disturbed beginning to her night's rest, she was in a sound sleep when Bea shook her awake the following morning.

'What's up?' she said in muffled indignation. 'We're not on duty.'

'So much for vain dreams, my girl,' said Bea, whipping sheet and blankets smartly to the foot of the bed. Jenny shot up, pulling them back, then paused in doubt at the sight of Bea thumbing the door over her shoulder.

'But we're not …' she wailed.

'Oh, but we are,' said Bea. 'There's a delivery of new aircraft. They're flying in this forenoon and it's our watch.'

Jenny groaned. How was she to let Perry know? She couldn't ring this time of morning. Despair engulfed her at the thought of his turning up at the gate and finding her not there. He might not come back.

'Oh, come on, kiddo. It's only for a couple of hours or so. We'll be back before lunch, even, I dare say.'

'But I'm expecting someone at ten. He's taking me sailing and I was so looking forward to it.'

'For crying out loud, all you've got to do is leave a message at the gate,' Bea pointed out. 'You can't help it if you're on duty. He'll wait, won't he?

Jenny dared not confess that she was afraid he might not. She could just imagine Bea's scornful response that no man was worth getting *that* het up over. She therefore left a message in an envelope at the gatehouse, addressed to Nance.

What with Bea being offhand and Jenny's worry and disappointment – which made her silent and withdrawn – they hardly spoke the rest of the morning. The silver lining to this cloud, however, was not having to explain to Bea why she was stopping off at sick bay on the way back for her clothes. They were clean and dry, even if looking somewhat the worse from whatever kind of treatment they had been put through.

Enquiring at the gatehouse if there had been any call for her, she was given back the envelope she had left there still unopened – something more to think about. Back in quarters she tried to hot-press her clothes into some kind of reasonable appearance, foregoing dinner in case Nance arrived in the middle of it.

Her restless alternation between her bed space and the door to look down the road, hoping for some sign of the blue jalopy, was bound to raise comment sooner or later. And it did: first in an exchange of knowing winks between her immediate neighbours, Babs and Dillys, then with teasing observations. So far no one in the hut knew who her new boyfriend was, but it was evident that he had her on tenterhooks. By half-past one it was also apparent she had been stood up, which caused the subject to be abandoned in sympathetic silence, making it worse.

Ten minutes later, however, the door flew open to admit a girl who could not forbear shouting the exciting news down the whole room.

'Guess what, girls! Jenny's unknown – he's an officer!'

Jenny blushed to the roots of her hair, but even in the wonderful profundity of relief she felt, at not having been stood up after all, she was aware of a scandalised hush that that descended on the Debs. The immediate and unmerciful but good-natured ribbing that broke out was abruptly cut short by Claire's raised voice.

'Good God! Does she really imagine she can go out with an officer looking like that? I do think she might have put something decent on, don't you, Chloe?'

One could have heard a pin drop in the silence that descended, while Jenny, only too aware of her appearance, wished the floor could have opened up and swallowed her. Bea, hitherto wordless and laying flat on her bed reading, laid the book aside with careful deliberation and rose to her feet.

'Come on, Jen,' she said, 'Thought you were going sailing?' Her remark at least vindicated Jenny's attire if it didn't do much else.

'Gosh!' squealed Dillys, 'Wish you had told me. I know you've not had time to get those things cleaned properly, and I've the dreamiest roll neck sweater I'd have insisted on your borrowing.'

Babs jumped to her feet. 'Well, get it out, then. Don't leave the girl waiting. And my new blue slacks are just the thing to go with it.' And promptly rooted in her locker to produce them.

Jenny was left with no alternative but to submit to the chivvying. A few minutes later, and feeling highly self-conscious, she was sent forth clad in a pale blue jersey, navy slacks with a knife-edge crease, and her head wrapped in a gaily coloured 'kerchief, with much laughing advice and instruction.

*

Ten minutes may not seem a long time, but having expected Jenny at the gate by the time he turned the car round, it was long enough for Nance to begin wondering if it was not deliberate on Jenny's part for his late arrival. Since the delay had been caused by his being summoned before his CO to meet some visiting brass hat who confronted him with a newspaper article, his quick temper was ready to flare. Such behaviour was not something he was going to take from Jenny as she was. He was on the point of pressing this point home by driving off, when she came in sight – and he blinked. Her trim, smart appearance was certainly something worth waiting for. This, along with the wait, suggested a startling overnight development in self-possession. He found it hard to credit, but did so in the profound belief that he himself had somehow inspired it.

The last thing Nance then wanted was to hear was any apology from her. He was not only given one, as she climbed into the beside him, but treated to a description of the furore his arrival had caused:

'... All I had were those things I'd just collected from sick bay, and Claire was outraged to think I was going out with an officer dressed as I was. But Babs and Dillys were bricks. As soon as they realised, they made me change into these things between them.'

It was an eye-opener for Nance. He thought he knew Claire. It was a shame the girl hadn't found it in her to quietly do the right thing herself, even if her remark had at least inspired the others to rally round.

Making no comment, he half turned to reach into the back seat for a newspaper which he dropped in her lap. 'Seen this?' he asked.

It was that morning's edition and carried the banner headline: *Flying saucer lands in Eire*. He watched her scan the article quickly, but there was nothing in it about her, the Captain or the CPO. The article set only the scene of destruction and some opinions on what on what might caused it.

Having allowed her time to absorb it, Nance went on: 'What happened, for heaven's sake? I was called in for a session with the Old Man this morning – which is why I'm late, by the way. He didn't say much, probably because there was a brass hat present, but I rather gathered he expected this to break. About all I got was a grilling from the brass hat and an unofficial pat on the back for my initiative in investigating something I didn't believe existed.' He could have added that Captain Mansett had spoken in even higher praise of Jenny's initiative in the matter, but left that out for the time being. 'Well, come on,' he urged, 'I'm dying to know the details.'

As Jenny told him about their encounter with the bird watcher, Nance creased up. He laughed so much he was in danger of running the car off the road.

'Jennifer, Jennifer!' he chortled, wiping his eyes as he envisioned his Captain's embarrassment. 'I'd have given a month's pay to have seen it! God, what a story … and I can't breathe a ruddy word of it! He must have been absolutely livid.'

'I can't see why you should think it so funny,' said Jenny.

He glanced at her. 'Never mind, my sweet, you wouldn't understand.' He chuckled again. 'But believe me; I'd have given anything to have been there.'

They were quiet for a time, and then Jenny said, 'Pen, I hope you won't mind something I've let you in for tonight?'

He looked at her with a grin. 'Depends what it is. I can usually go a basinful of what most people do at night.'

'This is serious,' she said. 'This woman rang. She said her name was Mary Little and she was doing research into flying saucers. She said she had read an account of my sighting in the evening press last night, and asked me for an interview. I reckon that bird watcher was even craftier than we thought for her to identify me so quickly. I told her I wasn't allowed to talk to the press without permission. And then she said I was quoted. Quoted! I ask you? And I've not said anything to anyone – 'cept you. And then she starts getting nasty. She said she knew I'd found something at the site and threatened me with telling the Captain. Didn't you tell him about it, Pen?'

'Actually, no,' said her companion. 'I limited the whole thing to what I saw with my own eyes. So what did you say then?'

'I told her I could meet her at The Shaun Hotel tonight, about seven. I didn't tell her that you would be with me. You'll know how to deal with her better than I can.'

'That's rich, getting *me* to protect your find. But don't worry, she might not turn up.'

But Jenny wasn't inclined to be so optimistic. 'Oh, I think she will. She ended by saying that I shouldn't talk to any stranger I might meet, no matter how innocent they might look. She said there's a very dangerous man after me.'

'Well, you're safe for the moment. But then you *are* going to have to tell the Captain.'

When they arrived in Londonderry, he had to find a parking space in the high street near the shop he was after. He had spent some time going over the pros and cons of what he intended doing. While on the one hand he was none too sure of the wisdom of it, on the other there was the promise he had made her the previous morning – as well as his determination to get hold of the shoe. After all, he told himself, if he was successful and the shoe *was* what he suspected, he could certainly recover the expense.

Switching off the engine, he said quietly: 'Now look here, Jennifer, there's something I'd like to do but, as you know, I can't do a lot in the way of walking around. I'd like to have taken you on a good old wander about to get some idea of what you like from a wider selection of places. But since that's out and I have been assured on the best authority that this establishment …' he gestured the dress shop a little further on ' … is the 'tops', I'd like to treat you to something to wear for tonight.'

Jenny stared, open mouthed, then exclaimed: 'But I couldn't possibly. I mean, it's very nice of you, and I hope I've not hurt your feelings, but I couldn't possibly accept. I know I said I hadn't got much in the way of civvies with me, but I can easily borrow something. Besides, my uncle sent me a cheque for my birthday – I can get something with that.'

'No, Jennifer,' he said. 'You see, I asked you out to dinner tonight quite forgetting what you had already told me about the state of your wardrobe. So, as a belated birthday present, I want to make amends, and I'd like to see you in something of that will be your own choice … not somebody else's.'

'I'm sorry, I truly am,' she said, 'but I cannot possibly accept.'

Her refusal hardly surprised him. He would have been shaken if she had said yes.

'Truly cannot?' he asked softly, 'or just a frightened child that can't accept sweets from a stranger?'

'Well, yes, I suppose it *is* a bit like that,' she admitted.

'Yet you've already said that you didn't feel I was a stranger,' he reminded her, going on persuasively, 'I've asked you out with me tonight and you need something to wear. It's as simple as that, and it would give me great pleasure to present you with it.'

'I don't know what to say,' she answered, helplessly overwhelmed. 'It's very—' He interrupted her with a finger on her lips.

'Just say,' he said, with mock sternness, '"of course, Pen, I wouldn't dream of denying you the pleasure." Come on, say it.'

She giggled, and obeyed. With that settled, he reached for the stout walking stick he had in the back of the car.

When it came to the shopping, however, Jenny was awkward and nervous. He suspected she'd grown up a bit of a tomboy, without a care for clothes, and without the kind of feminine influence which would have helped in this situation. He could tell she was afraid of saying, doing or choosing the wrong thing – especially in front of the shop assistant – so he took the lead and directed her choice.

With his guidance, she chose a light suit in lavender and white dog-tooth check, to which was added a white lacy blouse, court shoes and gloves.

It was with growing exasperation, however, that he either hovered at her back under a growing load of parcels strung on one arm with which he refused any assistance. Regardless of what his motives were, and he dismissed them, he felt piqued at her lack of excitement. Not once had she volunteered an opinion of her own, either of what she did or did not like. To hell with taking his word for it to please him, if only the girl would let herself go and enjoy the opportunity he was giving her. The whole thing was a great strain on them both. Something had to give, and it did when they were back in the car.

Nance asked whether she was pleased – pointing out she had given him very little encouragement to assess her preference

'Yes, thank you very much, everything is really, really lovely,' she said. 'But there is one thing I think you need to understand ...' Nance's eyebrows rose thinking he saw what was coming, only to find himself mistaken. 'with all due respect,' she went on, 'I didn't choose the situation. You insisted on it, *and* took it for granted that I would know how to act in it. But I didn't. I haven't had that kind of upbringing which is embarrassing enough, but the shop assistants knew it. And heaven knows what they must have thought you were up to, or what kind of girl I was.'

'All right, Jennifer, calm down,' he said with a sigh. 'You've made your point.' He nosed the car out into the traffic. 'But you got entirely the wrong idea. The last thing I wanted was to embarrass you … I simply wanted you to enjoy yourself. I rather imagined – mistakenly so, it appears – that we had achieved that kind of understanding before we started. Apparently, you just haven't got what it takes to accept something in the spirit it's given.'

He knew it wasn't true. What was true was his failure to humble himself. But damn it! She simply wasn't his kind. If he thought he was going to get anywhere, he might as well chuck it in here and now for all the progress he was making.

Why had he started it in the first place? It actually took him a moment to remember the shoe, and he realised the girl's personality had taken a deeper hold of him than he imagined. Well, he should put a stop to that now. He should tell the Captain about her precious glass slipper and let him sort it out. Then he realised what it was that was so barbing his thoughts toward her. He had become possessive and could not abide the thought of anyone succeeding where he failed. It was humiliating, but if he was to redeem anything at all from the mess, he was going to have to apologise.

He reached out his hand for hers, while keeping his eyes on the road. She had remained quiet since his speech.

'I'm sorry, Jennifer, I truly am. I've been crass and ignorant. Am I forgiven?'

Of course he was. A quick glance aside showed him Jenny's blue eyes as bright with happiness as a clear sky, and her ingenuous look of adoration went a long way to salving his pride.

He began to thaw more fully when she began asking questions about the dinghy sailing and what would be expected from her.

Nance was glad to be reminded himself, and gave her a general outline of terms she would hear and the particulars of what he would want her to do. A turn in the conversation, however, brought a discussion about the right of way of other craft in the lough – and he remembered the USS *Chimera*.

In common with a number of his friends, he intended to take a closer look at the sub that afternoon – if it surfaced at all – and it had sparked the memory of something he had forgotten.

'Who was that American you were with last night?' he asked.

Jenny coloured. 'Just someone I met.'

'You make a habit of it?' he asked, well aware he was being thoroughly nasty, but needled by a small demon.

'Habit of what?' she said.

'Being picked up by American seamen?'

'That's a horrible thing to say,' she answered in a low voice.

'How would you like me to put it then?' he said. 'You can't associate with men like that and not expect people to think the worst.'

'Well, if that's what you're thinking, you can put me down right here and I'll find my own way back to camp, thank you!' Jenny burst out.

Nance promptly brought the car to a stop. He watched her struggle with the door, then placed his hand firmly over hers, preventing her from opening it.

'Did anyone ever tell you how lovely you look when you're really angry?' he said. Then he was laughing.

'I hate you,' she said vehemently.

'And I think you have an irresistibly attractive spirit,' he said, still chuckling. 'Now sit up and dry your eyes, or we shall be late and the last of the dinghies will be gone.'

'You said something really horrible to me a moment ago,' she reminded him.

'I know, and I apologise hands down. It was pretty beastly, and I can't say fairer than that. You're a sweet girl, and I'm sorry I upset you.'

Things were quite cheerfully happy again by the time they turned in at the boatyard. They were barely out of the car, however, when another drew up alongside and Jenny saw with dismay that one of its occupants was Claire of the Debs trio.

CHAPTER NINE

Tackle and Tactics

If Claire was surprised or annoyed at seeing just who it was that Jenny had nabbed, she did not show it. Ignoring her, she descended on Nance with a little squeal.

'Pen, *darling*, what *have* you got yourself into?' she cried, 'It wouldn't be so bad if it wasn't positively *awful* with the oofuls of official smokescreen that's gone up round you with the discovery of that UFO thingy. You don't know how *relieved* I am to see you in one piece: there are the most awful rumours flying around. And then nobody, but nobody could say where you disappeared to this morning, except you were seen in the vicinity of the CO's office. We thought you were lost to us forever. Isn't that true, George?' She turned to a rather moon-faced man in yachting attire who had joined her.

He nodded, clapping Nance on the shoulder. ''Lo, Perry, old man. Claire's perfectly right, you know. Damn glad to see you're still with us. Lord knows what's going on. Sun wasn't over the yardarm this morning before your name was unmentionable, your movements under suspicion and you nowhere to be seen. Where on earth were you? Ted couldn't find you anywhere.'

'Thank the Lord for that,' said Nance. 'It's gratifying to know that no one has a complete list of my haunts. Actually my route lay from the CO straight ashore via sick bay … although I fail to see why no one could elucidate that simple itinerary from a sprained ankle and the desire – well voiced as I remember – to Edward to do a spot of the old heave ho—'

'Oh, you poor lamb,' interrupted Claire, spying his foot. 'How *did* you do it?'

'Well, darling ...' Nance beckoned her to him with a quick conspiratorial glance round, '... if you promise not to breath a word?' Claire nodded, her head close to his, eyes agog. Hand to mouth, Nance confided in a stage whisper, 'I slipped on the bath mat.'

While Claire giggled in disbelief, Nance steered the conversation off-course by shading his eyes at the sight of a short, dark-haired man approaching from the boathouse.

'Do my eyes deceive me,' he murmured, 'or is that really dear old Ham back off leave, already?' Raising his voice, he called out, 'Hello there, Hammy! What happened? Wouldn't she ...? Or wasn't the sport good enough?'

'More likely the latter,' growled George Broome. 'As it always will be while he insists on thrashing the water to a fine lather and scaring the fish for miles.'

'Just to provide a little light entertainment, I'll pretend I heard that remark, George,' said Norman Hamble reaching them. Nodding a greeting to Claire his eyes came to rest on Jenny with an enquiring look. 'Excuse me, but surely we met last evening?' The remark made Nance glance at her quickly, but Jenny looked blank, which evoked a chortle from George, who turned to Nance.

'You've got to hand it to the old Turk, Perry – he never fails to open with a fast one.'

Ignoring the gibe, Hamble raised an eyebrow at Jenny. 'I'm sure I'm not mistaken,' he said. 'You were with an American.'

Jenny coloured as the penny dropped. 'Of course,' she acknowledged. 'I do apologise: the gentleman on the motorbike with the kitten. I don't know how I could have forgotten.'

'D'you hear that,' said George, while Nance stared again at Jenny. 'What have you been up to, Hammy?'

'First things first, old boy,' Hamble insisted, and looked at Nance. 'Come on, Pen; where are your manners? I still haven't been introduced.'

'I wasn't exactly given the impression it was needed,' said Nance sourly. 'However, this is —'

But Claire, who had no intention of having to acknowledge Jenny, walked off, calling back to George.

'Oh, come on, *do*, George … unless you intend standing there all afternoon; in which case I shall take the thing out myself. I'm perfectly capable of doing it, you know.'

'Believe she would, too,' muttered George. ''Scuse me – see you fellows later.' He hurried after her with a passing wave to a man smoking a pipe who was coming to join them.

Nance introduced him to Jenny as Edward Rye-Smith who at once recognised Jenny's name.

'Ah, the UFO spotter,' he said. 'Perry told me he had made your acquaintance —' he broke off, regarding his pipe with disgust. 'Bally thing. That's the fifth time it's gone out.'

'New, is it?' divined Hamble.

'My first,' he confessed. 'Present from dear Great Aunt Matilda, so I've just got to be "with it" by the time I next see her.'

'Takes breaking in,' said Hamble, 'be all right in a fortnight or so.'

Nance sniffed cautiously. 'What on earth have you got in it, Edward: Dead Sea Twist? It'll kill you.'

'Think it already has,' Edward said ruefully. 'Had to get the thing started somehow, and George offered his favourite "Three Nuns".' He put the pipe away. 'But back to the point – I suppose you have seen today's papers? Would I be wrong in assuming the news might have something to do with the CO's sudden and overwhelming desire for your company this forenoon?'

'You wouldn't,' replied Nance. 'He pointed out that it might put an entirely different slant on things if the Eire authorities substantiate the report … pending which he's postponing the enquiry and having me flown to London tomorrow afternoon for a thorough overhaul on Monday.'

Nance spoke quietly and neither of the other two made any joking comments. Their colleague's predicament was now common knowledge and its threat to his career too close to disaster for ribbing. It was also apparent from the others who had joined them that Nance was popular with his fellow officers, and their unspoken sympathy made him the centre of attention.

Jenny, who had neither part nor place in their easy familiarity, soon lost track of their conversation when it turned to an enthusiastic discussion of the merits and performance of a new dinghy that the club had acquired. Left to herself she fell into absent observation of Norman Hamble. It was clear that he came from a different background to the rest. His self-possessed and lively personality combined a warmth and vigour with boyish enthusiasm in contrast to the others, whose laidback attitudes reflected vague contempt. Its effect on Hamble, however, was water off a duck's back. He caught Jenny looking at him and gave her a wink.

She was startled out of her reverie in time to hear Rye-Smith say, 'Well, what are we waiting for, then? Where is she?' at which the group went off to view the new addition to the *Fairy Class* sailing dinghies they had been discussing. This left Jenny with the alternative of either trailing after a fraternity deep in its particular interest, or staying where she was until collected. It wasn't even as if there was another girl with them she could have accompanied. Claire and George were already aboard their boat, the *Fairy Dancer*.

Hamble, who had disappeared with someone else over the quayside to crew the *Fairy Mantle*, reappeared a moment later and shouted to her.

'Here: catch!' He threw the end of a rope to her. 'Hold tight.'

She felt a strong tug as he disappeared into the dinghy again, then swung himself up on the concrete ledge to take it from her with a friendly grin. 'Well, are you coming? Tupper and I could do with an extra hand for'ard.'

She excused herself with a vague apology of commitment to Nance. Hamble dismissed it out of hand.

'Don't worry about him,' he laughed, taking her arm. 'We can be twice around the lough by the time he gets his nose out of the *Fairy Gleam*.'

'Hamble!' They turned to see Nance hobbling towards them as fast as he could. 'Lay off this instant, you lecher, or you'll find my armament outclasses yours any day!' And waved his stick in demonstration.

'Oh, 'Scuse me and all that,' said Hamble in mock despair, 'my cue for exit stage right. See you Sunday.' And had dived for his dinghy almost before she saw him go.

He might have been joking with Hamble, but Nance was clearly angry with Jenny as he practically pushed her back the way he had come.

'Why are you mad at me?' she asked.

'Mad? Furious would be a better description. Why the hell weren't you with us, instead of making me look like one fool in pursuit of another?'

'But you went off and left me! How was I to know what to do, or how long you'd be? I thought you'd gone to look at a new boat.'

'If you'd been paying attention to what was said, you'd have known we're sailing her – not looking,.'

He led her to where the dinghy lay rocking gently alongside the quay. On the edge stood a rating with a boathook, patiently waiting and listening to three of his superiors who were engaged in an animated chat with Rye-Smith in the boat below.

'… denied he was out of touch with the rank and file,' one was saying. 'It was the rank and file who were out of touch with him!' He turned to greet Nance. 'Hello, old man, so you rescued her all right from the handy Hamble, did you?' He turned to Jenny, 'Narrow escape there, m'dear … attracts women like flies.'

'And who wants women like flies?' quipped the second man, giving Jenny an appreciative look. 'No, Hammy's one of the best, really. It's just that maidens should take an old Arab proverb to heart where he's concerned: "If a stone falls on an egg, alas for the egg. If an egg falls on a stone, alas for the egg."' The straight face with which this was delivered brought a roar of laughter from the others; even the rating permitting himself a faint smile.

'That's the best I've heard Hammy summed up yet,' chuckled the first. 'Know what? I once lent him a biography of Oscar Wilde. He returned it with the comment that that the man really should have been a Christian.'

Feeling a need to defend Hamble in his absence, Jenny said, 'I don't think you can have understood what he meant. I believe Mr Hamble must have meant that if Oscar Wilde had been a Christian he would have understood St Augustine's meaning when he said, "Love God and do as you like" because Wilde believed in absolute freedom …'

she trailed off, seeing they were all staring at her: Nance in astonishment, but also with a wince when she said 'Mr Hamble'.

'Which, as I've always maintained,' said one of them, 'really goes to show there must be nine-tenths of Ham below the surface to the bit we see —'

He was cut short by the first man shouting to Rye-Smith. 'Steady on there, Smithy. In case you haven't noticed it, that's a brand new suit of sails: you can't set 'em that far yet.'

'And if *you* didn't need your eyes testing, Duggie, you'd see I'm not trying to,' retorted the man in the dinghy. 'You might be in charge today, but we're not all idiots.' Then to Nance, 'For heaven's sake, Perry, can we get under way before I commit murder?'

'He can't go aboard here,' Duggie pointed out authoritatively, before shouting, 'Take her down alongside the slipway, Smithy —'

'Nuts,' said the man nearest Nance with a quick signal to the third man to take their lame duck between them. 'Jeremy and I can swing him over.'

'Like hell you will,' swore Nance, 'I'm quite capable …' but he was seized bodily and lowered away.

In the effort it seemed to Jenny as if all three were in danger of ending up in the water. A life jacket was then thrown to Rye-Smith for Nance. Jenny was also given one and strapped into it before being handed a little more gently by Jeremy and his companion down to join Nance and Rye-Smith in the boat. She took a seat in the bow. Nance had already told her that she could take charge of the jib sheet, and to 'mind her head' whenever he ordered the boat to come about.

Rye-Smith sat by the mainsail near Nance at the tiller, and signalled the rating to cast off. The resultant cheers were soon lost on a freshening sou' sou' west breeze which sent them dancing over the choppy, sun-flecked water. Nance sailed as close to its wind as possible without allowing the edge of the sail to flutter.

'It's known as close-hauling,' he yelled up to Jenny. 'See you keep the jib the same way.'

Jenny was enchanted. Green she might be, but there was nothing to be afraid of or find puzzling about this. It was easy enough to keep the jib, or foresail centre, without its edge 'luffing' – or fluttering.

When Nance gave warning of his intention to cross the wind, she ducked as he put the helm down and she let fly the jib sheet, or rope, allowing the boom to cross above her head as she dived for the other side. The dinghy came around quickly, the mainsail going over at the same time with Rye-Smith ducking across, while Jenny pulled her sail close to luff up on the new course, or tack. The manoeuvre brought an exchange of approving glances between the two men. Their new crewman was no passenger. Their craft was fairly skimming the surface as Nance allowed himself to reach further into the wind.

A moment later, Hamble, with his crewman Tupper, in the *Fairy Mantle* was astern and hailing them with a challenge to race. Nance accepted, and the two dinghies made for a cone buoy as a start point, while Rye-Smith set the newly stretched sails far nearer their true marks.

From the buoy the two craft separated rapidly as each helmsman sought the wind according to its advantage, and Jenny became conscious of a change in Nance and Rye-Smith. Plainly there was no room for errors or mucking about when honour was at stake. The challenge was deadly serious and the race pursued with ruthless concentration. Its enjoyment could wait for the mulling of a post mortem afterwards.

The quickest way up the lough was to run before the wind; it was also the most difficult and dangerous. Let the helmsman allow the wind across his stern and there would be no time for warning: the least any crew could expect was to escape with badly bruised heads. The lie of the land, with valley and mountain on the port side and the sweep of the headland to starboard, was also a force to be reckoned with when they came abreast of it with the possibility of an unforeseen pattern of wind lying in wait.

The difference in character between the helmsmen of the two craft soon became apparent. Although both were fairly racing through the water with exhilarating speed, Hamble was three or four lengths ahead. Like a bull at a red flag, and probably because he was more familiar with the performance of the *Fairy Mantle* than Nance could allow himself with the untried *Fairy Gleam*, he turned first, fast and far too quickly for safety – and got away with it. All the same, if Nance's finer judgement and finesse had little to play with on the straight, his skilful handling and tacking into the wind once they had made the turn soon ate up the distance between them. Taking it steady, easing round and bringing the helm over while the dingy still had way, he sent her flying along at knots on her ear, gaining vital length. Hamble's charges, however, often brought him too far over before being able to luff up on his new course.

Jenny's admiration for Nance, little though she could yet appreciate the finer points of his seamanship, was boundless as she and Rye-Smith dived from side to side, feet pressing under the seats, to lean out against the strengthening wind. It was backing to west-nor-west and covering them with a fine spray one moment, only to be dried by a sun that still held warmth despite a swiftly darkening sky.

Nance had his eye on that change in the weather. It could spell disaster with its promise of sudden gusts. Hamble was also keeping his eye on it. It was not surprising, however, that Nance should meet it with rather more prudence. His sight of a dark scuffle racing across the water towards them caused him to prefer risking a loss of way by bringing the *Fairy Gleam* back close to the wind, than waiting until it struck.

If Hamble saw it, he did not take the same precaution. He held his course, and signalled his crewmate to let fly the mainsheet a split second too late … and over they went.

It happened so suddenly that Jenny could hardly believe her eyes. The *Fairy Mantle*'s graceful career was over. Like some great butterfly abruptly sucked to a watery end, she lay on her side, the hitherto beautiful taut stretch of her sails now no more than a limp bedraggled mass of cloth awash on the surface.

Jenny's gasp of dismay nearly meant her own disaster. She almost failed to hear Nance's yell in time before he came about to the rescue, and only just missed a stinging blow to the side of her head which could have floored her. Fortunately the other two had their attention on Hamble and Tupper, and missed her carelessness. By the time they reached them, Hamble had swum round to the keel and clambered on his dinghy's centreboard, and joined a moment later by his companion's weight, the sails began to lift. Jenny could hardly believe that such a load of sodden material could ever respond, but it did. Slowly, then suddenly, as the two breathless men crawled inboard over its lifting side the dinghy was righted.

Nance, knowing the once capsized the craft could keep going over, kept pace as Hamble close-hauled the wind to near starvation while his companion bailed furiously. It was a leisurely progress back in contrast to the excitement of their going, with a good deal of banter between the two boats, and Hamble giving back as good as he got.

The weather being bad, it was almost inevitable that the *Fairy Mantle* should capsize again, which it did as soon as Hamble tried to ease it a little more to the breeze. Yet even as the craft heeled, Nance cried out, 'Lee-oh', and veered suddenly to give place to a long grey shape that rose unexpectedly between them and the *Fairy Mantle.*

It was the *Chimera*: huge, sleek and powerful, and barely above the waves before Hamble and his crewman were being taken aboard, and other round, white-capped sailors quickly righted the dinghy, furled its sails and attached it with a tow line to their own vessel.

The speed of the unexpected intervention, and neatness of the operation, left the onlookers speechless.

Nance recovered first. 'Well, I'll be damned! Aren't we safer in the lough now, than tucked away in our lily-white hammocks aboard our unsinkable stone frigates?' he said bitterly.

'What on earth's biting you, Perry?' asked Rye-Smith. 'They'd never have made it back under their own steam. They'd have been up and down like Tower Bridge, and we'd probably have had to call out ASR.'

'I'd rather drown than be taken back like *that*,' said Nance. 'I tell you Edward, this is the last straw; I'll never sail this lough again while those lousy bastards are here, so help me. Can't you just hear them?' He imitated an American drawl. '"Extra lookout today, men, them darn boys is out playing at boats again." It makes me want to throw up. Whose bally lough is this anyway?' He broke off at the sight of Hamble who, after shaking hands with one of his rescuers, was pointing to the *Fairy Gleam*. The American immediately gave them an enthusiastic wave and a hail that was lost on the wind, but evoked prompt recognition from Jenny in the bow.

'It's Don!' she cried returning the wave enthusiastically, full of her ability to recognise and identify a link with their rescuers and quite forgetful of the hostility it would rouse in Nance.

To their helmsman's disgust was now added the barb of jealousy. Nance looked – and felt – murderous.

'Ready about!' he shouted, signalling Rye-Smith to loosen the mainsail. As the dinghy leaped forward past the submarine he cupped a hand at Hamble and yelled: 'That's the spirit, Hammy. And don't forget to say thank you to the nice kind gentlemen. Mustn't let them think we aren't *ever* so grateful, must we?'

'See you later, Nancy boy,' Hamble yelled back cheerfully. 'And thanks for the race. Knew you'd make it: all that native cunning—'

'And about!' snapped Nance to his crew, putting the helm hard over to send them careering before a broad reach of the wind and scudding away from the scene of his discomfort. With the darkening sky and first spots of rain on the wind, he headed for home and dry.

Jenny didn't hear much of Nance's exchange with Rye-Smith above the wind from where she was seated nearly fifteen feet away, but was grateful for the latter's presence. With someone laughing over the affair as Rye-Smith was, it helped restore a balance in which the shattered joy of the afternoon became more bearable.

*

Rye-Smith teased Nance for his ill-humour 'Come on, Perry, we know it's rather like climbing Mount Everest and finding a snack bar at the top, but that's Americans for you. Where's your sense of humour? Ham will dine out on this for months —'

'It's not that at all,' Nance interrupted. 'It's this high-handed attitude of theirs that gets me. I ask you, Edward, wouldn't Ham have blasted off at us if *we* had so summarily taken him in without so much as a by-your-leave or a "like a hand, old man?" You know damn well he would, and rightly so. No, we heave-to and keep him company in case things get sticky, but at least pay him the compliment of presuming he's capable of getting back by himself. But not these Yanks. We don't know what we're doing and have to be rescued whether we like it or not.'

'Don't talk wet, old man,' said Rye-Smith. 'Granted Ham had no options, but that's what makes it so funny. There he is, in no real danger, but gets rescued willy-nilly by the might of the American Navy. I tell you it's a scream if we can't put a toe in the lough without being in danger of having it "*yanked*" out for salvage! They've no doubt got a lot of keen young aspirants in training all gasping for a chance to prove themselves. Hell, does it matter all that much if they practice on us? I'm damn sure Ham's not grumbling – he's probably guzzling whiskey in the ward room while we have to wait until the bar opens.'

After a moment's grudging silence, Nance threw back his head with a laugh. 'Trust you to cut things down to size, Edward. What say we capsize the *Fairy Gleam* and join him?'

'All for it, old man – only I reckon you've rather loused up our chances of being picked up, now. It'll be, "Let him go, let him tarry, let him sink or let him swim: he doesn't care for us – and we don't care for him, either".'

'Aye, you could be right at that,' agreed Nance. 'Pity, really. I'd rather like the opportunity of meeting a certain party and hanging one on his nose.'

'Good lord! What on earth for?'

'A stitch in time, you might say. You've heard what the American matelot is like. Well, a warning shot across the right bows to keep its distance from my affairs now could save a lot of trouble later.' His gaze shifted to Jenny.

'I say, old man,' Rye-Smith lowered his voice on seeing the look. 'You're never serious about her, are you?'

'One doesn't have to be serious before one can be fastidious, Edward. I like the girl; she's a good kid. I simply prefer she stays that way, and since I'm aware of the danger she's in, I feel a certain responsibility in the matter.'

'And you're prepared to mix it with this American purely out of a platonic concern for a young girl's morals? Most creditable – if it were credible, Perry. You only met her yesterday. How do you know you're not too late, anyway?'

'It had better not be, that's all.' Nance's mouth set in a grim line.

'You'll pardon my horse laugh if it is, and you knock him for six and then find he isn't the guilty party. The girl's a wren, old man, and charity, they say, begins at home – especially that kind. What's wrong with you? Only the other day you were saying, and I can quote you verbatim: "Perhaps I'm cynical but out of the 350-odd girls on this station alone, I wouldn't rate the number of virgins higher than can be counted on the fingers of one hand." You're probably dead right, but you don't have to look further than your own navy to account for that state of affairs.

'If you're so keen on starting a one-man crusade to preserve the few, I'd advise you to lock 'em up in tin pants before sallying forth to deal with American windmills. No, Perry, I know you too damn well to be bamboozled by an attitude like that. And what's more, I'm not sure that I don't take exception to it. Your interest is your own affair, of course, but I think I've a right to a little more honesty from you than being fed a load of codswallop, especially when I'm damn sure your intentions can't be honourable. Your pursuit of the opposite sex has never yet been platonic – and you can't be considering marriage in this instance – so let's have it on the level – and allow me to remind you that fraternising with the lower decks *is* the quickest way of winning them a draft, *and* PRs noted accordingly.'

Nance brought the dinghy round on another tack before answering. 'Aren't you forgetting I've precious little left to lose, anyway?'

'So you are serious?'

Nance made no reply, so his friend shrugged and changed the subject. 'She's turning out a good little sailor, anyway. What about giving her a turn up here while I take the jib? Give me a chance for another crack at the pipe … there's more peace for'ard.' He got up, stooping to make his way to the bow, when he stopped and pointed the stem of his pipe. 'I say, what's going on? That bally U-boat's cast off the *Fairy Mantle* and submerged.'

'They probably don't think she's worth the salvage money,' said Nance. 'Either that, or Ham and Tupper have asked for political asylum.'

'Look's queer to me.' Rye-Smith shook his head and went over to Jenny. 'I'll take over here, Jennifer,' he said. 'Skip wants you aft. Keep low in the boat, don't stand up.'

Jenny looked none too happy. 'But I won't know how to manage that sail.'

'Nothing to it,' he disagreed. 'Perry'll be right beside you to keep things on course. You can't fail.'

'I'm not so sure,' she confessed. 'I'm bound to do something wrong and Pen can be very scathing.'

'Lord, you don't want to let that worry you. It's just that he's under a bit of a cloud at the moment and has another of his headaches ... I had to cart him down to the MO last evening again. Can't take any chances with that blackout of his. Which reminds me,' he added, taking more tobacco from his pocket, 'Perry pointed you out to me last evening. You two soon got together, didn't you?' The question seemed more of an accusation than an observation.

'Er, if you'll excuse me ...' Jenny started to edge away. 'I'd better be getting down to the other end–'

'No, stay a moment.' his tone took on an underlying authority. 'Perry'll be all right, and I'd rather like a word with you.' He fell silent while he filled the pipe and lit it. 'How long have you been in the WRNS, Jennifer?' he asked at last in between puffs.

'Just over a year now,' she answered.

'Long enough to know what's what, eh?' he observed, flicking the spent match into the sea and lighting another.

'I suppose so, yes. Why?'

'You and Perry. Do I have to dot the i's and cross the t's?'

'Pen asked me to come; why should I refuse?' she replied defensively.

'No reason at all, m'dear,' he said lightly. 'Sailing trip, perfectly all right ... nothing in that.'

'Then why are you saying this?' she asked.

'Well, let's put it like this, shall we – and forgive me it if sounds a little hard – Perry isn't really himself at the moment. I suppose you realise his naval career may very possibly be at an end?' Jenny remained silent. 'It's a possibility, but it just might not happen – one must never give up hope – which is why I'm not prepared to stand by and watch him throw everything overboard–'

'And about!' yelled Nance. They ducked, Rye-Smith taking the jib sheet from Jenny and pulling it home with the half eye and hand of expertise, as Nance called: 'What are you two finding so much to natter about? Have you forgotten I need a hand aft?'

'Right with you, old man,' Rye-Smith called back. He turned back to Jenny. 'In a nutshell, Jennifer, Perry isn't your métier. Don't encourage him.' And nodded her forward.

*

Nance was proving well able to control mainsail and tiller together as he would had his ankle been sound, the only difference being that he was allowing the *Fairy Gleam* only enough wind to enable him to keep his seat without having to go over the side to hold her.

Jenny was overly conscious of Rye-Smith's presence, even though he appeared not to be watching them. Nance asked what his colleague had been talking to her about. Jenny replied truthfully that he had warned her to stay away from him.

'Oh, spinning the yarn that I was a big bad wolf, eh?'

'No. You're an officer, I'm a wren,' she explained simply.

His lips tightened. 'And you intend taking his advice?'

Jenny was caught. All the time there was any hope that Nance himself had no intention of regarding Rye-Smith's advice, she was not prepared to admit that she should take it.

'I don't know,' she confessed.

'What do you want to do?'

'I want to go on, but—'

'No buts,' he said firmly. 'If that's your course, stick to it.'

'What about what Edward said?'

'I rather think that what Edward said is my concern, not yours, and I shall certainly have something to say to him on that score later. So forget it. How did you meet Norman Hamble, by the way?'

Jenny told him, omitting that Hamble had offered her a lift for the Sunday, but earned herself another reproof by referring to him as 'Mr Hamble'.

'Ham, Hammy, Norman, or the bloke on the motorbike,' corrected Nance. 'But not *Mr* Hamble, please.'

The *Fairy Gleam* reached the slipway where Duggie greeted them with concern. 'Fine old Barney you've been having out there, haven't you? What the hell happened?'

'You mean Ham and Tupper being rescued by the American Navy?' replied Rye-Smith. 'Nothing earth shattering about it. All rather neatly done, I thought. Tidy operation.'

'No, I mean the *Fairy Dancer*. Do you mean you didn't see her go over?'

'*Fairy Dancer* … that's George and Claire. Oh, pull the other one, Duggie. George isn't one for sailing on his ear, he's as steady as the Rock of Gibraltar.'

'Wouldn't care to bet on it, would you?'

Rye-Smith waited until Jenny and Nance were both ashore before demanding, 'Right, come clean, Duggie. What's the gen?'

'Message came through from the US patrol that both *Fairy Mantle* and *Fairy Dancer* had capsized and that they had taken the crews aboard but were leaving us to collect the dinghies.'

'You mean they aren't bringing them back?' asked Nance. He and Jenny were out of their lifejackets, and he was reaching for the walking stick Rye-Smith was holding out to him.

'I've got news for you, brother. They aren't bringing back the shipwrecked mariners, either … not until eighteen hundred hours, at any rate.'

'Why on earth not?' said Rye-Smith.

Nance chuckled. 'Sounds as if I was right after all, Edward. Now if you layabouts don't mind, Jennifer and I will push off. Make my excuses for dinner tonight, will you, Edward?'

*

In the car, Nance asked Jenny if she would object to his seeing her mysterious glass slipper that evening, adding, 'I told you I didn't mention it in my report to the Captain,'

'Yes, you did, and thank you. I'd like you to see it.'

'Well, bring it along with you when I pick you up at seven, okay?'

It was getting on for five by the time she eventually got into the hut, and laden with parcels as she was, wondered how she was going to explain them. To her surprise however, her arrival was met by disappointment.

'Didn't you go sailing after all?'

'We were relying on you to fill us in with the latest buzz, Jenny,' complained Dillys. Jenny had to confess ignorance of what they were talking about.

'Well, if you've been shopping, of course you won't know. The Americans have been on the rampage, capsized all our dinghies – '

'Because they got in the way of their manoeuvres,' put in Babs.

'And seized the crews–'

'And you'll never guess what,' Babs again interrupted, 'Claire's one of them.'

Jenny unloaded her stuff on the bed and sat down. 'Trust you lot to get hold of the wrong end of the stick.'

she hooted, and told them what had really occurred. '... but we didn't hear about the *Fairy Dancer* until we got back. That was the one with Claire on board. More than that, I do not know.'

'Well, the way we heard it – from the MSO,' said Dyllis, 'it's nothing short of an international incident! The American Captain has sent our CO a top priority, unclassified signal with an oversize in rockets.'

'Wow!' breathed Jenny. 'I wonder what caused that?'

'Personally, I would imagine it'll be more a case of *who* caused it,' said Babs, with a pointed a look at Claire's bedspace.

'But she would have been with George Broome,' Dyllis objected. 'He'd be the last person to cause an international uproar ...'

CHAPTER TEN

Breach of interservice good faith

The *Chimera*'s Captain, Joseph Dachas, had been inclined to be somewhat annoyed when Gene 'Legion' Gauss had arrived on board the previous evening demanding an immediate security check on his men. The Captain's voice, like the edge of a rasp at the best of times, positively grated in his disgust.

'Hell, they've all been through a fine-tooth comb to even set foot in this fish and cleared to death by your people. If they can't be trusted we'll never have a man who can.' But they both knew he had no choice.

Gene wanted to start with whoever had been ashore that evening. Dachas denied there had been any leave at all, reminding Gauss that they were still in the middle of Lough Foyle. Gene persisted, and two were found to have gone on legitimate detail to Derry Down: the bosun and a photographer.

Before he had them in, Gene went through their papers.

'This guy, Rossini.' He tapped one of the documents almost accusingly. 'He was on USS *Eldridge*.'

'So what?'

'Did you know it was an experimental ship?'

'Sure. So's this, in case you haven't noticed.'

'So what's he do?'

'Like it says,' Dachas nodded, keeping his patience under control. 'The guy's a photographer.'

'So he would be in on the cine-assessment film development for Project Jump?'

'I wasn't informed you were in on that,' said the Captain. 'Your job's security; not technical assessment.'

'I have to know what I'm looking for. Why was he sent to the Royal Naval Air Station at Derry Down?'

'Because they have a pilot who saw the collision; then lost his memory. Initial enquiries by their CO, Captain Mansett, established an anomaly at 11:52 hours: the time the incident took place. The officer in charge of their radar unit reported no bogey, but an inexplicable ten minute displacement of an aircraft was noted and thought to be their equipment at fault. Subsequent checks found nothing amiss. As the only other friendly radar in the area that might be able to substantiate the displacement, Captain Mansett then asked me if we'd had registered anything.'

'So?' prompted Gene.

'So the guy was right. There *was* a displacement of an aircraft. I sent Rossini with a copy of the cine footage—'

'You did what!' Gene almost exploded out of his chair. Dachas smiled, knowing exactly what he was thinking.

'—Suitably edited,' he finished. 'It's called interservice good faith where cooperation, makes for good relations. They won't know it was anything to do with us. Of course, we had the whole thing on radar – but that's *our* business. We were also filming, so it was no big deal to have *Arctic Tern*'s Captain given an edited copy. There's a guy's career at stake here.'

'So what's it show actually happened?'

'There's been no report of any missing aircraft, so the footage we sent them doesn't show one of their aircraft vanishing into thin air: there one moment, gone the next. Just radar records and confirmation of a ten minute blip. If I knew what it all meant, they wouldn't have needed to put you on the job, would they? You say you saw the records; you tell me.'

'Okay,' Gene settled back, 'I'm no mathematician, so we'll ignore the physics of the thing. But our missile was special, okay? No more than a shell, mind you – no warhead, minimum guidance system – but gets itself magnetically displaced from A to B – which is here – without a trajectory. You were to retrieve it from a watery comedown, hence the sub.'

'No, we weren't,' corrected Dachas. 'We were monitoring. A chopper was on standby for retrieval.'

'Whatever.' Gene dismissed him with a wave. 'So what shows up? Not one missile but two … and those two are half the size of the original and equal to it in mass. An aberration, I suggest, caused by a beam of resonating frequency forcing the missile initially into two parts, which are then under as much pressure to reunite as one object, which they do at speed, and *pow!* Annihilation. At the same time anything else flying in the area is affected; that is, the missing aircraft seen on the film could have *jumped* – backwards or forwards in time, I don't know – at least none is reported missing, for which we have to be thankful.

'Now I don't think it needs a mastermind to deduce a spot of constructive sabotage on the part of the Russians,' he went on. 'It's my remit to presume they've learnt about Project Jump, found out our material's peculiarities, capabilities *and* resonating frequency, and so discovered a way to affect it … not by a large difference, it's true as yet – it came down the other side of the lough instead of in it, but that would certainly suit me as a beginning.'

'Yeah, and just how do you figure they'd do that?' Dachas was plainly an non-believer. 'You can't have a man pointing some kind of trigger at something he can't see.'

'If he knew *where* he was supposed to be looking, he could plant the trigger within the parameters he'd been told it might be effective, such as the woods the other side of the Irish border. It doesn't have to be anything large, and he wouldn't have to plant it himself: that vanishing aircraft could have dropped it itself, and promptly disappeared on the rebound.' He shrugged, 'I don't know. What I *do* know is that you had two men ashore last night, one of whom is directly in the know about this.'

Dachas threw up his hands wearily. 'Okay, okay. You get to see them …'

*

The summons puzzled Abe and Don, although they answered Gene's questions readily enough.

Yep, they'd had a couple of hours to kill before they could get transport back to the sub. Yep, they had called in at Derry Down's NAAFI. Yep, they had met a couple of wrens … their names? Sure, Abe had taken up with a Bea somebody – he couldn't remember her surname – and Rossini with the other. Don could remember her name, all right: Jennifer Howard.

The bosun was dismissed, and Gene got to work on the photo-assessor.

Three hours later, Donald was allowed to go; appalled, shaken and sore. Where had he blotted his copybook? He hadn't been through a session like that even when he was being screened before and after the USS *Eldrige*. And over what? Because he had been ashore that evening and met a wren; the very one, apparently, who had seen the disappearance of their project. So what? She had said nothing about it, and he certainly hadn't shot his mouth off. Project Jump was under strictest wraps.

The interrogation had gone on until he was dismissed without explanation for any of it, except to a possible link to the *Eldrige*. Could he ever forget *that*! As a direct effect of the experiments carried out on the ship, a number of her crew had suffered physical ailments, ranging from dizziness and lack of concentration to severe neurological and circulatory disturbances due to the diathermic effects. His own reaction had been nothing serious – or so he had thought up until now when Naval Intelligence seemed to be insinuating a delayed reaction: a possible amnesia that made him a security hazard; that he had somehow kept a prearranged assignation with Wren Howard, about which he could remember nothing.

What would the next thing be? Suspension on medical grounds? Dismissal? Gene's interrogation had reduced him to a wreck.

*

Back in his cabin, Dachas was also somewhat disturbed. His orders were to cooperate with Gauss over the investigation, but it had been asking a lot to stand by and see one of his men taken apart as ruthlessly as Gene had done with Rossini. The agent was relentless. Clinically and analytically, he had got Rossini to spill everything that the man could under a hail of contradiction, innuendo and accusation: every word that had been spoken that evening by the girl Jennifer Howard. He had been merciless, but he could now be reasonably sure that Rossini was in the clear; which was something to be grateful for – as he reminded Dachas.

'I told you my men were clean before you started,' retorted the Captain. 'I'll tell you something else, too. You intelligence guys get so twisted; you can't believe anything could be just as plain straight and simple as you got from Rossini.'

'Gullibility comes expensive in my profession,' said Gene mildly. 'What I'd really like to hear from you is some constructive way of getting hold of the girl.'

Dachas refrained from the ribald comment he was tempted to make, and asked what was wrong with allowing Rossini to go ahead and bring her aboard as the man had proposed. '… but you can think up your own excuse for getting her aside for a heart to heart and body search,' he added.

'*Then* will be too late,' said Gene.

Dachas felt a degree of asperity 'Well, you heard what the guy said,' he reminded Gene. 'The dame's dinghy sailing in the lough tomorrow. Why don't you tell me to go knock a hole in her boat and bring her in for salvage?'

Gene glanced up with interest. 'You could do that?'

Dachas was incredulous. 'No, I blamed well could not, sir!' he said. 'You really take me to be as plumb crazy as yourself?'

'Accidents do happen between sub and surface craft,' Gene pointed out.

'Not under *my* command, they don't.'

*

However, taking the *Chimera* into the lough at periscope depth the following day, Dachas watched the little drama of the *Fairy Mantle's* capsize, and abruptly decided he could perhaps work a compromise for Gene on the basis of a now bona fide rescue operation. It could be the girl's craft, and if not, well, nothing lost, but a precedent set to repeat the operation if necessary. He could get Rossini in on the rescue team to identify her, or which dinghy she was in. The photographer had already been referred to him that day by his First Officer. Not surprisingly, it seemed Rossini had made a number of inexcusable blunders since the commencement of operations that morning. So much so, Commander Trasker had become progressively surprised and deeply concerned about a hitherto utterly reliable crewman.

Dachas had Rossini summoned to his cabin for a private word.

'I suppose it's last evening that's really bugging you?' he asked kindly.

Don admitted it had unsettled him.

'Well, forget it,' Dachas said firmly. 'I can assure you, you're one hundred percent physically and mentally okay in all respects. But you know the drill these days: it's check, recheck and check again. You can't be too careful, but you, the poor sod at the other end, has to take it.'

Dachas outlined his plan, and Don, responding like a wilting plant soaking up fresh water, was more than happy to be part of the rescue detail that Dachas ordered for Hamble and Tupper.

'You said the girl you met would be sailing this afternoon, didn't you?' Dachas reminded him. 'Well, give her a wave, too, if you see her.'

*

Of course, Hamble had recognised Don at once as he assisted him aboard. He held out his hand chuckling, 'Hard lines, old man, your girlfriend's in the other dinghy.'

Don responded promptly with a cheerful wide-armed signal to the indicated craft in which he recognised Jenny, then said to Hamble, 'Captain's compliments, and I'm to escort you below, get your clothes dried and restore your spirits with whatever suits you in ice-cream, thirty-five flavours to choose from.'

'You don't say,' said Tupper in astonishment. 'Thirty-five!'

'Very considerate of him,' said Hamble as he turned to give a thumbs-up to the officer he could see on the bridge.

Once below, out of their wet gear and feeling warm and dry in borrowed jersey, trousers and deck slippers which Donald brought them, Hamble introduced the other half of his crew.

'Charlie Tupper,' he gestured. 'Tup, old man, meet—' The rest of his sentence was drowned by the blare of a klaxon and a man's voice ordering all hands to diving stations.

'Diving!' Tupper's head jerked up in alarm. 'Hey, what about our dinghy?'

Don grabbed hold of a passing sailor to ask what was going on.

'Don't ask. The Captain's acting like a bear with a sore head. Another of them dinghies has capsized. Some guy said the *Fairy Dancer* I think.'

'*Fairy Dancer* – that's George!' said Tupper. 'He took Claire with him, didn't he, Ham?'

The listening navy man gave them a grin. 'Then she must be the dame they're saying caused it,' he said as the speakers hummed again, this time summoning Rossini to the control room. He made his excuses and raced off to find the officer in charge of the rescue team waiting to hand him charge of the other two soaked arrivals.

'Get these stowed, and fast,' he was ordered.

'What about my dinghy?' protested George, as Don bundled him and Claire down a corridor. 'You aren't going to cast it adrift—?'

'Guess we must be!' Donald shouted above the hum of engines and noise level.

Claire was delivered into the care of the medics with apologies from Don that they had no other facility that could be adapted for ladies, and George, a few minutes after drying and changing, met with Hamble and Tupper in the wardroom.

'Hello,' Hamble greeted him with a grin. 'We were told you were on the way. What happened?'

'It wouldn't have if Clare had had her wits about her,' George said. 'Of all the clumsy idiots—' He broke off as his erring partner appeared in the doorway looking rather pink-faced and appealing wrapped in the dry massive thickness of a seaman's jersey and bellbottoms.

'George, I simply can't tell you how sorry I am. But isn't it wonderful the way these gorgeous Americans turned up in the nick of time? I wasn't the least bit scared after seeing the way they dragged Hammy out of the drink.'

'Gorgeous be damned,' swore George. 'What about our boats? That's what I'd like to know.'

'A good question,' came the voice of Dachas, who stooped to enter the room. The three men automatically shot to attention, recognising the insignia of a senior American naval captain. 'My apologies for the somewhat abrupt action, gentlemen. However, I was given little choice. When I picked up Lieutenants Hamble and Tupper, I did so in good faith, believing they were in genuine distress.'

The two named men who were looking at him wonderingly, nodded affirmatively. Dachas went on: 'But I found my action misinterpreted. I was therefore compelled to set the *Fairy Mantle* adrift instead of towing her to shore, as was my original courteous intention. In short, gentlemen, I have a schedule to meet, and have no time to waste on skylarks. Do I make myself clear?'

'Not to me, sir, you don't,' said George. 'I was *not* skylarking.'

'Your craft was not capsized by accident, Lieutenant Broome. It was intentional—'

'Intentional!' George exclaimed.

'—by your companion,' finished Dachas calmly.

'Me?' cried Clare. 'How can you say that?'

'You deliberately rolled the craft in circumstances which you knew would inevitably lead to capsize.'

'But that's absurd.'

'No more absurd than your reason for doing it,' said the Captain. 'No doubt you watched the rescue of the *Fairy Mantle* and decided you would enjoy the same excitement and be entertained on board an American submarine by its obliging personnel, providing yourself with a talking point for days to come.'

'I've never heard of anything so preposterous,' Clare said in obvious confusion.

'Lieutenant Broome will be held responsible for the incident.' Dachas looked at George again. 'This sort of thing has to stop right now. It should not need me to point out that it's dangerous, time wasting and does nothing for our operational needs, to say nothing of relations. I am therefore making an example of the incident and shall be forwarding the facts to your Commanding Officer with the request that it be treated as a breach of interservice good faith.' He looked at their dismayed faces, and added, 'Don't be unduly concerned about your dinghies, gentlemen. I at once advised your people, who will undoubtedly take the necessary steps to recover them. Good afternoon.' He turned abruptly and walked out.

Tupper gave a whistle of dismay. 'This *is* going to raise a stink.'

'He'll never make it stick,' Clare cried, thoroughly alarmed. 'He can't prove that I did it on purpose.'

'Well, at least the dinghies are all right,' said Hamble. 'That's got to be a relief, George.'

'Relief!' George buried his face in his hands. 'I'm trying not to think what our Old Man'll say after he gets this stinger. My name'll be mud.'

'So will Clare's,' said Tupper. 'After all, she's not a novice. She must have known.'

'It *was* an accident,' Clare insisted.

'It wasn't, and you know it!' George turned on her. 'You've been out often enough to know this is no weather to be mucking about in and, dammit, *I'm* the last one to take risks. Now I come to think of it, it *could* only have been deliberate.'

'If you're going to stand there and say such nasty things to me, George, I'll never speak to you again,' Clare said vehemently.

'That's the kindest thing I've heard you say yet. It's me who's in the can, remember? I was skipper. About all you'll get is a reprimand.'

This depressing verdict was greeted with silence. Their spirits weren't lightened by the news they were being kept aboard until six that evening. It seemed an interminable time with nothing to do but sample thirty-five different kinds of ice cream carried by every ship in the US fleet, which was dry. They asked Don if they could be shown around the *Chimera*. He didn't seem very hopeful, but forwarded the request all the same.

Dachas, feeling they had seen enough of his rough side, gave his permission with strict provisos on what they were not to be shown. After all, there was little point in taking it out on them any more than he already had. His little plan had been scuppered simply by the unforeseen hazard of a girl's prankish behaviour.

'Women!' he muttered vengefully to himself. From now on, Gauss could go and chase his own.

CHAPTER ELEVEN

The Importance of Homework

In good time that Saturday evening, Mary Little entered the lounge of the hotel, neatly dressed in a perfectly tailored suit which meant she didn't escape notice. She looked good in any language and she was out to create an impression.

She chose a table in the corner of the room near one of the windows from which she could survey the whole room. She was only just in time. Within a few minutes an apparently endless procession of men and women poured in, the men solidly packing the bar with the women making for every available table. Mary tilted the backs of the other two chairs against her own, smiling regretfully in response to every approach. She had seen these pub crawls before – a wedding party or a minor civic function had just terminated and the celebrants were rounding off the occasion with appropriate enthusiasm.

She had a sufficient description of Jenny to identify her almost immediately as she entered the room, but her escort was a complication. He had 'naval officer' stamped all over him, civilian suit notwithstanding, and she could only speculate on who he might be. Why he was accompanying the girl, however, was clearly a defensive move by Jenny – either that or he was in on whatever she was a part of.

Both appeared put out for a moment by the throng, but after a word from her companion who had spotted the apparent vacancies at Mary's table, Jenny hurried towards the corner set upon grabbing the spaces only to come to an embarrassed halt when she saw the tilted chairs. Mary set one upright and indicated it with a welcoming smile.

'But aren't they reserved?' asked Jenny shyly.

Mary laughed. 'Be my guests,' she invited. 'It just happens I'm a little choosy and don't fancy being too close to any of these roisterers. I came here for a holiday, you see. Is it very naughty of me?'

Jenny appeared grateful. 'Oh, no, not at all, and thank you very much. I'd never have thought of it myself.'

Sitting down, she placed the small brown paper package she was carrying on the parcel ledge under the table, before looking back to see how her officer friend was progressing in the crush, but he was hidden in the crowd.

Mary spoke. 'I beg your pardon, I know I'm being unforgivably rude, but I'm sure I can't be mistaken. Aren't you from the naval air station at Derry Down?'

'Yes, but how did you know? We haven't met before, have we?'

Mary noted the complete innocence of her expression. There was not the slightest hint of wary apprehension that an agent might be forgiven for betraying, even minutely, at such a greeting. Unless, of course, the child was a consummate actress, and she appeared a little young for that.

'No, we've never met, but put yourself in my position. Don't you think *you* would recognise a familiar type – psychologically speaking, of course – even after you had left the service?' Mary fibbed. 'I was a wren during the war, and stationed at *Arctic Tern* for a spell myself.'

At that moment Nance appeared, shouldering his way out of the crowd.

'Oh, damn! So sorry, Jennifer, I've spilt a little.'

Mary put the other chair upright with a casual invitation as he set the glasses down and Jenny looked at him with excitement at her discovery.

'Pen, this lady has just been telling me she was a wren during the war and stationed at Derry Down. Now she's here on holiday.'

Nance took it in his stride. 'A testimonial if ever there was,' he commented, wiping his fingers on his handkerchief. 'What are you drinking?' He made to pick up Mary's empty glass, but she covered it with her hand.

'Please, I wouldn't think of intruding. If my memory serves me right, and Irish drinking habits haven't changed, these pub crawls are timed to the minute. There's bound to be another table vacant soon.'

'On the contrary, I insist. Birds of a feather, you know.' He received an obviously pleased shrug of compliance.

'An Irish whisky then, thank you.'

Although Mary had every right to feel pleased with her little stratagem that allowed her to take stock of Jenny incognito, she had too much to occupy her to waste time in self congratulation. Seeing the girl for herself, with her officer companion, opened up a completely new set of considerations. It was obvious the child was no undercover agent. It was almost painfully obvious too that she was not the type that a young man like her companion would normally be seen with. It therefore seemed that he was the agent and had used the girl to go to the site for him.

With the poor child so patently sweet on him, one would imagine he was finding it an embarrassment having to accompany her.

Mary's threat to advise Mansett of Jenny's find had certainly hooked a fish she hadn't expected. Thinking along these lines, she passed a congratulatory smile to Jenny.

'He's charming,' she said.

'Oh, yes, he is,' replied Jenny enthusiastically. 'Only I think he finds me a bit of a strain at times.'

Mary hardly doubted it. Outwardly, she expressed sympathetic understanding.

'No need to feel that way, my dear. And anyway, when a girl's in two minds on a point of that kind, she can be reassured the fellow's gone the deepest yet.'

Jenny's eyes widened in delight. 'You really think so?' she asked.

Mary realised at once that her meaning had been misunderstood. The girl really was a congenital innocent. She would have to go right back to the tonic sol-far. 'I mean the deepest with *you*, my dear,' she corrected gently.

'Oh,' Jenny's face fell. 'I thought you meant Pen. I know all right how I feel about him.'

'Then let's start with that. You can't make up your mind whether he can really be serious towards you?'

Jenny nodded 'Yes, that's exactly it. You see, he's an officer and I'm only ... well, you know, you were in the WR —'

'Later,' she was interrupted softly. Mary gave a significant nod to the bar counter. The revellers had begun to drain away, leaving Nance isolated, waiting for them to pass. He arrived back at the table eventually with Mary's drink.

'Thank you,' Mary said. 'I really ought to introduce myself, oughtn't I? The name's Mary Little, and I'm researching flying saucers here in Ireland —'

Jenny's mouth had opened in a startled 'Oh!' and Mary affected surprise, glancing enquiringly from one to the other of them. 'Have I said something?'

Jenny swallowed hard. 'I'm Jennifer Howard,' she confessed, her face colouring. 'And this is —'

'Perry Nance,' he introduced himself.

'Now isn't that a coincidence,' said Mary, hardly surprised that the man should turn out to be the very pilot concerned in the affair. She turned to Jenny. 'Do forgive me. I was expecting you to be alone.'

'And I'd no idea what you would look like,' returned Jenny. 'It was silly of me. I didn't ask for any identification.'

'There's nothing lost,' Mary said, smiling. 'In fact,' she went on, 'I think we've got to know each other rather better this way, wouldn't you say?'

'Jenny told me she was expecting to meet you here, and why,' put in Nance, proffering an open cigarette case. 'But surely I understood you to say you were on holiday?'

Mary waived the case aside. 'If you don't mind?' she said, smiling at him sweetly, and produced a cigarette case of her own. 'It's so often the case with work like mine, Mr Nance, that one finds oneself on a busman's holiday.'

'Perry, please,' he said, passing the cigarette case to Jenny, who shook her head. He continued to Mary: 'Seems you were on the spot at the right time for this one?'

Mary laughed. 'Quite coincidental, I assure you. It's an extraordinary thing though,' she went on. 'I've found time and time again, some sighting or fresh piece of evidence invariably turns up just when I need it most.'

'And what do you make of this one?' Nance thumbed his lighter and leant over to light Mary's cigarette.

'Not much at the moment,' she admitted, drawing at the flame and sitting back as he lit his own. 'It seems that ever since the story broke in the press, half the population of Ireland appears to have turned up to view the area and stayed on to trample across the evidence.'

Nance looked distracted, and frowned at his cigarette.

'Something wrong?' asked Mary politely.

He shook his head. 'No, nothing … I was going to say, imagine if the thing belonged to some foreign power – Russia or America – what a damn good way of destroying the evidence that might have betrayed its country of origin? The man who gave the story to the papers in the first place, I wonder if he can still be traced.'

Mary gave an incredulous half-laugh, and mentally kicked herself for even doubting it before – it had to have been Gene after all!

Jenny was looking at Nance. 'You mean the bird watcher?'

Mary looked interested. 'Bird watcher?'

'Jennifer,' Nance's tone was warning. She quietened at once with a guilty-looking blush, and Mary glanced from one to the other with a raised eyebrow.

'Oh dear,' she said, 'have I started a private war?'

'Not at all,' replied Nance quickly. 'May I be curious and ask what made you choose Northern Ireland for a flying saucer hunt, Miss Little?'

'Mary, please,' she insisted, and reminded him sweetly, 'I didn't. I'm here on holiday.'

'Yes, of course.' He nodded. 'What I really meant was, that with such an unusual interest, I couldn't imagine you not combining the two things–'

'Of course,' cut in Jenny, 'Cuchulain!'

Nance and Mary looked at her, both mystified.

Jenny explained. 'He's a legendary Irish hero renowned for his prowess in war and "feats of thunder". Mary must have come to visit the site of his supposed stronghold.' She turned to her. 'The earthworks aren't far from here, are they? Just outside Armagh. They call them the Navan Rings.'

'We live and learn,' murmured Nance, saving Mary from comment. 'But do tell me what an Irish hero has to do with flying saucers will you?'

'It's all part of flying saucer history,' said Jenny. 'They're not new, you know. Accounts of sightings have been found in early Egyptian papyri; in the sacred writings of the Mahabharata and Ramavana, and in the Samar, where it says that by means of these craft, men could ride up to the stellar regions and heavenly beings could come down to earth. Much later, in France—'

'Hang on,' said Nance. 'You're going a bit too fast for me, Jennifer. We're still in Ireland, and I thought you were going to tell us about this Cuckoo … whatever-his-name-is?'

'Cuchulain,' she replied. 'Well, it's said that he also possessed an "enchanted chariot", that it was light and airy, flew faster than any bird, and "had not a horse to pull it".'

'And just where did you get all that from?' he asked derisively.

'My guardian made a special study of the subject, along with other things,' she said defensively. 'He went through the war as scientific advisor to Lord Charwell. It was when he was asked his opinion on flying saucers that he became interested in researching them historically.' She looked to Mary for support. 'You must know what I'm talking about,' she said.

Not a muscle betrayed Mary's inwardly shaken composure. One of her very good reasons for posing as a flying saucer investigator were the odds against the girl being an expert herself in the field. So much for statistics!

'What an amazing girl you are, Jennifer,' she said. She turned to Nance. 'She is absolutely right, of course, Perry. Flying saucers have a most fascinating tradition. One could go on for hours citing historical data.' This had to be true if Jenny's guardian had spent so long at it. 'One has to beware, though,' she added with a gentle smile at the girl, 'that one doesn't bore other people who might not be so interested.'

'I must admit my interest lies solely within the possibilities of modern day technology,' agreed Nance. 'And since any future war looks like being a largely air and submarine affair, I'd put my money on someone, somewhere, developing a device able to detect sound and movement under the sea over a large area. An eye and an ear in the sky – your flying saucer if you like – would quite fit the bill. But please, don't let me stop you two comparing notes on your interest.'

Mary smiled at him. 'Thank you, I'd really love to do that, but I'm afraid I've already taken up too much of your time.'

'You're not going, are you, Mary?' Genuine disappointment showed in Jenny's eyes.

Mary could have assured her that her disappointment was no greater than her own. But there was no sense in staying to have her cover blown.

'I'm sorry, Jennifer,' she said sincerely. 'Yes, I really must. It's been most pleasant meeting you both, though, and I haven't even taken down those details you were going to give me. Perhaps we could arrange another meeting?'

'Why, yes, of course,' Jenny said. Mary saw her receive a nudge from Nance. 'Er, that is, I mean I would love to, very much, Mary, but I never know what my duties will be so I can't say when I shall be free—'

'What Jennifer is really trying to say,' cut in Nance, 'is that she would love to discuss the history and possible origins of these things with you, but as a member of Her

Majesty's Forces she's not free to discuss anything she might have seen or heard in the course of her duty … *whatever* it might be.'

'Oh, come now, Perry,' said Mary archly. 'I find it hard to believe that Jennifer could be classed as being on duty the other side of the Irish border.' She laughed quietly. 'I'm afraid you'll have to wave a bigger stick at me than that. But I'm not here to fight about it. As I've already mentioned, half the population of Ireland has now trampled across the site and left it useless. But Jennifer here actually saw it in pristine condition, and I would greatly appreciate her comments on what she saw—'

'And I would like to know just how and where you came to hear that Jennifer had been anywhere near the site?' countered Nance. The steely note of authority in his tone made Jenny fidget with embarrassment.

Mary met his eyes in a cool stare, then shrugged easily. 'It's quite a story, actually,' she said truthfully. She took out her cigarette case, handing it round. Jenny accepted one for Mary's sake, Nance refused, but brought his lighter into use for theirs.

Jenny inhaled hers with a smile of surprise. 'These are nice, Mary. What brand are they?'

'A personal make,' she answered, smiling, 'I told you I was choosy.'

'You try it, Pen.' Jenny held hers out to him. He took it warily and drew at it cautiously.

'Different,' he allowed, 'But no flavour.'

'It's got a lovely taste,' Jenny objected. 'Fresh, and sort of … minty.'

'If that's fresh and minty,' he snorted, 'I've got hay fever.'

'Is that why you were sniffing your drink a moment ago?' enquired Mary.

'No, I did that because it was tasteless. I shall take it back in a minute.'

'Try it again, first, will you?'

He did so and stared in surprise. 'It's all right now.'

Mary took the cigarette from him and waved it under his nose, and he looked amazed. 'What the …? I can smell it now. What's going on? Is it some kind of drug?'

Mary shook her head firmly. 'I assure you it most certainly is *not*.'

Nance apologised. 'Well, what is it then? Why should it affect my sense of taste and smell?'

'Did it?' Mary handed the cigarette back to Jenny and regarded Nance with enigmatic eyes. She knew the menthol cigarette was special – but not that special. So unless Nance was laying a very clever red herring there was something radically wrong with him, after all. In any case, the incident was certainly going to have to be mentioned in her report back to MI5.

Nance, now thoroughly suspicious, reminded her that she had not answered his question about how she came to hear that Jennifer had been on the flying saucer site.

'I've a friend on the staff of a paper here,' she lied smoothly. 'I happened to be in his office last evening when the story came in. Naturally, knowing my interest, he immediately let me to have an on-the-spot interview with the man. Well, to cut a long story short, what he told me of what he had *not* put in the article proved every bit as interesting as what he had – but quite unprintable. It concerned two men and a girl he had seen at the site, and whom he was quite prepared to swear on oath were British naval personnel … in fact, he recognised the girl, which clinched it. He gave me your name, Jennifer. I'm sorry I had to lie to you over the phone.' And lie to her now, because she had learned Jenny's name from Mansett's report. 'But I was quite sure that if I had admitted that I knew there were others involved, you would never have agreed to meet me and I should certainly have had no chance of meeting them. It's a simple as that.'

'Since you already have a detailed account from this man concerning the site, I fail to see there's anything that Jennifer can add to it,' said Nance.

Mary smiled sweetly. 'Corroboration *is* an important part of my work,' she reminded him. 'The more witnesses I can find the better and in this case, from what I was told, it seems the site had been visited and disturbed by someone prior to my man. Now I don't know who, or how many prior people there might have been, but it does seem that Jennifer was one of them … maybe even the first.' She turned to Jenny. 'The question I would like to ask you, my dear, had the place already been disturbed when you first saw it?'

'Don't answer that,' ordered Nance immediately, but Jenny was looking genuinely puzzled.

'How on earth would I know if anyone else had been there first?' she asked.

'Footprints …?' suggested Mary.

'I didn't look for any,' she answered truthfully. 'I was so staggered by it. I just stood and stared. I never saw any reason to question the evidence of my own eyes, and never thought of anyone else finding it before me. It never even occurred to me that I ought to takes notes in case I was questioned. It was all there, plain enough for anyone to see with their own eyes.'

'And you took nothing away from the site?'

Nance promptly pushed back his chair and rose with a nod to Jenny that they were leaving, telling Mary briskly, 'You must excuse us, Miss Little. We do have a dinner date, and it's time we went.'

He pulled Jenny by her hand and they were gone.

Mary watched them go, lost in thought. There was no doubt in her mind now that Jenny was an innocent and still in possession of whatever she had picked up from the site. She suspected that Nance knew of it, was after it himself and, the fact that he had not reported it to Mansett, made him the one to pursue.

It was time to contact the CO of *Arctic Tern*. As to where she would go from there would then depend rather much on the good Captain himself.

CHAPTER TWELVE

Interlude for dinner

'That woman's a menace,' said Nance, as they adjourned to the dining room.

'I thought she was incredible,' confessed Jenny a little wistfully, still somewhat subdued by her companion's open hostility.

'You're too impressionable, Jennifer. It's a good thing you had me with you or heaven alone knows what she would have got out of you.'

Jenny forbore pointing out that she had made the arrangement with Mary for that very reason. They sat down and he handed her a menu. One glance was sufficient to assure Jenny the prices were astronomical, and Nance was going to have to best judge of what he could afford. She returned it to him with the assurance that whatever he chose would be fine by her.

He frowned, and apparently reminded of their shopping spree, but let it go with a shrug. It was obviously not worth the fuss of forcing an issue out of all proportion to its size, and so he placed an order for both of them with the waiter. On the man's departure he turned back to her.

'You never told me what your guardian was during the war?' The way he spoke it sounded almost like an accusation.

'Why, what difference does it make?' she asked. 'There are tons of things I don't know about you.'

'Me? I'm ordinary enough.'

As if she were peculiar, Jenny thought rebelliously. In an attempt to divert another argument, however, she reached out a hand.

'Pen, do we have to quarrel?' she begged.

He covered her hand with his. 'Of course not, but you're a funny child … and an amazing one. One moment you have me floored in a daze wondering what sort of person you are, and the next you're giving yourself away with both hands.'

It was most unfair, this continuing attack, and she prickled under his criticism. 'I can't help being myself, Pen,' she returned defensively.

'That's the whole damned point of it,' he said impatiently. 'You're not. Listen to me, Jennifer,' he insisted, tightening his hold on the hand she tried to draw back. 'I like you, I like you an awful lot, and I'd like to make something of you—'

'Well, thank you very much!' she said in low-voiced fury, snatching her hand away and shooting to her feet. 'But your kind concern for me is more than I can possibly accept. You must excuse me; I'll find my own way back to camp. I'll return the things you bought the first opportunity I get in the morning.'

Nance rose to his feet. His tone was icy and his words scathing. 'I am well aware that what I said was unforgivable without your need to ram it home and advertise the fact. If you have any courtesy in you at all you will oblige me by sitting down at once.'

For a moment she stared at him, and then sat down as abruptly as she had risen, suddenly conscious of the attention they had begun to attract from other diners.

Nance sat down in his own chair more slowly. Tears brimmed in Jenny's eyes as she sought for a handkerchief. Once again he offered his own, but she shook her head.

'What's the use?' she replied in as low a voice, her eyes unseeingly on the bowl before her. 'You still meant it, so what difference does it make? It just proves what a complete fool I've been to think you were interested in me for my own sake, instead of being a specimen for some kind of experiment, and not a very good specimen at that. That's the thing that beats me: what on earth it was you ever saw in me to make you think it was worth your while.'

Nance made no attempt to do answer her, instead telling her to eat her soup before it got cold. Jenny felt it would choke her if she did but made the effort for the sake of appearances, keeping her eyes steadfastly on the plate lest sight of the lean tanned features across the table cause a renewal of the tears she was struggling to hold back.

*

Nance appreciated that the situation may well have become too much for Jenny, but that was no reason why they had to share the entire meal in silence. His effort at light conversation, however, was a mite too cheerful an approach. All it won him was an aggrieved glance that intimated she did not think much of this callous display of indifference to the misery he had just inflicted.

The pilot's temper flared again. She was not the only one unhappy and he at least was trying his best.

'Jennifer, surely to God it isn't completely beyond you to make some kind of effort?'

She promptly burst into tears, and that made him even more annoyed.

'Listen, Jennifer,' he said, 'either you dry up, or so help me, I'll–' He stopped, more at loss for what he could do than for dramatic effect. But Jenny had gone so round eyed with alarm that it abruptly struck him as funny. As quickly as he had lost his temper, he regained it, but keeping as straight a face as he could, finished: 'I'll… I'll take back my handkerchief!'

For a moment she gazed at him uncomprehendingly, then a giggle escaped her, which turned into helpless laughter as he broke into a chuckle as well.

It began to be an enjoyable meal after that, especially when Nance commented that he had never asked her where her home was. When she told him it was near Corsham in Sussex, he was astonished. 'Good Lord, I've a married sister lives there.'

'We live in a village called Polhurst,' she said.

'Know it,' he grinned triumphantly. 'My brother-in-law took me there to ramble round while he chased a pair of Jacobean glasses someone had found in their attic. He's an art dealer. He was invited to make an offer for them—'

Listening with widening eyes, Jenny cut in. 'Your brother-in-law wouldn't be a Mr Getty, would he?'

'Why, yes,' he said in surprise. 'You know him then?'

'My uncle does, very well,' she replied. 'I've only met him once or twice when I've been with Uncle Jay on one of his visits to Corsham and he's called at your brother-in-law's antique shop. Your brother-in-law would always let uncle know when he found some curio he thought might interest him. I remember once, though, he found something but wouldn't tell uncle where he'd found it.'

'Sounds like Frank, alright.'

'I don't remember ever having met your sister, though.'

'Probably not. Maggs is more often at home. She's quite a bit older than I am, and I'm an uncle three times over myself. You'd like her. She's a grand soul. Just goes to show doesn't it?' he went on. 'Small world and all that. My home's in Lancashire – Newby Bridge.'

'I know a Newby Bridge at the lower end of Lake Windermere,' she offered. 'We went on holiday there, once. But that's in Cumbria.'

'Not at all,' he chuckled, delving into his pocket and bringing out pencil and notebook. 'Here, I'll show you,' He drew an outline of the lake showing where the border ended halfway down its side at Bowness. 'And the rest is good old Lancashire,' he explained, filling in details at the southern tip of the lake. 'Here's Combe Hough, that's our place.' He planted a dot near Newby Bridge. 'And the grounds go right down to the water.'

'Sounds lovely,' she said. 'Boating and fishing on your own doorstep and all those lovely mountains to climb.'

'Steady on. Those mountains can be pretty grim at times in places. As for fishing, it's all pike and perch in the lake – not to mention eels.'

'Oh, yes of course, you'd want fly fishing, wouldn't you?'

Nance glanced at her. 'Not at all,' he said. 'I was trying to correct your impression that I live in some kind of perpetual paradise. I enjoy coarse fishing. It's just that for fly one has to go a lot further afield, that's all. Of course, it is lovely there, and it's home to me. But you have some equally great scenery down your way.'

'Used to, you mean,' she corrected. 'There was once the most beautiful forest – Weir Forest, it was called – stretching from Polhurst to Three Weirs Village and miles beyond.'

'I know,' he agreed with a nod. 'Frank – that's my brother-in-law – told me about it. His father knew Sir

Edward We'ard, the Forest Warden. It seems the old boy spent nearly every penny he had on a campaign to preserve it from being cut down and turned into a dormitory town.'

'Yes, but accidentally or on purpose, it got burned down, and they started building on it,' she said, adding wistfully, 'There's a poem of Shelley's I think would make a good epitaph:

'Now the last of many days
All beautiful and bright as thou
The loveliest and the last, is dead:
Rise memory and write its praise!
The epitaph of glory fled
For now the earth has changed its face
A frown is on the heaven's brow.'

'You like poetry?' Nance asked.

She nodded enthusiastically. 'And you?'

He smiled. *'What difference? But thou dost possess the things I seek, not love them less.'*

'That's his *Invocation*,' she exclaimed, her face mirroring her delight. And going on: *'Rarely, rarely, comest thou.* I love it all, but my favourite verse is:

'I love snow, and all the forms
of the radiant frost.
I love waves, and winds, and storms,
Everything almost
Which is nature's and may be
Untainted by man's misery.'

'Good for you,' he said admiringly. 'You really do know your Shelley, don't you?'

'Not really,' she confessed, 'Those are verses I just happen to like. They say what I feel.'

'And the rest,' he said with a grin. Jenny returned it happily. Nance was pleased. It was quite something to have successfully coaxed this other side of the girl to emerge from the rather tense, awkward one he had known up until then. But Jenny was in her element. Books, poetry and music were things she loved and knew well, therefore it was easy to talk when she discovered she had someone to share with.

So they ate, talked and laughed in an exchange of opinions and ideas until Nance at length remarked on her evident enjoyment, and she told him that she hadn't realised until then how much she had missed having such discussions. 'I've not met anyone interested in talking books in the mess,' she explained.

'What do you talk about, then, in the mess?' he asked. 'You must talk about something.'

'Not much that I'm any use at,' she answered. 'The girls like to talk about boyfriends, films, hair do's, the latest gossip, and I'm not much good at that ... not that the girls aren't the best,' she added hastily. 'They are. It's just that, somehow, I suppose there isn't time, or place to do more. Coming off duty is like being set free. You want to shout, sing, let off steam – anything. No one wants to sit and talk. I expect,' she concluded a little daringly, 'we save it for our boyfriends.'

'Ah,' he said lightly, wiping his lips, 'so you think I qualify?'

Jenny blushed and lowered her eyes to the tablecloth. 'I think you're wonderful,' she said in a low voice.

Nance sighed. 'It was meant as a light-hearted remark,' he said with kindly exasperation. 'A "you'll do", or "I'll think about it", or even "you might, if you're lucky!" is more the kind of response one expects – not something that's going to embarrass the poor fellow.'

Jenny was abashed. 'I'm sorry,' she answered, 'I didn't mean to embarrass you. It's been a lovely evening, the dinner was beautiful, and I've enjoyed talking to you very much. I just wish it was proper to say how much I liked you as well.'

'It's a rule evidently designed to protect women from themselves,' he joked. 'Where *did* you go to school?'

He discovered then that she had never been to school, and was incredulous. His own education through prep school, public school and Oxbridge, made it difficult for him to credit that Jenny could exhibit a similar level of knowledge without the same background. But she had been allowed to run free and taught as and when her interest in a subject demanded it, her guardian tutoring her himself in academic subjects, his housekeeper in all practical necessities.

This insight explained a lot of what Nance had found such a mystery; it also worked a subtle difference in his attitude. Like it or not, an ingrained sense of class distinction was an inescapable fact of life for Nance. People were either you, or they were not you. It was a distinction reflected by his brother officers and himself, reinforced by naval tradition, towards Hamble. Hamble had come up through grammar school and polytechnic, so he was not one of them. Nance had also looked on Jenny as definitely not being one of them. Now she was revealed as someone within his parameters, no wonder he had been annoyed for misjudging her.

'What made you join the WRNS?'

'The war,' she replied at once. 'I wanted so much to be in it but wasn't old enough. As soon as I was, though, I nagged Uncle Jay until he allowed me to join on my twentieth birthday. And I've enjoyed it tremendously. It's been a terrific education.'

'He must be a strong minded man to have held out so long against you,' commented Nance glancing at his watch, surprised to see how late it was. Although Jenny's pass did not expire until midnight, he thought it was high time he was getting her back.

*

The night air was chilly on their emergence from the hotel a few minutes later: it was also pouring with rain.

'Glad I put the hood up before leaving the car,' said Nance wrenching open the offside door. ''Scuse me if we don't stand on ceremony.' He bundled her into the further side before diving in himself to fish out a rug he carried in the back and wrapped it around her. Leaning over with an arm behind her head to adjust its folds with his other hand, brought his face close to the pale oval of her own, and he kissed her.

It was intense enough for Jenny to vividly recall the first time he had kissed her and was suddenly struggling to free herself.

'The shoe,' she gasped, drawing breath. 'I've left it in the hotel!'

'Hell.' He drew back resignedly. 'All right, I'll get it. Whereabouts?'

'Under the table where we were sitting,' she told him. 'But I'll get it. I know exactly where it is—'

'I have said I'll go,' he vetoed. 'It doesn't need the pair of us.'

Jenny watched him hobble off, then realised she had forgotten to tell him whether it was under the table in the dining room or in the lounge. She slid out of the blanket and hurried after him.

Nance, heading straight for the dining room, had already disappeared by the time she reached the door so, rather than waste time advising him of her presence, she ran into the lounge straight to the table there where they had been sitting. But the brown paper package was gone. She frantically searched the adjoining tables in the hope that they might have been switched, murmuring apologies to the people she disturbed, until one of them suggested she should try asking if her property had been handed in at the bar.

She was found by Nance just as she was waiting – in a daze of relief on being informed that a lady had given in a parcel answering her description – for it to be produced. Before she could say anything, however, the barman's head reappeared from beneath the counter with abject apologies. He was unable to find it there now.

'But you said you had it,' she insisted, on the verge of tears.

Nance interrupted. 'Leave this to me, will you?' and told the dismayed man to fetch the manager.

But the shoe appeared to be lost without trace. The only hope the manager could hold out was that one of the staff who had gone off at nine o'clock might know something about it. He reassured them that he himself would most certainly call on and question each one the following day, and would notify Jenny of his findings when she called in the next day. In the meantime, he would continue a thorough search of the premises.

*

Nance was as concerned as Jenny. His one examination of the shoe had assured him it really was a tiny shoe made from quartz crystal as she had said, and very beautiful. It had also made him determined to win it from her by any means for expert examination. It should not take a proper authority long to identify the origin of its mineral – terrestrial or otherwise – although he was quite certain it could only be the former.

Jenny was inconsolable. 'How could I have forgotten it?' she said on their return to the car.

'I could say the same myself,' he told her, settling into his seat with an unwonted air of defeat. 'I'm damn sorry about it, but there is no point in grieving.' He started the engine and nosed the car onto the road. 'The shoe isn't beyond hope yet. Look, if it's any help at all, I'll ring the manager myself tomorrow lunchtime, and if he's had any joy, I'll run you in straight away to pick it up. How's that?'

'It's kind of you, but I already have a promise of a lift in, so I'll be able to do it myself quite easily, thank you.'

'Please yourself, of course.' He shrugged and said no more, but mentally assuring himself he would be there all the same.

A few minutes later he was aware she had fallen asleep against his shoulder. Wrapped in the warmth of the rug, he could the guess the excitement and emotion of the day had taken its toll.

He slid the car quietly to a halt in order to adjust her head to a more comfortable position, before lighting a cigarette and regarding her by the illumination of a streetlight. The composure of her features, in contrast to the animation which lit them so constantly when awake, affected him oddly. So much he knew, so little he could only guess at, but one thing was certain he had undergone a profound change towards her since the time they had first met just thirty-six hours previously.

He drove on again, deeply preoccupied with its effect on his future behaviour. What was he going to do? What could he do in view of the professional crisis looming in front of him? The blackout he had had could mean anything. Heaven knew what the psychiatrists and medics would make of it. Suppose they found something physically wrong with his brain? At best it might mean a major operation, at worst maybe even the stigma of mental instability. What kind of future had he to look forward to in either case? How could he contemplate a future of any kind with a loveable innocent like Jenny? It looked impossible whichever way he looked at it.

A little short of her quarters, he stopped in order to give her time to wake up. But because she had gone off to sleep so deeply, Jenny did not seem immediately aware of her surroundings or any memory of the evening, only that it was Nance who was trying to rouse her.

'Oh, Pen, I do love you,' she sighed drowsily, nestling closer to his shoulder.

'You're dreaming, Jennifer,' he said with a brusqueness that made her sit up, fully awake.

'I'm not … and I do,' she declared, drawing away from him.

'You've a funny way of showing it then,' he said

'I don't understand … why should it matter to you how I feel?'

'Because it does happen to matter. Very much,' he answered. 'I'm not as unfeeling as you seem to think me. I do care about you. I care a lot.'

'But you said you never wanted to see me again,' she said accusingly.

'Pardon me; I said nothing of the kind. I was under the impression that it was you who found my company unbearable.'

'But I don't,' she insisted. 'How can I? I've told you that I love you, and I do. But what's the use if you don't feel the same about me?'

He looked at her. 'Did I ever say so?'

Jenny felt her heart would burst with the strain of holding its emotion. 'Then you do?' she asked, gazing at him in with an expression of disbelief.

Before he could say anything he was distracted by a rapping of knuckles on the window beside him. Seeing the shadowy outline of a figure in the white cap and belt of a naval patrol, he turned down the window. 'Yes, what is it?'

'Duty watch, sir. Sorry to disturb you but I must warn you that the wrens' approach is a dangerous place to park this time of night without sidelights.'

Nance flicked the lights on and turned back to Jenny as the man returned to his beat. The interruption had provided him time to think.

'Cigarette?' he asked, offering his case. Jenny declined, and watched as he lit one himself. He drew on it deeply, then eyed the glowing tip. 'I care about you too, Jennifer. But it's quite impossible for me to make plans or promises concerning anything at the moment. My whole future is in the balance. I just don't know what's going to happen to me.'

'But, Pen, what differences can that make? I'll still feel the same about you, whatever happens.'

'I believe that, Jennifer. You're so heart-whole. But one of us has to keep their head ... and that's why I can't commit myself to any kind of definite assurance. It wouldn't be fair to either of us.'

'All right,' she said bitterly, 'you needn't go on. I've got the message. I'll say goodbye now and not embarrass you any further. It's your fault though for leading me on as you have.'

'I'm sorry if you see it like that, Jennifer, but it's pointless arguing with you any longer. You're obviously tired, overwrought and in no mood to be reasonable. I suggest the best thing you can do in the circumstances is to go to bed with a hot drink and a couple of aspirins. You'll feel better in the morning. I'll give you a ring around noon.'

'I shall be out,' she said. 'I promised Don Rossini I'd meet him tomorrow.'

'That's that then, is it?' said Nance his lips tightening. 'In spite of the sentiment you've just expressed towards me you're still intent on going out with him.'

'I don't see why it should concern you. You keep saying you've no intention of committing yourself to anything with me.'

'Oh, for heaven's sake, woman!' he burst out angrily. 'Why must you keep on trying to force the issue? I can't possibly make any decision one way or another until I know where I am. Doesn't it mean anything to you that I'm facing the end of my career?'

'Pen, of course it does,' she said. 'It's just that I can't see why it should make any difference. Unless what you really mean is that, you can't go on seeing me if you do remain an officer …'

'God give me patience,' he said, exasperated. 'Listen, Jennifer, when I say the end of my career, I mean just that. If I'm not discharged on medical grounds for whatever they can hang on me, it's a certainty I'll never be allowed to fly again – and I couldn't stand that. No, I should simply resign my commission and strike out into the blue after something else. I've always had a yen to take up car racing seriously, but that's neither here nor there at the moment. Now, if you don't mind, I think we'd better both call it a night. I really have got a headache.'

'Oh, Pen, I'm sorry, I forgot. I'll say goodnight, then, and thank you for taking me out.'

'It's been a pleasure,' he said. 'And I mean that, even if it hasn't been exactly what one could call an entire success. At least it's been a very memorable day – for me at any rate – and although I don't know when, where or if we ever meet again, I can assure you of this: I shall never, ever forget you, Jennifer. You are one incredible girl.' He leaned over and opened the door for her.

Jenny got out of the car, then turned. 'Goodnight, Pen.' She hesitantly held out her hand. 'I wish you all the best in London.'

He took her hand and unexpectedly pressed it to his lips. 'Thanks, Jennifer, I shall need it.'

CHAPTER THIRTEEN

The Shoon of Cladich

It is said that all men are boys at heart, and Derry Down's first allocation of jets appeared to rouse all the youthful enthusiasm associated with a new toy in those concerned with flying the six Supermarines which were to perform their fly-past on Sunday morning.

Captain Mansett was not best pleased at the prospect of having to postpone their takeoff time. Whilst Lieutenants Broome and Tupper could be put on hold until Monday morning, Mary Little's telephone call the previous evening was something he could not ignore. Nance was unavailable and the Captain had had to leave a message for the pilot to report to him first thing that morning.

Not really believing the summons could have anything to do with Mary Little's threat to Jennifer, Nance was taken aback when Mansett demanded to know what Wren Howard had found on the site that had not been handed over with his report.

'I find it unbelievable that you, of all people, should deliberately withhold something like this,' he stormed. 'Quite incredible! Or maybe you're going to tell me that it escaped your memory, along with the unidentified flying object you've forgotten you were chasing?'

Nance defended himself. 'Sir, I was limiting my report to you to what I had actually seen with my own eyes. Wren Howard insisted that what she had found was a glass shoe, and refused to part with it, or allow me to see it. I've now seen the artefact with my own eyes; last evening. It is exactly as she had described. A small glass shoe, probably of ancient Celtic origin, apparently thrown out or up from wherever it had been buried by the explosion.'

'And where is it now?' demanded the Captain.

'In Londonderry, sir.' Nance could be the soul of brevity when it suited him. 'I'm hoping to collect it later today.'

'Good.' Mansett nodded. 'Just see that you do, and let me have it when you get back.'

Nance delayed his run ashore to watch the display, albeit with some bitterness and envy. If it had not been for the cloud he was under, he would have been among those flying in it. Knowing Jenny was on the duty watch for it, he had all the time he needed to nip into Derry and enquire about the shoe before Jenny could get there herself. The ethics of the matter hardly troubled him; he was quite sure it would be returned to her ... eventually.

Nance arrived at The Shaun Hotel by midday and made at once for the reception desk. At first he gave the tall fair-haired US Navy man sitting in the corner of the foyer no more than an incidental glance, then looked again as something familiar about the man struck him, and he recognised Jenny's escort to the music circle. If the navy man recognised him, he didn't show it.

When the manager appeared, he approached the pilot with an outstretched hand.

'Ah, Lieutenant Nance, I'm glad you've come. If you'll kindly step this way, please ...?'

Nance was agreeably surprised. It sounded promising, and it was. The first thing to catch his eye as he followed the manager into his office was the twinkling quartz of the lost shoe on the desk.

'Oh, good show!' he exclaimed, picking it up. 'You found it.'

'Indeed, sir,' the manager said, somewhat ruefully. 'It appears we have a young idiot on the staff. The bar boy came across it – loosely wrapped as you described – and presumed it belonged to the hotel. Apparently he had heard of champagne being drunk from slippers, jumped to the conclusion that we kept this glass one for the purpose, and set it aside for washing up. It then got put it away with the tankards.'

'Damn,' swore Nance under his breath. The explanation meant that any small particles of dust which would have proved it to have been found on the site of the crash would now have been removed.

The manager, not understanding the sudden frown, was profuse in his apologies for the mistake. 'I sincerely hope it hasn't suffered any damage?' he said. 'It seems perfectly all right to me. A most beautiful and unusual ornament. I have never personally seen anything like it in my whole life. Pure crystal, I would say –'

'Thank you,' said Nance, cutting him short and made for the door only to pause outside and turn back with a request for some paper or small box in which to put the thing. As the man hurried off, Nance became aware that he was the object of regard by the American still waiting in the foyer. As their eyes met, the navy man nodded at the shoe he was holding.

'Say, that's a mighty pretty piece you have there.'

Nance thought he could just detect a faint Scottish burr beneath the American drawl. The man went on: 'I'd be mightily obliged if you could tell me how you came by it.'

'And I'd be "mightily obliged" if you'd kindly mind your own business,' Nance returned coldly.

'Now from where I'm looking, I reckon it *is* my business,' said the American. 'I reckon I could tell you more about what you've got there than you might know yourself.'

'I'd be damned interested if you did,' Nance replied, his annoyance overcome by astonishment, adding: 'Might your name be Donald Rossini by any chance?'

'Just call me Don,' he said, rising and holding out his hand. 'You must be Lieutenant Nance?'

Nance wasn't sure whether he was meant to shake his hand, but gave him the shoe, then watched intently as the navy man moved with it into a better light. After a few moments careful examination, the pilot was amazed to see Don staring at him with a most odd expression.

'This is one of the *Shoon of Cladich*, he said, his tone accusing.

'And what, precisely, is that supposed to mean?'

'You don't know?' asked the American. 'There's only one other like it, and they're known as the *Fairy Shoon of Cladich*, or in the Scottish Gaelic, *Sliopairs mo ghaoil*, and belong to the McTears of Argyle.' He held it up to the light and pointed out the tiny lines of faint inscription.

'This is the left shoe, which means those characters can be translated: *Until the day break and the shadows flee* … which is completed on the other shoe as … *thy feet shall bring my peace*. Don't get me wrong,' he added quickly. 'I'm not saying I can read this script myself, and I sure don't remember much Gaelic now, but that's the legend as I heard it from my ma. My father was of the clan McTear.'

He handed the shoe back with obvious reluctance, while regarding Nance with intense curiosity. 'I sure would appreciate knowing you how you came by it?'

But Nance was profoundly disappointed. What he had heard was intriguing, no doubt, but nothing like what he had hoped for, which was something to account for its connection with the flying saucer.

He made up his mind abruptly. If there was anything in this American's story, it should be capable of being corroborated or disproved. If he hurried he still might have time to hunt through the station's reference library. Failing that, there was his brother-in-law. It would be something to have the thing thoroughly researched by the time the Old Man saw it. But if he couldn't find the necessary information at the station, he would take it to England with him that evening and see what Frank had to say on the matter. After all, Mansett's instructions that he was to be shown it 'when you get back' could be as open to meaning back from Londonderry, as back from London.

All this flashed through his mind in the gap between Don's question and the reappearance of the manager, who saved him having to answer by producing a large brown paper bag, with apologies for keeping him waiting.

'Quite all right,' Nance said absently as he wrapped the shoe into a parcel and pocketed it in his raincoat.

With a nod to Don and a brief, 'Thanks for the gen,' he was halfway through the door before the navy man realised he was actually leaving.

'Hey there,' he called after him.

'Sorry and all that, old man,' Nance said over his shoulder. 'I've a plane to catch.' But the American caught him up. Sprinting down the steps he turned to face Nance, barring his passage to the car parked at the pavement's edge.

Taken aback by his behaviour, Nance tried to hide his surprise behind an icily lifted eyebrow. At that precise moment, however, the roar of a motorbike made them both turn to see Hamble with Jenny and a friend, both in uniform, as passengers on his pillion.

For a split second Nance was torn between the consequences of going, or staying to surrender the shoe. The decision he came to was the inevitable one. He darted past the waiting Rossini and round to the other side of his car while Don, taken off guard, let him go.

*

Jenny could hardly believe her eyes at seeing the two together. It seemed quite in character, however, that Nance should go off in a huff as soon as he realised her arrival tied in with the American's presence. Then she realised why Nance would have been there.

They dismounted and the other passenger, Bea, thanked Hamble for the lift, while Jenny anxiously asked Don if he had seen Nance collect anything up from the hotel.

As Hamble roared off out of sight, Don told her what had happened and Jenny could hardly believe the coincidence that it was Scottish and that he had been able to identify it.

'But I found it over the border in Eire, where that flying saucer came down. The explosion blew it out from wherever it had got buried, so how could it have got there?' she asked.

'There's a legend that the Shoon walk,' he said. 'But, Jenny, if you found the Shoon, it's yours. That guy sure shouldn't have gone off with it.'

Bea immediately volunteered to find the nearest telephone and have Nance apprehended as soon as he arrived back on camp.

Jenny greeted the idea with horror. 'We can't do that!' she cried. 'It'll lead to the most terrible trouble!'

'Listen, honey, the shoe's worth a million,' said Don. 'You're not going to let him get away with it, are you?'

'It's all right,' she insisted, trying to sound firm and reassuring. 'Pen will either give it to me when I see him next, or he'll have left it at the Wrennery gatehouse for me to pick up tonight. The only reason he's gone off like this is because he wasn't going to stay here with me seeing you, Don.'

And with that they had to be satisfied. But as she appeared to be on the verge of tears, Don felt bound to take issue with the manager. He shot a look at Bea and nodded they should take Jenny inside. Between them they propelled the miserable girl firmly into the foyer. Don went after the manager, and by the time the young American had finished pointing out to him that he had had no right to return Jenny Howard's property to anyone but herself, the man was heartily sorry he had ever set eyes on the thing.

In placatory spirit, he offered them a pot of tea in the privacy of his office where they might care to discuss what should be done. But all Jenny wanted was to return to camp. Rubbing at her smarting eyes with her knuckles, she went with Bea to find the cloakroom and wash her face, and bumped into Mary Little who emerged from the powder-room as they arrived.

Surprised and pleased to see Jenny, she exclaimed, 'Jennifer! Did you recover your property last night? It was yours wasn't it – a glass shoe in a paper bag left under the table?'

'You mean it was you!' gasped Jenny. 'They said a lady handed it in. But I never thought—'

Bea excused herself past them into the cloakroom.

'I guessed it might be yours,' Mary went on. 'I spotted it as I got up to leave. I would have come after you, but time was so short, I had to leave it with the bar staff with your description.'

*

In actual fact, leaving it at the bar had been the only tactful course open to her. When she hurried to the dining room to find Jenny, it was to see her and Nance deep in a stand-up row and had deemed it more tactful to leave it with the management. With Nance so hostile, she had wondered if their tiff might have concerned herself. She was curious about the shoe, and had been as surprised as the manager at its obvious value and careless wrapping.

'You wouldn't think me too awfully nosey, would you, if I asked how you came by such a beautiful objet d'art?' she asked.

'I found it at the flying saucer site,' answered Jenny.

Mary blinked unbelievingly and kicked herself at the thought of having had the thing actually in her hands. Her mind then raced – accounting for what might have happened in as little time as it took to nod with just the right amount of astonishment and interest in the girl's story while thinking the shoe was a perfectly innocent cover for the instrument of damage.

A quartz shoe; flawless, approximately twelve centimetres in length, or twenty-four centimetres wavelength of resonating frequency. Given velocity over wavelength where velocity equalled the square root of density over elastic modulus, intensified propagation of wave frequency between the crystal and something in the missile tuned to the same frequency building up to destruct-point and complete disintegration.

The mind boggled with the questions it posed. Even more pressing, did Gene know that the girl had found such a crystal? If he did, and he was the man who had leaked the news of the flying saucer site to the press in the first place, it all added up to Gene throwing up a very clever dust cloud to conceal what he was really doing, and who he really was working for.

Not a flicker of the turmoil showed in her friendliness towards Jenny; only the warmth of her delight in the other's good fortune as she asked, 'I suppose you wouldn't allow me another look at it?'

But Jenny was regretful. It appeared Nance had already collected it and returned to camp without realising she was on the way in herself to pick it up.

'Unfortunately,' Jenny continued, 'he's flying to England this afternoon and I might have to wait until he returns before I get it back.'

Mary thought it high time that Jenny was told something of the truth. With a finger on her lips, she drew the girl further down the corridor out of the possibility of any earshot.

'Listen,' she said urgently in a low voice. 'This shoe is a crystal made to look like a shoe to disguise its real use, which was a device to interfere with a highly secret operation being carried out in the lough last Thursday. It now seems evident that Lieutenant Nance dropped it in the required zone when he was flying over it that morning. Fortunately, or unfortunately, depending on one's point of view, the nature of the whole operation caused a temporary blackout for him. It was very convenient for him, therefore, that *you* found it as you did. Now he has obviously recovered his memory of what it is, he has taken it to return it to whoever gave it him to do the job in the first place – which is hardly going to be Captain Mansett, is it?'

*

Jenny gazed at her incredulously, not knowing whether to laugh at what surely must be a joke, or make agreeing noises as one did with someone who was obviously mad.

She was rescued by Bea emerging from the cloakroom wondering where she had got to.

'Thought you wanted the loo, Jen?'

'Yes,' said Jenny quickly. 'Thanks, I do. Please excuse me, Mary.'

'Goodbye. And remember what I said.'

Jenny assured her she would.

By the time she rejoined Bea and Don, she had made up her mind that she had to see Captain Mansett as soon as possible and confess everything. After all, if Mary was so sure that Nance was a Russian spy – which had been the implication – the woman might just tell the Captain and that would land Jenny in hot water.

Bea wanted to know who Mary Little was, and how Jenny had met her. Jenny told them both about the previous evening's meeting with the woman and her flying saucer research. But that was all. She was becoming so confused as to what she had already said, to whom, plus what she was supposed to know, and what she was supposed to keep secret, that she simply stuck to the conversation they had had at that time.

'And the flying saucer site is where you say you found this glass shoe of yours,' exclaimed Bea, remembering what she had said on hearing Don's news. Jenny nodded unhappily in answer, and turned to Don.

'You called it the Shoon of something or other?' she asked.

'Cladich,' he replied. 'The Fairy Shoon of Cladich. They're as legendary as the Fairy Flag of the MacLeods, or the Luck of Edenhall.'

'Oh come on,' Bea scoffed. 'What do you mean by that?'

'That's the legend,' he insisted. 'It's said that a Scottish chieftain, Duncan the Red, first of the House of McCladich of Argyle in the sixteenth century, had been befriended by a glaistig or elf-maid – a kind of fairy being – who had attached herself to him …' And Don went on to relate that due to the troubled times of the period, Duncan's death was brought about by treachery, and the story went that the fairy girl had declared a doom on the man who betrayed him that would last forever. The Shoon then went into the possession of the Clan McTear through marriage. The odd thing was that in the ensuing four hundred years one or both of the shoon would go missing from time to time; but always mysteriously reappeared until a rumour had grown up around them that they 'walked' in search of Duncan, or his betrayer, and returned when they had found neither. That was the legend that had grown in a country and out of a time when a belief in fairies and their mysterious power over human destinies played such a part in folklore.

Jenny was very taken with the story.

Bea was more practical. 'How can you possibly know it was the same shoe? And how come you know so much about it anyway?' she demanded.

Donald explained his origins. '… but the legend of the Shoon is well enough known in Ayr and Argyll for any Scotsman to have remembered it if he saw what I saw.'

Bea turned to Jenny. 'Well, that's that, then,' she said. 'And now, if you two don't mind, I'm supposed to be meeting Abe–'

Don hit his head. 'Gee ma'am, I'm sorry!' he apologised. 'Abe got caught for extra detail and asked me to see you back to the ship with Jenny.'

'You go, Bea,' begged Jenny. She turned to Don. 'I'm very sorry, Don, but I really *do* have to get back to camp and see our CO.'

Bea tried to dissuade her but Jenny reminded her that she didn't know the full story, and that it had become imperative she should see Captain Mansett himself as soon as possible.

Bea gave up. 'She *is* serious,' she assured Don.

Getting back to *Arctic Tern* on a Sunday afternoon, however, threatened to be difficult with buses few and far between and none of them stopping anywhere near the camp, but Jenny was no stranger to hitchhiking. Persuading the others that she would soon get a lift, she set off walking.

CHAPTER FOURTEEN

How one thing leads to another

When Gene saw Don arrive on the dockside with a wren, he had to assume it was Jennifer Howard. Since the one and only time he had previously seen Jenny was through the he fuzz of pebble-thick lenses he did not normally wear, he had not had a very clear image of her. It seemed she was gazing at what she could see of the submarine's superstructure, apparently waiting for Don to come back for her.

Deciding to take her by surprise, he came up on her from behind: 'Interesting, isn't it?' he said using a cultured accent to contrast his look of destitution.

She turned quickly, and blinked. 'Who are you?' she asked, staring back at his grinning face.

Gene was taken aback. He had hoped his appearance in disguise as the bird watcher would be recognised with something of a shock. The girl's amused gaze, however, held nothing but curiosity. Gene did a lightening rethink of his approach.

'Civilian supernumerary, m'dear,' he said. 'A bit of the ballast they had to dig out of the bilges to make up the numbers. Ex-naval type with the thoroughly traditional name of Hardy. Yours wouldn't be Nelson, would it?'

The girl chuckled. 'No, and it isn't Emma, either.'

'Pity,' he said, realising he must have either made a completely wrong assessment of the girl's personality or she wasn't the one he thought she was. 'Never mind, I'll just call you Jennifer, how's that?'

The amusement in the dark eyes gave way to surprise. 'How did you guess?' she asked in with apparent astonishment.

'Intelligence,' he replied, and made an inviting gesture at the submarine. 'I'm quite a fellow, really, you know. Come aboard. I'll show you some etchings of mine.'

The girl laughed again. 'What's that on your sleeve?' she asked. 'Paint?'

'The girl's got it.' he observed admiringly. *And how!* he thought. 'Yes, I'm a ship's painter; fourth class.' He again indicated the submarine. 'See those rectangular blotches on the deck, there? Well, it needs a pretty artistic and steady hand to differentiate those without it being too obvious. They're a new type of escape hatch that works a damn sight quicker than the old. Has anyone told you what lovely long eyelashes you've got?'

'One or two,' she answered. 'You seem to know a lot about this sub?'

'Why not?' he replied, adding in a whisper, 'I'm a master spy in the employ of never-mind-who. It's my job to discover these things.'

'You're a liar,' she giggled. 'If you did know what they were, you wouldn't be telling me.'

'Oh, Grandma, what big eyes you've got.' He looked into them. 'Nice eyes, honest eyes, generous eyes …'

'Oh, give over,' Bea said, but it seemed she was succumbing to his charm. She certainly appeared to be looking at him more closely, and he knew that in spite of his irregular features, he wasn't unattractive. Her response pleased him, it was what he had angled for.

'You really must allow me to introduce you to the Captain,' he urged. 'He's a great friend of mine, and licensed for marriages!'

'Do you make these things up as you go along?' she asked.

'No, it's in the ship's regulations, actually. I have unfortunately had to adopt a rather more roundabout way to assure my future. But you could help me. What *did* you find on that flying saucer site?'

'A glass slipper,' she answered at once.

'Original,' he replied dryly and without humour. 'Whose foot did it fit?'

'That's just the hell of it,' she answered lightly. 'I'll never know because Prince Charming is on his way to see my CO with it.' She looked at her watch. 'I should imagine he'll be trying it on his foot by now.'

Gene showed his surprise. 'And why should Prince Charming want to do that?' he asked. 'Doesn't it belong to you?'

'Of course it does. But how did *you* know I picked anything up?'

'I watched you – but I couldn't see what it was; my glasses were too thick.'

'And now you know …?'

'It explains a lot, and I'd very much like to see it myself.'

'So go and ask our CO to show it you, why don't you? If you want to see it that badly—' Her eyes had suddenly switched from his to someone emerging from the submarine. 'Hi, Abe,' she called, waving for his attention, and hurrying off.

Gene was left gazing after her with the realisation that he had been very neatly hoodwinked by a girl who was no more Wren Jennifer Howard than he was – although obviously in league with her.

He sped after her and caught up in time to hear her asking Abe who the 'nutter' was that she had just been talking to.

Gene answered for himself. 'The "nutter" in this case is security,' he told her. 'And I'll trouble you to show me your ID.'

'Oh, yes?' she challenged, 'and how do I know you're who you say *you* are?'

'The guy is who he says he is,' vouched Abe wearily.

'Thank you, O'Riley. Please?' he held out his hand to Bea. 'The USS *Chimera is* a restricted area.'

Bea produced her service book, and Gene noted her name.

'You don't have to answer,' he said, 'but why did you let me think you were Jennifer Howard?'

'Because the kid needs a friend, that's why,' she said without apologising.

'And not because *you* wanted to find out what she has got herself involved in?' Gene guessed.

'Look here, I don't have to answer your questions.'

'I never said you did; you are completely free to go.' Returning her service book to her, Gene tapped her confused companion on the shoulder. 'But *you're* coming with me, O'Riley. Inside, pronto!'

Abe groaned. 'Aw, what've I messed up now?'

'You'll see.'

'Hey,' objected Bea, 'That's my date you're marching off with.'

'If you're choosing not to answer my questions, then I have to get my answers somewhere,' he replied reasonably.

'But Abe wouldn't have the first idea what you're talking about.'

'I know that,' he replied, and saw the penny drop.

'All right,' she admitted, 'So I was … am curious. There's no crime in that. I would like to know what the kid's been getting into. She needs help.'

'And you're just the person provide it?'

'If I have the right answers, yes,' she answered.

'So what would you like to know?'

'Why *you're* after her, for one.'

'I'm not after her,' he spread his hands. 'You've already told me all I wanted to know.'

'What was that then?'

'What she found on the flying saucer site. You did say a glass slipper, didn't you?'

'Yes, a genuine hallmarked glass slipper as old as the hills, and the kid's jolly upset that her boyfriend's gone off with it without so much as a please, thank you or by your leave.' There was no denying the truthful tone of Bea's statement.

'Thank you,' said Gene with a smile, 'That's all I wanted to know – nothing else.' He stepped back from Abe, before addressing them both, 'I hope you two have a really great afternoon. Enjoy yourselves.'

He watched them go well satisfied.

He had not been truthful with Dachas when he said he had suspected Russian sabotage. He had only said so because it was the one sure fire thing that would guarantee the Captain's cooperation. It was the last thing Gene himself believed to be true.

Now that he had heard a corroboration of what he had suspected all along: that the incident had been purely fortuitous – an accident occasioned by an unforeseen crystal presence that had happened to be of the right size and frequency to have that effect.

All he had to do now was to gain possession of the shoe for essential analysis; an analysis which would prove of inestimable value to himself and all those whom it concerned.

CHAPTER FIFTEEN

Escort for a pilot

Jenny had not very got far when the roar of a motorbike and sound of its horn made her glance back to see a now familiar figure in black leathers pulling up beside her.

'Met Bea and Don and been sent to the rescue,' Hamble informed her cheerfully. 'Like a lift? Don said you're on your way back to camp.'

Jenny was horrified. 'But you can't waste your time taking me all the way back to camp.'

'It's where I'm going,' he assured her. 'I'm flying Nancy boy to England this afternoon.'

As she mounted the pillion with grateful thanks, Hamble remarked casually, 'They told me you found one of the Shoon of Cladich at that flying saucer site?'

'That's what Don said it was,' she answered, 'He was born a Scotsman.'

'Me, too,' yelled Hamble over his shoulder above the noise of the engine he was revving up to move off.

Nothing more was said until they neared the camp when Jenny shouted into his ear that she needed to contact the Station Duty Officer, preferably where she wouldn't be overheard.

'I don't want to use our gatehouse phone: the girls on duty will hear me.'

Hamble brought the bike to a halt so they could hear each other properly.

'You want to get Nance, eh? Look, I'll take you to the SDO if you really want me to, but you don't want to be too upset about Perry. He's done you a favour, really. The Shoon are cursed.'

It was so unexpected and out of character, Jenny was astonished. 'How can you say that?' she asked.

'Take it from one who knows,' he answered darkly. 'Do you still want the SDO?'

'I shan't be complaining about Pen,' she assured him. 'But I do have to see the Captain – urgently.'

When they finally found him, the SDO wanted to know the why, and the wherefore of what it was that she needed to speak to the Captain about. And Jenny had to lower her voice out of earshot of the waiting Hamble, to tell the officer he should tell the Captain that it was urgent and had to do with the previous Friday afternoon.

The SDO went to telephone her request. A few moments later, and evidently impressed with the importance of a message that could break the Old Man's Sunday afternoon without so much as a snort of impatience, he said the Captain would see her at his house.

Hamble dropped her off there and then roared off back to camp as Mrs Mansett met her at the door.

'My husband is in the garden,' she said kindly, leading Jenny into the lounge. 'Take a seat. I'll tell him you're here.'

Jenny sat stiffly on a straight-backed chair against the nearest wall. When Mansett entered, she nervously jumped to her feet, even though he was not in uniform. He crossed to the fireplace and knocked his pipe out on the grate.

'Come and sit down,' he invited.

'I'd rather stand, if you don't mind, sir, she answered, twisting her fingers and wondering how on earth she was going to tell him what she had come to say.

'All right,' he said easily, coming upright and standing in front of the hearth. 'Take your time. I was given to understand that this has to do with our little jaunt last Friday? What's happened – somebody found out about it?'

'Oh, no, sir,' she answered, shocked. 'I mean, yes – well, in a way that is – I found someone else who knows all about it and I hardly know where to begin.'

'Then don't!' he advised crisply and pointing the stem of his pipe, ordered: 'Now take off that hat and come here, sit down, and relax!' He crossed to a cabinet. 'Do you drink? Well, whether you do or don't, you're going to have one. You look as white as a sheet.'

He handed her a small glass containing brandy, and went on. 'Now, when you feel ready and able, just go ahead.'

The spirit made her cough, but warmed and helped her to feel less nervous. 'It's like this, sir …' she began, and carried on to confess how she had found the shoe, and why she had not reported it. '… It was the Oghamic script engraved on the sole, sir. I knew it had nothing to do with the UFO.'

'And you've not brought it with you?' he asked. 'Don't you think I would have been interested in seeing it?'

'Oh, yes,' she agreed at once. 'But that's just the awful thing. I haven't got it any more …' And it all came out: how she had shown Nance the shoe the evening before, had then mislaid it and how he had collected it that morning, but not before an American sailor she had met had identified it as a four-hundred-year-old Scottish family heirloom.

She continued on to what had happened afterward: how she had been told by a lady researching flying saucers named Mary Little that Lieutenant Nance had used Jenny to recover it from the site. '... Sir, she said Lieutenant Nance was a Russian agent, and that the crystal shoe was a very clever disguise for an instrument that had caused terrible interference with some American operations in the lough. I wanted to laugh, it seemed so silly. But Miss Little appeared very sure, so I was afraid she might telephone you and accuse Lieutenant Nance of being a Russian spy, which is perfectly awful and not true at all. Which is why I've come to tell you what really happened.'

*

Jenny did not know until later that the only new thing in her story that Mansett had not already heard was the shoe's identification as a long-lost Scottish heirloom. Mary had not mentioned it being a recognised heirloom when she had rung earlier that afternoon to warn him of Nance's defection with the item. Mansett had assured her that he had interviewed the lieutenant regarding the shoe that morning, and it was on *his* orders that Nance had not waited to return it to Wren Howard, but was reporting straight back with it to himself. He was therefore expecting him at any moment. Greatly relieved, Mary had asked him to keep hold of the artefact; she was on her way.

That had been an hour and a half ago. Mary had arrived, and was being entertained by his wife in another room at that moment. Jenny had arrived with another piece of the jigsaw, but of Lieutenant Nance there had been nothing.

Mansett thanked Jenny for what she had told him and left the room excusing himself, but leaving the door open.

He picked up the telephone and asked for the officers' mess. 'Lieutenant Nance returned yet?'

'He came in, picked up his bags and left straight away, sir'

'Did he leave an overnight address? … Yes … wait.' He tucked the receiver under his chin to write down what he was given, '… Mr Getty, 1 Chadbrook Close, Polhurst. Telephone number …?'

'I couldn't help overhearing you, sir,' Jenny said on his return to the lounge. 'Mr Getty is Lieutenant Nance's brother-in-law. My guardian knows him. As Lieutenant Nance has to fly to England today, he may be having the shoe verified: his brother-in-law deals in antiques.'

'Thank you, m'dear. That sounds like an excellent explanation. More things in heaven and earth, they do say. Thank you … and thank you for everything you've told me. Now you get back to camp, and I hope it won't be long before I can give you some good news, *and* be able to congratulate you on a most remarkable and valuable find. Until then, be patient. I'm sure this will all sort itself out, given time.'

*

Having returned to the station by one-thirty, Nance had picked up his bag and checked out of the mess, leaving an address and telephone number where he would be staying in England. He then found someone who could open up the station library for him and searched through it with no result. By then it was too late to even think of seeing the CO.

The Anson he had been told would be taking him to a service airfield near London was due for take-off at three-thirty.

Making his way to the airstrip, he found Hamble, clad in flying jacket and parachute over his normal uniform, waiting for him while a mechanic in overalls busied himself with some last minute checks on the engine.

'Your girlfriend's a bit upset, you know.' Hamble greeted him. 'She's gone to see the CO.'

'Pull the other one, Ham,' Nance said wearily, 'I don't believe it.'

'Yours truly chauffeured her, old man, all the way back from Derry, and on up to the Skipper's residence … via the SDO.'

'Well, thanks a million. That's really made my day, that has—'

'If you've really got the Shoon with you,' Hamble cut him short quietly. 'I would thoroughly advise dropping it into the middle of the English Channel as we fly over. I thought *I* had chucked it in the lough last Thursday – it evidently wasn't big enough, nor wide enough.'

'*You* threw the shoe in the lough?' gasped Nance.

'I *thought* I had,' Hamble corrected him, 'Seems I missed it by a mile or more.'

'But how come *you* had it? Where did you find it? What were you doing with it?'

'Questions, questions, questions. It's a long, sad story, old man, like you don't want to hear – and anyway, here comes my other passenger.'

Nance turned to see none other than Mary Little approaching over the tarmac.

'I don't believe it,' he breathed, shaking his head. 'I just do *not* believe it!'

'You know the lady?' Hamble queried with interest.

'We have met.'

'So, we meet again, Perry.' Mary greeted him with a smile on reaching them and holding out her hand.

Nance ignored it. 'And may I ask what you are doing on this flight?'

'Here, steady on, old boy,' reproved Hamble. 'That's hardly the way to speak to the CO's guest passenger.'

Mary quickly rescued the dumbfounded officer. 'Don't worry about it, Perry, please,' she said sweetly. 'It was hardly the time or place last night to tell you that Captain Mansett and I were old friends.'

No wonder the Old Man had known all about the find. The question now was why she was on this flight. Had Mansett told her that it had turned out to be a glass shoe that Jenny had found? Had he told her that he, Nance, should have reported in with it as soon as he returned from Derry? Nance decided it was unlikely. He might be in for a carpeting for not getting straight back, but the Old Man would never let that be known by anyone until he had heard what Nance had to say, first. It seemed logical, therefore, that he would not have told Mary what Nance had told him that morning; that Jenny's find had been a glass shoe.

*

His reasoning was only half correct. Mansett had certainly not discussed what had passed between his officer and himself that morning; neither had he said anything of what he had learned from Jenny. Mary, on the other hand, had substantiated the fears voiced by Jenny by telling Mansett that the girl's find, in the shape of a crystal shoe, had been instrumental in wrecking an American project. It was therefore vital to their enquiry. The fact that Nance had gone off with it from The Shaun was also highly suspicious.

Mansett feigned astonishment, saying he found it difficult to believe – which was true – and asked if the

Captain of the *Chimera* wouldn't be interested in the artefact. Of course he would, Mary had agreed, but she was the one who knew where it was and, with Mansett's help, was in the position to act quickly and retrieve it before it was too late.

'I see,' mused the Captain. 'Plus we get the benefit of learning what the Americans are hiding?'

She nodded. 'That also.'

'Very well,' said Mansett, deciding he would give Mary the opportunity of getting closer to Nance. If she was right, she had her chance to prove it. If wrong, Nance would be reporting back to him with the shoe the following Thursday.

*

As soon as Hamble had assisted Mary aboard the Anson, Nance passed him up her luggage to stow safely, followed by Hamble's and his own holdalls, their caps and raincoats.

When Hamble then took his place as pilot he found he had another unexpected passenger; an American in Royal Navy uniform sitting beside him in the co-pilot's seat.

*

After leaving Abe and Bea to wander off together, Gene Gauss had gone in search of Donald Rossini.

'Thought you were seeing Jennifer Howard this afternoon?' he asked.

Don explained that he had gone to The Shaun to meet Jenny, but Nance had turned up and asked for the shoe, which Don had recognised straight away when he saw it.

Questioning him for every specific detail, Gene asked if he knew if Jenny had been contacted by anyone else.

'She did say something about meeting a woman who was researching flying saucers here last night,' he offered.

Gene rang The Shaun and found Mary Little had already checked out, which could mean she had been shown the shoe and decided it had nothing to do with the crash, or had recognised its potential and gone after its present bearer.

Gene's next target was Dachas.

'… And I'd appreciate you getting in touch with *Arctic Tern*'s CO and finding me a seat on whatever flight that young man is taking back to England: the Captain owes us a favour.'

Dachas phoned and checked.

'*I wondered how long it would be before you were in touch,*' said Mansett. '*But be my guest; there are still a few seats left.*'

'What's he say?' queried the waiting Gene.

Dachas repeated the response.

'May I?' Gene held out his hand for the phone. There was no trace of the bird watcher's tones as Gene introduced himself.

'Good afternoon, sir, Gauss here. Gene Gauss, US Naval Intelligence. Good of you to give me a lift. I understand one of your pilots, Lieutenant Nance, has hold of an artefact found at the UFO site?'

'*If you mean the crash site where some project of yours met an untimely end, then yes, that is correct,*' Mansett agreed.

It confirmed that Mary Little had seen it and spread the joyful tidings.

Which is just great! thought Gene grimly. Aloud he said: 'Then you will understand why we are particularly interested in having a look at it?' *An understatement, if ever there was – it was vital*!

'*Absolutely,*' replied the Captain. '*I have been informed that the Russians could have been responsible for it, although, somehow I doubt it.*'

'You know what the artefact is, then?' asked Gene. 'You have seen it?'

'*I have not seen it myself, as yet,*' Mansett conceded. '*I fully expect to do so on Lieutenant Nance's return when he has completed his research into its history, but from everything I've learned, it is simply a very ancient and valuable family heirloom; Scottish in origin.*'

'That's about the gist of it,' Gene said. 'My interest lies in preventing the Russians from getting wind of it, and working out its properties themselves to interfere with our project.'

'*Then you have no need to worry,*' Mansett assured him. '*One of our own agents from MI5 is keeping a close watch on it.*'

'If you mean Mary Little,' said Gene, 'I'll just bet she is. Mary Little *is* the Russian agent!'

The upshot of the conversation meant that Gene took his place aboard the Anson disguised as Hamble's co-pilot with Mary none the wiser, and Hamble listening to his CO's voice from Flight Control to vouch for the man beside him.

*

The few seats in the dimly lit interior allowed enough space for Nance not to have to make conversation with Mary. It hardly deterred her, however.

She promptly engaged him in an apparently innocent discussion about aircraft which meant he had to sit closer to hear her to hear what she said above the noise of the engines, so that by the time they touched down at Elstree, Nance had, reluctantly, been forced to revise his opinion of her. He had found her bright, entirely charming and an extremely interesting woman to talk to; not in the least put out by his initial hostility for which, by then, he felt obliged to apologise.

'Not at all,' she assured him. 'You were only doing your duty, protecting Jennifer. I really should have known better, having been in the Service myself.'

'But aren't you packing your holiday in rather sooner than you expected?' Nance enquired. 'I didn't get the impression yesterday that it was your last day.'

'Never look a gift horse in the mouth, Perry. When I discovered James Mansett was your CO, I naturally called him for old times' sake and told him what I was doing here. We had quite a conversation, and he gave me a lead – an exciting lead, but confidential – on this flying saucer affair. Can't talk about it, you understand? Means I have to follow it up in England. Jimmy was kind enough to allow me on this flight since it was leaving more or less straight away. Kind of him, don't you think?'

'Very,' Nance said, wondering what on earth the 'confidential lead' could be. Unless, of course, it was a deliberate red herring to lead Mary away from interfering with whatever conclusion the authorities might have come up with over the UFO.

CHAPTER SIXTEEN

All the way to morning and halfway back again

Hamble's curiosity about his cockpit companion was given short shrift by Gene, who discouraged questions with terse, monosyllabic answers. On their arrival at Stanmore the man disappeared – or that was how it seemed to Hamble. One moment he was there, the next gone into the night. Mary bid Nance adieu and, on being helped out of the aircraft, appeared to vanish very nearly as quickly.

'It's more than likely I shall be giving you a lift back on Thursday, old man,' Hamble told Nance, giving him a hand with his luggage. 'Leave me your telephone number, and I'll give you a bell.'

Nance gave him the number, gathered his things and went to find a kiosk from which he telephoned for a taxi to take him to Edgware Underground Station for the Northern line to Waterloo, before ringing his sister with news of his estimated time of arrival at Corsham Station. She promised him Frank would be there to meet him.

At Waterloo, Nance found himself face to face with Mary Little.

'Good heavens,' he exclaimed, 'how did you get here?'

'The same way as you?' she suggested with a smile. 'I have to change here. What's your excuse?'

*

She gave no hint of knowing his route home, getting to the underground first while he was on the phone, then hanging back out of sight to see which part of the train he was boarding, before choosing a compartment well away from being seen by him.

Before the pilot could answer, however, she cried, 'Oh dear,' her expression altering abruptly as she looked about her in dismay. 'I've left my handbag on the train.' And she truly had, having first packed her valuables in her suitcase and pocketed the key to her flat. The train was gone, of course. Mary put on a good act. 'My purse! My ticket! I haven't even tuppence for a phone call.'

Nance's concern was immediate. 'Please, allow me. How much do you need?'

'Well, if you *could* lend me tuppence, I'd be enormously grateful. I could phone a friend of mine and get her to come and pick me up. She has a car.'

'Do you live far from here?' he asked.

'Well, no, actually,' she answered, 'just up the road in Lambeth—'

'Then, look,' he interrupted, 'that's not far out of my way. Please, let me see you home.'

She hesitated a moment, as if making up her mind before smiling brightly in agreement. 'That's awfully sweet of you.' She was quite touched by his solicitude, even if she had banked on it. 'All right, I'll accept your kind offer.'

'Come on, then,' he said, shifting his case to his other hand with the walking stick in order to carry hers. 'What are we waiting for?'

Mary eyed him with some amusement. 'I'd like to inform the station master here about losing my handbag,' she reminded him.

With her loss reported, Mary began to feel that things were working out even better than she had hoped. His spontaneous suggestion to see her home had solved a number of problems in one. She could afford to relax a little, although not entirely.

Nance hailed a taxi for the short ride into Lambeth, and by the time they arrived at the address she gave, was completely hooked by a hint of excitement that was seductive. Mary palmed her key, making it appear as if it was a spare one secreted behind a loose brick by the main door.

It seemed only natural she should invite him in for a coffee, which easily led to a meal, given the length of their journey without one. By then it was getting late, so she suggested she put him up for the night. She could make up a bed on the sofa in the lounge with no trouble.

Nance hesitated. The offer was tempting in more ways than one with his having to be in London again in the morning, but he had never been in a situation quite like this before. 'I couldn't possibly put you out to such an extent,' he said, 'quite apart from compromising you with the neighbours.'

Mary laughed at him indulgently. 'Good heavens! If *I'm* not going to let the neighbours worry me, why should you? We're both adults, aren't we?'

By then it was gone ten in the evening and the train Frank was meeting was due in at ten-thirty. Not before time, Nance availed himself of Mary's telephone and rang his sister. Telling her he had been unavoidably delayed, he said he was altering his itinerary and would be with them in the morning.

Margaret had two messages for him. One was from Lieutenant Hamble asking her brother to contact him as soon as possible, leaving a number which Nance noted down, and another from someone who had not left his name but had promised to ring again later. Nance couldn't imagine who it could be, and wasn't too minded to care.

Mary's flat was small, neat and compact. The tiny hall, just big enough for a small table to hold the telephone, opened into a kitchenette, a bathroom, one small double bedroom and a lounge.

When they had arrived, Mary had put his uniform cap, naval raincoat and suitcase on the bed in her room, there being nowhere in the hall – something for which he was to be thankful later that night.

As she kept her spare linen and blankets in the top section of a built-in wardrobe in the bedroom, she had to climb on a stool to reach it. Nance stood by to receive the things she handed down, and she slipped. He broke her fall, but staggered back under the impetus which sent them both sprawling on the bed. Mary giggled.

'Now I know what they mean when they talk about being thrown together!'

'My mother used to say it was the way she made her best cakes,' he replied.

She looked at him speculatively with a little smile, and ran a finger down his nose to his lips, 'And what sort of mixture would you say we'd make?' she asked.

The effect was quite electric. 'It's something we could always find out …' he answered softly.

It took a long time for Nance to come to his senses one way or another when he opened his eyes an hour or so later. He did not know what it was that had awoken him – the light had been on when they had fallen asleep. Perhaps it was the soft sound of the zip of his holdall being opened that disturbed him. Whatever it was, it was hard to believe that he wasn't still dreaming when he saw Mary knelt on the floor in her slip going through his possessions.

He was on the point of demanding to know what she was doing, when the doorbell chimed. He immediately closed his eyes, knowing instinctively she would look to see if it had woken him. He heard her softly reclose the zip and move to put on a dressing gown before leaving the room.

No sooner was she gone, he shot out of bed, throwing on his clothes and straining his ears to what was being said in the hallway. Glancing at his watch he saw it was a quarter to midnight.

Mary's tone was low and startled. 'Gene! What are you doing here?'

'I could ask you the same question, ducky!' a man's voice replied and, from the sound of it, its owner was pushing his way past her as he went on curtly: 'Where's the shoe?'

'What shoe?' demanded Mary, managing to make her voice sound as astonished as Nance felt himself at hearing such a blatant lie. He had confided in her that very evening that the shoe she had found in the bar was what Jenny had found at the UFO site.

'Cut the play acting,' the man said. 'We both know what I mean: a pure quartz crystal in the shape of a shoe. You discovered Nance had it, so you went after him. He hasn't turned up to where he was going, so what's happened? Did he take fright when he saw you? Have you done him in? Or …' he paused, '… have you got him here?'

Nance heard her open the lounge door. 'Does it *look* as if I've anyone here?' she said indignantly.

Nance, completely dressed by now, waited to hear them both go in the lounge, then, cap on, holdall and stick in one hand, shoes in the other, he crossed the hall to the kitchenette where he put his shoes down and soundlessly opened the back door. Just as he had hoped, there was a fire escape outside. Collecting his shoes and, still holding them, he made his way silently down the iron stairway, his mind in complete turmoil.

He arrived at his sister's house at two in the morning after hitching a lift on a late-night lorry en-route to the coast. He had no worry about how he was to get in: Margaret had given him a key in case he ever arrived on leave unexpectedly.

Once more without his shoes, he stole upstairs to the room he knew his sister would have made ready for him, slung his stuff on the bed, then sank into an easy chair by the still open curtained window to think.

He was in a state of shock. For all his apparent maturity, Nance was still only twenty-two years old and a woman like Mary had never come on to him before.

He had believed in her – as profoundly and trustingly as Jenny had believed in him. Even now, he could still feel Mary; the warm, soft, silky smoothness of her body against his own like an actual physical presence – and all she had wanted was the shoe!

The blow to his ego was shattering, especially to find that whoever 'Gene' was, he was also in league with her. God, how she must have been laughing at him, believing she was investigating flying saucers as she had said she was.

In the end, it all came back to the shoe – the entire cause of his present wretchedness. What had Hamble said? Throw it in the Channel. Nance realised somewhat belatedly that he not even checked that it was still safe in his possession. Although he had caught Mary opening his bag, she could have already been through it once, and reopened it for some other purpose … maybe to replace something she had left out, because the shoe had been in his raincoat.

He drew the curtains, switched on the light, and went through his raincoat pockets. No shoe.

There was a certain grim satisfaction in contemplating his next course of action. Firstly, though, he had to wake

Frank. He disliked the necessity, but he had done enough hitchhiking for one night, and he needed to move fast.

Fortunately, his brother-in-law slept in a room on his own – not through any breakdown of the marriage, but of necessity where Margaret was concerned: her husband snored. Nance woke him as gently as he could, but it took a lot to soften his shock at being woken at two-thirty in the morning.

'It's all right, old man,' Nance whispered, 'it's me, Perry. I've just arrived and remembered something terribly important. Can I borrow your car, please?'

'Oh, Good Lord,' Frank groaned. 'Can't it wait till morning, for heaven's sake?'

'No, I've mislaid some top secret material, and I've got to go back for it *now*.'

'Oh, all right,' he agreed testily. 'You'll find the keys on top of the chest of drawers there ... and Perry?'

'What?'

'Try and be back in time for me to get to town in the morning, will you? I'll need the car.'

Motoring the seventy-odd miles to and through London in the early hours had its advantages: near empty roads. In just under two hours, as dawn was breaking, he was parked down a side street in Lambeth and remounting the fire escape down which he had fled four and half hours previously.

He had thought that getting back into the flat was going to be rather more difficult than it had been getting out. To his surprise, however, the windows showed all the lights were on and, when he tested the back door, it opened.

The place was utterly silent, empty it seemed. He walked to the entrance into the hall and stopped, stunned with the horror that met his eyes.

Blood seemed to be everywhere. Staining a pillow and blanket lying on the floor by the telephone table, it marked the bright yellow rug that was pushed against the front door, and carried on in a sequence of smeared hand prints along the lower part of the cream walls and floor to the bathroom.

Feeling sick at the thought of what he might find, and guilty that he had abandoned her to fate for which her late night visitor appeared responsible, Nance had to force himself to follow the trail into the bathroom.

Mary Little lay against the side of the bath, her face drained of colour, but her slip red with blood from the blades of a pair of open scissors embedded in her chest.

CHAPTER SEVENTEEN

Paranoia

Gene's priority had been getting to Nance without being seen by Mary when they had arrived at Stanmore. His difficulty lay in not knowing what might have passed between Mary and Nance during the flight over.

When he saw her getting straight into a taxi and being driven off, it seemed logical she had probably arranged to meet Nance some other time the following day – certainly not that night.

It made his job easier, for all he had to do then was to tail Nance to a telephone kiosk and loiter outside as if waiting to use it himself, while listening to the man giving the time of his train from Waterloo to Corsham to his sister.

There was a delay, however, when it came to following Nance to Edgware underground in another taxi. When Gene eventually got one, it was in time to see the train with Nance on board leaving the station. But Gene remained unworried. Underground trains being extremely frequent, he was sure he would catch up with the pilot at Waterloo Station.

When the Corsham train pulled in for boarding, however, Nance had failed to show at the ticket barrier. Gene waited until after the train had left, hoping the pilot might still show up, but to no avail.

Mansett had given him the address and telephone number where Nance would be staying, so Gene rang and spoke to the pilot's sister in case her brother might have found alternative transport. When told he was still expected off the Corsham train, Gene had some hard thinking to do, and his conclusions all added up to the deviousness of women – Mary in particular – and a mystery: Why, if she *had* waylaid Nance, hadn't she shared a taxi with him to Edgware? Why keep her meeting secret unless she suspected Gene was following her? Surely Mansett wouldn't have said anything. The Captain had been cooperation itself in getting him kitted out and onto the aircraft.

The pilot, Norman Hamble? Had he said something unwittingly to Mary? It would have needed the barest humorous mention of having had had a slightly odd co-pilot for her to have been alerted.

So how and where would, or could Mary and Nance have got together?

He had no idea where she lived, but he knew a man who did. It took two or three hours to track him down; eventually, however, Gene had her address.

As soon as Mary opened the door, Gene knew he had succeeded for once in catching her off guard. He was the last person she expected, and she hadn't time to think straight.

They both knew her denial concerning the shoe was not the most intelligent thing she could have done. It stood to reason that Gene wouldn't be there were he not aware that she must be lying to say she had no idea what he was talking about. If Gene was surprised not to find Nance with her, the state of the bed, however, betrayed the fact that two people had been sleeping in it.

Convinced now that she was in possession of the shoe, there was no trying to tell Gene otherwise.

If he had to take the flat apart, he was going to find it, but why go to all that trouble when he still had a trump card?

'Hand over the shoe,' he said softly, 'or I let Sergev in on what you've been doing.'

Mary paled.

Gene knew she had been playing a double game with the Russians; he and she had worked out the details between them. If he were to implement his threat, her days were numbered.

'I've often wondered just how nasty you *could* get,' she answered, 'but since I *haven't* got the shoe, where's it going to get you?'

He looked at his watch, saying flatly, 'You have one minute precisely.'

'You wouldn't …'

'You have only to wait and see,' he promised.

'Gene, look,' she said, 'I promise, you're making a terrible mistake. *I have not got it.*'

'Thirty seconds,' he answered, moving into the hall.

Mary suddenly sped past him to the kitchen, grabbed a pair of scissors and tried to get behind him. He saw what she intended to do: she wanted to cut the telephone wire. But he was too quick; he was also strong and wiry. Catching her wrist and keeping her hand at arm's length as they struggled fiercely in the little hall while she tried desperately to reach the hanging cord. The next moment the rug slipped from beneath their feet on the polished floor. Mary fell forward; her hand hitting the wall jerking the open scissors round and back towards her, and Gene's weight collapsing on top of her pushed her down on them, driving the blades completely into her body.

Gene was horrified when he saw what had happened. He knew better than to attempt to remove the blades, though. The released flow of blood could be fatal in minutes.

He brought a pillow for her head and a blanket to cover her now shivering body.

'I only … wanted to cut … the telephone wire,' she gasped.

'I was bluffing,' he admitted. 'You should have realised I've as much to lose as you with Sergev.' Then with imperative urgency he added, 'But you must know where the shoe is?'

'I had … Nance here … it wasn't … on him … I couldn't find it.'

'If you'd only had the sense to say so at the beginning,' he said. 'None of this might have happened.'

'Wouldn't it?' asked Mary with a sad smile. 'Would you really … have … believed me?'

'Probably not,' he admitted, rising. He dialled 999, and asked for an ambulance. When answered, he said: 'There's been a very bad accident. Please send help,' and put the phone down. Like many people in situations like this, his mind was too preoccupied to remember to give either name or address and the call went unanswered. In later years the emergency services were to find procedures to catch up to this all too human failing, but they came too late to save Mary in 1954.

Gene's next thought was where the shoe could have got to. Mary had admitted she had been unable to find it on Nance, and he believed her, which left three alternatives. Either Nance had taken it to his CO as soon as he had returned to camp, or it had been passed to Hamble during the flight or to someone else at some stage of his journey to Waterloo station.

If Mansett had it, then Gene guessed he had every right to keep schtum and let Gene chase his own tail … he would have done the same himself in similar circumstances. Then again, if Mansett had had it, he might have used Hamble as a special courier to deliver it to the requisite authority in London.

Tracing Hamble might not be so difficult, either. Gene was still in British naval officer's uniform, and down as co-pilot. If he returned to Stanmore and pleaded for help with contacting Hamble saying he had forgotten to leave him a telephone number, he might just get lucky.

Assuring Mary that she was going to be okay, he unlocked the front door ready for the ambulance service, then left quickly by the back door.

*

Left to herself, Mary crawled slowly and painfully to the bathroom for her first aid kit, and collapsed against the bath.

Nearly four hours later, and barely alive, she heard Nance, and opened her eyes. He moved quickly, diving to the telephone and dialling 999, she heard him giving her name and address with disciplined distinctness. He then went back to the bathroom. He had to kneel, putting his ear close to her mouth when he saw her trying to speak, her words hardly more than a sigh of sound.

'I'm glad … you're … here.'

'Don't try and talk,' he said.

But Mary turned her head slowly from side to side. 'Listen,' she implored and, finding her words with difficulty, went on: 'The shoe … has … a resonating … frequency … with a top … secret American … project'

She saw light dawn in his eyes. 'So you're not researching UFOs?'

'No … MI5.'

'And this Gene person, who's he? Did he do this to you?'

'Gene's … US Intelligence … your CO met him … bird watcher. … Do you have … the shoe?'

'No. When I got home, it was missing. I thought you had taken it, which is why I came back.'

Again, she shook her head slowly. It was becoming such an effort to speak at all. 'Gene will try …. and get … the shoe from you … Please … you must go … to Benedict Brand … Bond Street. Identify yourself … say you have … *a new setting … for uncle's piece* … Tell him … all I have said … tell him how you … found it … tell him *uncle's peanut … is a … jumping bean.*'

'If the thing's affecting an American project, and this Gene is US Intelligence, why did tell him you knew nothing about it?'

'Don't you think … your own … country needs it, too?' She sighed, her voice tailing off, and closed her eyes exhausted with the effort it had taken to speak so much. All she wanted to do was sleep.

The front doorbell chimed.

*

Nance went with her in the ambulance to the hospital; it seemed the least he could do. At the hospital he was asked a good many questions he couldn't answer.

No, he wasn't a relative, he was a friend.

No, he had no idea how it had happened. Was she going to live?

They looked at him oddly and said they were sorry, but had he not realised she had been dead on arrival. They told him they had called the police and asked him to wait until they arrived. He gave them a false name and address and walked out, feeling dead himself inside.

It was nearly six in the morning. He found a callbox and rang the hotel number he had been given for Hamble, saying it was urgent. Nance was in dire need of a wash and tidy-up before he could think of returning Frank's car to Corsham.

The sleep-robbed Hamble forgave him the early hour and told him to come for breakfast. Nance hung up after getting directions to Hamble's hotel, telling him he'd be there in half an hour, after picking up Frank's car in Lambeth.

*

Hamble's eyebrows rose when he saw the state Nance was in.

'Good Lord, old man,' he exclaimed. 'There's blood all over you! Have you been in an accident; are you hurt?'

'Not mine, Ham,' he answered wearily, 'not mine. I need a bath, a shave, and valet service. I've a medical at ten hundred this morning, and am due before a board at fourteen hundred this afternoon. I've also somehow to return the car to Corsham somehow by eight-thirty … I'd be glad of some help.'

By the time Nance had made himself presentable, he found Hamble waiting for him in the dining room for early breakfast. On the table lay a package that Nance recognised at once.

'How the blazes …' he began.

Hamble held up a navy raincoat. 'You took mine instead of your own.'

'Well, I'll be …' Nance stopped lost for words. He didn't know whether to laugh or cry. After the events of the night, either emotion seemed equally appropriate. He managed a sincere 'Thank you, Ham, thank you, very much … you don't know what this means to me.'

'I'll drive the car back, if you like, old man,' Hamble offered. 'You'll never make it to Corsham and back in time for the medical.'

'That's good of you, Ham,' said Nance, relieved and grateful. The car was beginning to weigh as heavy on his conscience as exhaustion was on his stomach.

'But hang on, Ham,' he added, as the thought occurred to him. 'You're not here just to ferry cars around for me. You must have something else you were going to do. What are you doing in London, anyway?'

'Wangled a couple or so days' leave, old man,' he answered. 'Thought I might do some sightseeing and possibly fit in a show. Taking your car to Corsham this morning will be fun. I get a lift back, I take it?'

'Of course.'

Feeling so much better after something to eat, Nance voiced another thought he'd had. 'Ham, tell you what. If you're taking the car back for me, could you take the shoe as well and get Frank to have a look at it. The CO wants it verified. There are a couple of provisos, though,' he added. 'One, I'd rather Frank *didn't* involve a certain Professor Howard of Polhurst with translating the inscription—'

'He wouldn't need to; I know it.'

'Sorry, Ham. I'm sure you do if you say so, but this has to be all officially stamped and accredited genuine by the experts. You know the sort of thing?'

Hamble shrugged. 'Could've saved them a lot of trouble. What was the other?'

'He hasn't to leave it with *anyone*. I mean, I want it back in my hands when I get there this evening. You threw it away, remember, and Jennifer found it, so finders keepers, okay?'

'Am I arguing with you, old man?' Hamble said, spreading his hands. 'I'm the last person to want it back. I warned you about it didn't I?'

'Sorry,' Nance said. 'There seem to be so many people after it, I'm becoming rapidly paranoid.'

'You should have taken my advice and chucked it in the Channel when you had the chance.'

'I'm beginning to think it was damn good advice,' Nance said. 'But I'd love to know why you recommended it.'

Hamble ignored the question. 'What time shall I tell your sister that you'll be home?'

Before Nance could answer a waiter arrived and told Hamble there was a telephone call for him.

'Another!' he said, 'Well, what it is to be so popular.'

He returned a few moments later with a frown. 'That was my very odd co-pilot of yesterday. Saw him catch the same train to London as I did last night. Damned if I was sharing a seat with him, though; didn't want to give me the time of day on the flight. Now it seems he's back at Stanmore and dying to talk to me. Weird or what? Told him it'll have to wait till midday now and I'll meet him in the bar here. Wonder what on earth he wants?'

Nance shrugged. 'Very weird. I'd be interested to know what he's after.'

'I'll let you know. By the way, you never said what time I should tell your sister you'll be home today.'

'Heaven alone knows really. What with the physical this morning, and the board this afternoon, it'll probably take all day. Tell Margaret I'll ring when I know what train I'm catching.'

His estimate proved correct. The morning was a two-hour session of exhaustive clinical examination, before he was told to report elsewhere during the afternoon for an appointment with the psychiatrist. Subject to their findings, the board was being postponed until Wednesday or Thursday.

It seemed plain enough that he was going to be treated like a priority guinea pig: his physical report to be rushed through to the psychiatric department, who in turn would rush through their comprehensive evidence to the other powers who would hold his ultimate fate in their hands. Even then, he was unlikely to know the upshot until sometime later. There seemed nothing for it but the preservation of a stiff upper lip.

*

The afternoon appointment was all very quiet, informal and friendly to begin with. No obvious pressure was brought to bear, but the pressure nevertheless always there in the back of Nance's mind.

All it seemed he was required to do was talk; give opinions on politics, religion, inventions, his job, his friends, his love life; and give only a passing confirmation of what had happened during the flight of X-Ray Charlie which had been the cause of all the bother. He began to get irritated with all the questions and asked point-blank if he being given a security check.

'You can have one with pleasure,' he was told, 'but that isn't our particular objective. Would you like to make an application for one?'

'I might as well,' he said. 'It can't be worse than this. Okay ... so I had a black out. I admit that. I said something over the r/t for which I can't account. From the records, it's obvious I said I saw something and have no recollection of what it was. All I remember is making the usual request to land. Beyond that, I'm well and truly stymied.'

'So we've already gathered, which is why we haven't been pressing you about it.'

At the end of the session, and when the panel had conferred, he was told to report back the following afternoon.

It was around three in the afternoon, by then, which left him time to find the address in Bond Street Mary had given him before she'd died. It turned out to be a jeweller's where, to his amazement, he found his brother-in-law, Frank Getty, about to leave.

CHAPTER EIGHTEEN

Benedict Brand

Although Frank's business as well as his home was in Corsham, he often had to go to London on the trail of some antique or other, and leave his partner in charge. His partner, a much older man, was well used to these sudden trips and asked no questions. Young Getty was constantly rushing off to chase some last little piece of information on something he had been keeping up his sleeve until he had amassed a small file of evidence before producing his surprise. Sometimes, nothing more would be heard of the enterprise, but more often than not, after days or even weeks of research the junior partner would return with a real windfall, and looking at the shoe that Hamble had delivered to him that morning, along with his car, Frank believed he was on the verge of doing it again.

When he didn't want anyone to know where he was going, the British Museum was his favourite place to give as a destination, whether he intended going there or not, and today was no different.

Having returned Hamble to his hotel around nine-thirty, and then collected a piece of bric-a-brac he had been after for months and had finally persuaded the owner to sell, Frank went to Bond Street arriving there around ten-thirty.

Adrian Brand and his father Benedict were both well known to Frank Getty. Benedict, however, being semi-retired, left his son largely in charge of the business. Thus, when Frank called at the exclusive shop in Bond Street he was admitted at once to a private interview. After a few pleasantries, Frank placed the shoe on Adrian's desk without a word and awaited a verdict. Adrian Brand took it up and surveyed it carefully before examining the tiny diamonds through a jeweller's lens with a professional eye.

'Remarkable … quite remarkable,' he announced at last. 'Undoubtedly original and obviously one of a pair because it's quite definitely the right foot.

'But I suppose it's the diamonds that have brought you to me. You probably know more about the shoe itself than I do. Well, the stones are flawless and perfectly matched, too: they'd fetch a very good price on their own account. What's the inscription?'

'Oghamic, I'm told.'

'Ah, then that's another clue. I've only seen this type of setting twice before, and never in quartz. Judging from the other examples, I'd place the craftsmanship, at its latest, in the fifteenth or sixteenth century. I'd even stick my neck out and say that the trick was individual to one man only … whoever he may have been. Any help?'

'Quite a lot. I take it, from what you said, you've never come across a matching shoe before?'

'No, but my father may have done; it's just possible.' Actually Adrian was covering up his surprise. His father had told him about these particular shoes, the whereabouts of only one was known, the other had been lost for the past twenty-odd years. So either this was the known – which meant it had been acquired unlawfully – or its fellow, which made it priceless. He was not prepared to admit anything like that to Frank, though.

He approached the matter another way. Leaning back in his chair and turning the piece over in his hands, he said, 'You know, Frank, there's something about this which suggests it's quite unique, with its fellow of course. You know how you get a feeling about things? Well, I'd say this was something more than a curio – sounds mad, I know – but I'd place it in the same catalogue with the Edenhall Goblet or the Fairy Flag of the Macleods. So now for the sixty-four-thousand dollar question …?' He raised an eyebrow.

"Fraid I can't tell you, Adrian. All I can say is that it isn't mine and I'm not hawking it. So it's no use asking me where it came from.'

'Sheer artistic interest, then? Well, we all have our foibles, and I must admit I'm as interested as you are. You wouldn't care to leave it with me for a couple of days, would you?'

Frank shook his head. 'Adrian, I wouldn't hesitate to if time wasn't so short, but I must return it to the other party this afternoon.'

'Pity. I'm sure I could turn up a lot more about this, given time. Tell you what I could do. If you'll leave it with me for a couple of hours, I'll have it photographed and work from there. I'll send you copies, of course.'

Frank Getty settled willingly enough for that and made an appointment to call back that afternoon to collect it

*

It was when he was leaving after his second visit to collect the shoe, that he bumped into Nance on his way into the shop.

Nance might have been astonished at their meeting, but Frank was not.

'Oh, hello, Perry. Margaret tell you where I was, then? You're just in time for a lift home.'

'That's great, thanks.' Nance accepted gladly. 'Give me a moment, though. I've a message to deliver here; then I'll be with you. By the way,' he added quickly, 'did Hamble get the shoe to you?'

'Yes,' Frank assured him. 'And there's a couple of questions I'd like to ask you on that before we go any further with it. But thanks for finding someone to bring the car back. Your friend said you'd never have made it to the medical otherwise. How did it go?'

'Tell you on the way home,' said Nance. 'Let me get this off my chest first.' And Frank heard him ask the assistant for Benedict Brand, saying he had a new setting for uncle's piece.

Frank's curiosity had to go on hold when the assistant returned to take Nance into Benedict's office. And Frank wondered if his brother-in-law knew how lucky he was that Benedict was there that afternoon. It was only because Adrian had called him in to see the shoe. Frank also wondered if it was something Margaret and her brother had decided on for one of their uncle's birthdays … although Margaret usually asked her husband's advice first. Still, with her brother home, it would be natural to get him to make any alteration he wanted himself

'I'll wait for you in the car outside,' Frank said.

*

Benedict Brand, white haired and bespectacled, had arrived after a quick phone call from his son telling him he had the lost shoe in the shop, Adrian had concluded '... so if you want to see it before I have to return it to Getty, you had better hurry.'

Benedict came as soon as he could, and confirmed that it was, in fact, the lost shoe and therefore priceless.

The arrival of Frank Getty's brother-in-law with a password that identified him as 'Mary Little' was an odd coincidence. He had Nance ushered into his office, a dark-panelled sanctum that only he ever used. Seated behind a desk, he invited Nance to take an armchair in front of the desk, and waited for his visitor to speak first. He was surprised and immediately wary when Nance told him of a miniature crystal shoe; how it had been found, its history, and Mary's message of its value to British Intelligence – that 'uncle's peanut was a jumping bean' – plus all the details that Nance could relate of her brush with US Intelligence and the circumstances of her awful death.

A principle from which both Brands – senior and junior – never deviated was under no circumstances to volunteer information. Such confidentiality was sacred, even with members of the same family, unless they themselves broke it. As Frank Getty had not revealed the identity of the shoe's owner to Adrian Brand, so neither did Benedict now tell Nance that he had already seen it, but he needed to think about the information that had just been given him.

It was plain the young man in front of him was deeply affected by the painful details of Mary's death, and it called for a gesture. Making no comment, Brand rose and, going to one of the panels lining the walls, pressed a button, disclosing a softly lit drinks cabinet. From this he took a bottle of Cognac, and poured a measure for each of them. Closing the panel, and still without a word, he handed one to Nance, before reseating himself at his desk and gravely lifting his glass.

'In memoriam, Mary,' he said.

He could see that accepting her memory between them as a mutual friend, gave Nance a much needed and tacit recognition of the grief he obviously felt, and possibly been unable to share with anyone until that moment.

Nance returned the toast, drank slowly, and set the glass down. 'Thank you, I appreciate your thought,' he said.

Having pondered the thing from every angle he could in the time, Brand asked quietly, 'And you have the shoe with you, now?'

'No, I gave it to Frank Getty – my brother-in-law – I see he was just leaving as I arrived. Has he shown it you? My CO wants it verified. I was hoping Frank might have time to check it out with his contacts, and with the British Museum before I have to return.'

'I'm sure he will,' replied Brand, ignoring the question and adding nothing to what he had already said. 'I trust you will respect the need for keeping the contents of this meeting to yourself?' he reminded Nance,

'Mary's message, you mean? Of course. But what do you make of what she said about the shoe?'

Brand smiled. 'I'm only an information exchange person, Mr Nance: one who receives and passes on messages. Doing anything else with them, fortunately, is not my responsibility. I have no doubt the right quarter will evaluate all that Mary said, and take whatever action is appropriate in the circumstances. By the way, your brother-in-law, is he waiting for you?'

'Good heavens,' exclaimed Nance looking at his watch and standing up to leave. 'He'll be wondering what on earth's kept me.'

'Tell him Adrian was sharing a few anecdotal tales about his dealings,' Brand advised, smiling. 'But you've forgotten the details, if he asks.'

They shook hands, and left Nance left the office. And Benedict Brand, who had no connection with MI5, was left with everything he needed to pass on to the KGB.

*

As arranged earlier that day Gene, in naval uniform, met Hamble at noon in his hotel bar for a whisky and soda and asked if the pilot had seen or knew anything of a small crystal shoe.

Expecting Hamble to be cagey about it if he had, Gene was surprised when the pilot looked at him askance, saying almost sourly, 'Not you, as well! What do you want with it?'

'Simple, have you got it?'

'No.'

'Do you know where it is?'

'Listen, chum, when I tried to get conversational with you on the way over, you didn't want to know. So what's different, now?'

'One of your passengers; Mary Little? She's had a nasty accident.'

Gene's shock tactic worked well. Hamble's eyebrows rose. 'Why, what happened?' he asked

'She fell on a pair of scissors last night trying to cut a telephone wire.'

Gene could see from the way Hamble was frowning, and from his tell-tale sudden wariness and defensive stiffening, that he was wondering if he was hearing some kind of threat. Was he being told that an 'accident' was going to befall *him* if he didn't answer Gene's questions?

Guardedly, Hamble asked, 'Mind if we start this conversation again?'

'Fine by me,' Gene answered cheerfully. 'What were you doing with the shoe?'

'When?'

To Gene, the question implied that the pilot had had it in his possession either a long time, or more than once. 'When you first had it?' he asked carefully.

'I've been trying to get rid of it, basically,' said Hamble, 'but the blasted thing won't go away.' He tossed back his whisky and pushed the empty glass towards the barman for a refill.

'Meaning?'

'Meaning, every time I think I've got rid, it comes back to haunt me. Thought I'd thrown it away for ever at last, in the lough last Thursday, but here it is right back again. Only this time, thank heavens, somebody else is laying claim to it, and they're welcome.'

'At about what *time* would you have thrown it in the lough?' Gene deliberately gave the question a significance that made Hamble look at him sharply.

'Funny you should ask that,' he answered, 'because it was 11:52, and I'll swear that in a court of law because I always synchronise my watch before take-off. It told me that I landed five minutes later: 11:57 but the station clock read 12:07, and radar said they had an anomaly for ten minutes. Then there's the shoe itself. It was apparently picked up the *other* side of the border. Now if you can throw any light on that little oddity, then I'm all ears.'

'Did you say anything about it to anyone?'

'Do I look silly?' he asked, 'Don't you think if I had, that I wouldn't be in the same boat as Perry Nance, by now? By the grace of God, I kept my mouth shut. It's to do with that UFO, isn't it? It was 11:52 when someone saw the thing: same time as Perry blacked out, and my aircraft 'vanished' for ten minutes.'

'Possibly,' Gene was careful to make his answer noncommittal. Inwardly he was shaken, remembering the displacement of an aircraft in time on the radar screens, 'Where's the shoe now?'

Hamble looked at his watch. 'Hopefully I'd say it could be anywhere between here and Corsham. But, come on, I want to hear what you've got to say about my missing ten minutes?'

'Ask your radar officer,' said Gene. 'Has Lieutenant Nance got the shoe?'

Hamble shrugged. 'I haven't the foggiest,' he said truthfully. It was clear he beginning to feel he had done more than his share of cooperating.

His 'co-pilot' stared at him for a moment or so, thinking that if it hadn't been in either Nance' or Mary's possession the previous night, it must have been with Hamble, himself. '*You* took it to Corsham this morning, didn't you?'

Hamble 's expression became dead-pan and he again drained his glass: 'And who the hell says I've got to tell *you* where I was this morning?'

'Your CO okayed me with you for this,' Gene reminded him.

'He did no such thing,' said Hamble. 'As I remember, all he okayed you for, was for you to sit in as my co-pilot. He said nothing about answering a load of damned inquisitive questions. Now, if you think Nance has the shoe, why don't you run along and ask *him* about it?'

Gene tipped the remains of his drink down his throat and stood up. 'I think I might just do that,' he said, and left Hamble staring after his departing form.

CHAPTER NINETEEN

Surprise returns for 'Terns

'Wonderful, to see you Perry.' His sister greeted him with a kiss when he and Frank arrived home, and ruffled his hair. 'You haven't changed a bit. But I've an apology. What with one thing and another, and the children, I forgot to let you know there was another telephone call for you last evening. Your CO; he wanted you to ring as soon as you got in last night. He phoned again this morning. I told him you had stayed in town for the medical and we weren't expecting you back until late this afternoon. Mum and Dad called as well. I told them you'd ring back as soon as you could. Your friend Norman Hamble also rang. He wants you to get in touch with him as soon as possible too.'

'Popular, aren't I?' Nance joked, privately thinking it wasn't at all funny, and booked a personal trunk call to Captain Mansett as a first priority.

While he was waiting to be rung back with the connection, he asked Frank for the shoe.

'I thought you wanted me to investigate it,' said Frank.

'I want to know that you still have it in your possession,' said Nance. 'I know you people think you know who you can trust with your pieces, but I trust no one where that shoe's concerned.' It sounded rude and aggressive, but Nance was feeling sore, tired and distrustful.

He saw Frank and Margaret exchange glances that told him they thought his remark was very unlike his usual cheerful, devil-may-care self.

'A friend of mine picked it up somewhere,' Nance explained when Frank produced it. 'I promised I'd get a valuation if I could. Apart from that, I thought it might interest you since it seems so unusual. What do you make of it? Did you show it to Adrian Brand this morning?'

'Let's say I've got a feeling it ought to ring a bell somewhere, but in what room I simply couldn't say at the moment,' replied his brother-in-law sounding cautious. And Nance had to let it go. He knew Frank well enough to know he would be unwilling to say he had shown it to the jeweller if it meant he could keep hold of it for a day or so longer. Frank continued: 'It's pure crystal, of course—'

'You're certain of that?'

Frank stared at him. 'I'm not a nit, Perry. I do at least know the difference between quartz and glass.'

'What about the diamonds?'

'I'd prefer to get an independent valuation on those. And, besides, the way they're set looks unusual to me. I understand you know what these marks are underneath it ...'

'Oghamic script, I'm told,' said Nance. 'That's something else I'd like translated.'

'Well, you're in luck in that respect. There's a man I know in Polhurst who's an archaeologist.'

'Professor Howard, by any chance?'

'It is,' agreed Frank with surprise, 'John Howard, d'you know him?'

'Suffice to say he's the last person I want to ... I mean I'd much rather you got it from a recognised authority, Frank.'

'There's hardly a better one. What's wrong with you?'

'Nothing. I just want the thing done my way, that's all.'

'You won't get it done any way if you're going to be as obstinate as all this, Perry. I can't go chasing all over the British Isles on account of a single piece. Will your friend sell?'

'No. I'm certain of that. I think we'd better forget about it.'

'All right,' Frank soothed quickly, 'no need to get heated if you're all that particular. What I'd like to do is to have the stones assessed. Seeing as I have to go to town again tomorrow morning, I'll take it to Adrian Brand; that is,' he added sarcastically, 'if you have no objection to him?'

'I'm sure he'll be utterly delighted,' Nance assured him truthfully. 'Just see it doesn't leave your sight.'

'Do you want a lift up with me in the morning?'

'Thanks, but my appointment isn't until two-thirty.' He turned to his sister. 'Maggs, I'd like to sleep in, in the morning, if that's okay by you?'

'Of course you can. The children will be at school so you won't be disturbed–'

The telephone rang cutting her short. Margaret listened, then passed the receiver to Nance and, nodding her husband, they left the room quietly closing the door behind them.

Nance was asked to hold the line while he was connected to Mansett.

'Lieutenant Nance, sir,' he said when through. 'You rang.'

'Three times in total! What's going on, Nance? You should have been back here before your flight left. Let alone being unobtainable for nigh on twenty-four hours. I want a report.'

'Of course, sir, but there have been developments ...'

He paused. Just where did he begin? He decided to go straight for the truth. 'Sir, I should tell you first; your friend, Miss Little? I'm sorry to have to tell you this, but she died this morning on her way to hospital.' He could almost physically feel the reaction at the other end: shock, incredulity. Nance went on quickly. 'Sir, it was entirely accidental. I don't know if you knew this, but Miss Little was an MI5 agent. And the accident, involving a US Naval Intelligence agent, happened in her flat.' Nance paused, waiting for a lead. It was not slow in coming, and was razor-edged.

'*And just where do you fit in all of this?*'

Nance told him, beginning with finding Mary penniless at Waterloo, and ending, '… so I had to go back when I found the shoe was missing, and that's when I found Mary Little … dead.'

The almost imperceptible pause marked where he had been going to tell the Captain what she had said, but he decided against it. He knew she had meant him to keep it secret and, after all, MI5 were the people concerned.

'*And the shoe?*' asked Mansett.

'Sir, Lieutenant Hamble had it with my raincoat. I'd picked his up by mistake. The shoe is now with my brother-in-law.'

'*Good. Let's see what he makes of it, and I'll see you when you get back.*'

He responded politely 'Sir,' but the receiver was already down at the other end.

It was obvious to Nance that he had given his CO more than enough to think about, and it had taken a large amount of the heat off him, himself … or so he imagined, unaware of what was in the pipeline from another direction.

Leaving the room, he remembered he had not rung Norman Hamble, and returned to the phone absent mindedly leaving the door ajar.

Hamble outlined the conversation he had had with Gene Gauss that day.

Nance reassured him, 'Ham, you did absolutely right. The man's a menace. He's US Naval Intelligence and dangerous.'

'*So what's the Skipper doing giving him clearance with my aircraft?*' asked Hamble, his tone sounding justifiably annoyed.

'He's obviously pulled something with the Old Man,' said Nance. 'But take it from me, Ham, he's responsible for Mary Little's death. She was MI5.'

Hamble whistled '*Bloody hell! I hope you know what you're doing, and look out for yourself.*'

'I'll be all right,' said Nance. 'I'd be grateful though if you'd keep in touch.'

*

The rest of the afternoon and evening was pleasant enough with Margaret's children, William, eleven, Millicent, nine, and Gillian, seven, all making a big fuss of him. He was glad to let them drag him outside to play with them. They and the garden were a world away from the horror of the previous night.

The following day was Tuesday. Before leaving in the morning and while her brother was still asleep, Frank passed the shoe to his wife with instructions to take it to Professor Howard that afternoon *after* Perry had left for London. Although Frank had tacitly agreed he would not refer to that authority himself, he was so intrigued by the artefact he eased his conscience by doing it this way.

'It's the only way Perry's going to get it done before he has to return to base,' he told Margaret. 'And what the eye doesn't see, the heart won't grieve about.'

Margaret sent the children to school with packed lunches and a covering letter as they usually came home for their meal at midday. Nance slept in until eleven that morning, had a late breakfast and caught the noon train to London.

Margaret, who had already rung the Professor to ask if she could see him that afternoon, explaining what it was her husband wanted, had been invited to lunch at one, so dropped her brother off at the station on her way.

Margaret decided that John Howard reminded her of a bird; a bright-eyed, inquisitive looking, ring-necked pheasant with gravitas with his glinting spectacles, white collar above a blue shirt, and plum coloured waist-coat over his rounded form with its thin legs.

He called her 'dear lady' and insisted they had lunch before she showed him the artefact, '... or we'll not get anything to eat,' he said. 'The translation could take time, and my housekeeper has the meal ready for us.'

While they ate, he asked after Frank and the children, expressing an interest in anything and everything that Margaret had to say of their progress.

'Never had any of my own, dear lady,' he said when Margaret asked. 'I'm a confirmed bachelor. Just the one niece I inherited after my brother died. Twenty-one years old now, and in the WRNS stationed in Northern Ireland.'

'My brother's stationed at the Royal Naval Air Station Derry Down. Could be the same one? I've not heard of other shore establishments in Northern Ireland.'

'Must be the same then. Jennifer's is with HMS *Arctic Tern*. Did you know,' he went on, when she nodded, 'that the navy names all its flying bases after birds?'

'No,' she said, 'Perry's never mentioned that.'

'Yes, well apparently inland establishments are named after birds of prey, and shore bases are named after sea birds – my niece has become a mine of information on the subject. And now, dear lady, if you have had a goodly sufficiency, shall I take a look at this artefact that Frank's found?'

They left the table and went to his study where she handed him the shoe, which he examined with intense interest.

'Extraordinary,' he said. 'You know, dear lady, that husband of yours really has the most extraordinary luck. This is quite the most incredible thing I have ever seen in my whole life. Where on earth did he find it?'

'I have no idea,' she said. 'He didn't say.'

'He never does, does he?' he said with a chuckle. 'Now let me see. It's certainly Oghamic. He's quite correct there ...' He picked up a pencil and carefully copied the script onto a notepad, then looked up at Margaret, his eyes twinkling over the top of his glasses '... it's short but very poetic. If I'm not mistaken, it simply reads: *until the day dawns and the shades are gone* ... And that's it, for what it's worth—' a knock at the door interrupted him. 'Come in,' he called.

The housekeeper entered, followed by a girl in WRNS uniform who ran to the Professor, flung her arms around him and burst into tears.

CHAPTER TWENTY

Read All About It ...

Nance found the afternoon every bit as bad as he had anticipated, and the whole atmosphere very different from the previous day. Where the panel then had been two doctors and a psychiatrist, there was now just the psychiatrist and a civilian who was introduced as 'Jethro'. Both seemed to be looking at him rather oddly he thought, almost as if there was something new they had just learnt about him that they had not known before.

Their questioning, never straight to the point they were really aiming for, started by asking him to tell everything he had seen, heard or read about UFOs.

'About as much as anyone else in the Service,' he answered promptly. 'Obviously, we're all interested to some extent in the phenomena. That doesn't mean we all believe in the things, but it can't be denied that there are odd objects seen from time to time – by professional people, as well as the man in the street.'

He was urged, nevertheless, to remember and relate everything he had ever heard or read; who told him, where he had read it and his impressions at the time. He did his best, and it was soon obvious that the thumbscrews were only just beginning to be wound in.

'And that's all you've ever heard on the subject? You've never met anyone claiming to have seen one?'

What the devil were they after? He did some quick thinking.

'I did chance to meet a woman last Saturday evening at The Shaun Hotel in Londonderry,' he offered. 'Her name was Mary Little. She said she was researching the subject, but we never got round to discussing whether she had ever actually seen one.'

'Captain Mansett's report says briefly that you were not the first person from *Arctic Tern* to visit the scene of the UFO crash. You returned in company with …' The questioner made a show of consulting the papers he had before him.

'A wren,' said Nance. Mansett could hardly have omitted that – in fact he knew he hadn't for he had spoken highly of the girl's initiative. 'Her name's Howard. She had got in touch with me that morning saying she had been to the scene of the crash. I didn't believe her straight away, but then it occurred to me such evidence might conceivably have a bearing on what I was supposed to have said.'

'Why did she do that, do you think?'

'She told me she had seen the thing explode from the control tower. She was the one who had taken down everything I'd said, and believed it would help me if I saw the facts for myself.'

'Yet you didn't mention her when you were asked if you had ever met anyone who had actually seen a UFO. Why was that?'

He made a helpless gesture. 'I forgot.'

'Forgot!' 'Jethro' said, while the psychiatrist made notes. 'Isn't that rather remarkable? I would have thought it quite astonishing to meet a girl who not only shows you where the thing came down, but that she had even seen it before it did so. And yet you "forgot" all about it?'

Nance began to get irritated. At best they would probably interpret the omission as another glaring blackout. 'That's exactly what I do mean. If it's another black mark against my record, I can't help it. You were asking me about UFOs previously, and I was thinking *previous* to the present. I didn't … I don't think of Jennifer Howard in that way.'

'So in what way did you think of this girl?'

'I didn't. I'd never met her before.'

'But you did again, afterwards?'

Damn them. 'Yes, as a kind of thank you for the trouble she'd taken, I invited her to go sailing with me on Lough Foyle Saturday afternoon.'

'And then you took her out to dinner that evening. Where?'

Nance could have punched the fellow. They'd been saving this, of course.

'To The Shaun Hotel.'

'Where you met this investigator woman? Yet you didn't you mention before that this girl – who, I'll remind you, is vitally concerned in your case – was with you at the time?'

Nance took a deep breath. If he didn't control his feelings, he could make his situation even worse. 'I gave you a straight answer to a straight question.'

'But Jennifer Howard *was* present when you had this conversation with the flying saucer researcher. How did that start? Did you speak to her first?'

'No. It was in the lounge while I was getting drinks. Jennifer – Wren Howard – went to find a table, and the only one available with empty chairs was this woman's. When I came back,' Nance paused to think, 'Jennifer told me that the woman had introduced herself as having been …' *Oh God, I've forgotten that as well.*

'Having been …?' he was prompted.

'Having been a wren at *Arctic Tern* during the war. I'm sorry, I forgot to tell you that.'

'An amazing coincidence, yet again you forgot?'

The point was not pressed further. Instead they applied a full turn to the thumbscrews.

'I wonder, would you remember ever meeting the lady again after that evening?'

'Yes,' he answered levelly. 'She was a passenger on the flight I was booked on to Stanmore, Sunday afternoon. Apparently she was a friend of the CO's – Captain Mansett – and he arranged it.'

'And did you meet the lady again after that?'

Nance bridled. 'Look here, do we have to go into *every* detail of my private life?'

'Unfortunately, yes. You asked for a security check, which this isn't, by the way. This is merely a precursor, or what the Americans would term a fact-finding tour. We aren't concerned with intimate details. We *are* concerned with times and places of where you were, and with whom. Now suppose you tell us, taking your time and in your own words, the events of Sunday evening and Monday morning?'

Forget the thumbscrews – this was the rack! he thought, and wondered how much they knew. He tried proceeding on the premise that they could not possibly know that he knew of Mary's connection with MI5, or that he had gone to Mary's flat, or even, come to that, of Gene and his connection with the American Central Intelligence Agency.

Bad thinking. Their questions, the way they probed soon told him that they knew all about Mary, her death, Gene Gauss and his own presence in the flat. How on earth they had found out was a mystery until he realised Gauss could have told them some of it. *But would Gene have known he, Nance, had gone back to the flat?* He was asked no questions about the shoe, nor anything about an artefact being found at the site, which seemed odd. It was a bit dodgy, too, therefore, when it came to saying *why* he had gone back to the flat.

He got round it by telling them he had had an attack of conscience over leaving Mary as he had – because of Gene – and had gone back to check she was all right, which, as it turned out, fully justified his hunch because she wasn't. To his relief, this seemed to satisfy them. But as with everything, they went through it over and over again, attempting to trip him up, until by the time he was allowed to go, which was nearly seven that evening, he felt utterly drained. They told him he was to attend the enquiry at ten hundred hours Thursday morning … *and what a bloody awful affair that was going to be*, he thought bleakly.

Emerging from the underground at Waterloo, his eyes were caught by a banner headline of *The Evening News* board:

MYSTERY OF WOMAN FOUND DEAD IN BATHROOM

Buying a copy, he read:

The Soviet Union yesterday accused American Intelligence of being involved in the murder of one of their scientists, found dead in her bathroom on Monday.

They claim that the woman, twenty-nine-year-old Mary Little, was approached by an American agent shortly before her death at her London flat in the early hours of Monday morning.

Officially listed as working for the International Computer Organisation, Mary Little's office was at Woodgate Street, London.

The allegations published in the official Soviet newspaper, Izvestia, also accuse British Intelligence of trying to cover up the circumstances of her death and of tampering with the body.

A senior government source today dismissed the allegations as 'completely absurd' but in the shadowy world of espionage and counter-espionage, no statement can ever be taken at face value. It may never be known who Mary Little actually was. The Russians have long made a practice of infiltrating KGB officers into international organisations and trade missions where they possess an immaculate cover as well as, in most cases, diplomatic immunity. If a KGB agent, then the name 'Mary Little' would almost certainly have been a pseudonym.

The Russian version of the events of Sunday night and Monday morning in the small flat in Lambeth is certainly dramatic. Having been apparently tailed by her US Intelligence watchdog all the way from a holiday in Northern Ireland, Mary was found with a pair of scissors through her heart. The Russians claim that that British authorities carried out a hurried autopsy before a Soviet doctor could reach the scene, despite a promise that no examination would be made until the Russians arrived. Additionally, they say, Mary Little's passport was missing when her flat was searched.

'To this moment,' claims a spokesman for the Russian Embassy, 'the Soviet Union has received no reply to any of the questions put to the British Government by our ambassador: neither detailed results of the autopsy, nor copies of interrogation of witnesses, although it is known that Miss Little's body was found by a serving British naval officer who accompanied her in the ambulance to the hospital and then left after giving a false name and address.

The article immediately explained the reason for the suspicious nature of the interrogation that afternoon, but where could this misinformation have originated? 'Russian version of events' indeed! 'Hurried autopsies' and 'missing passports' ... it hardly sounded like Gene, and certainly not Captain Mansett.

So where had it come from? He went back over everything he had told Benedict Brand, and there it was. Only Benedict Brand could have given the KGB the kind of details that could have contrived this vengeful, clever tissue of lies and half-truths ... and what a stirred-up hornet's nest of revenge it was for Mary's death. The very fact there was no mention of the shoe also went to prove it. He had told Brand that Mary had said the shoe had a resonating frequency with a top secret American project. The Russians wouldn't want anyone to know that they had learned that. Had Mary really been working for the Russians? Or was Brand a double agent?

As if all that wasn't enough, his eye was caught by a smaller set of headlines further down the page as he was folding the paper.

WREN TOLD GUARDIAN DEAD, THEN FINDS HIM ALIVE

He went on to read:

When Jennifer Howard, twenty-one-year-old Wren stationed with the Fleet Air Arm in Northern Ireland, was told that her guardian had died, she was sent home on compassionate leave. When greeted by her guardian's housekeeper, however, and taken to see him alive and well, she was overcome with emotion. Speaking from the family home today, Professor J Howard – her mother's brother, who has looked after Jennifer ever since her parents were killed in a car crash when she was a baby – said: 'I shall never forget her face when she came into the room and saw me. She was completely shattered emotionally. She simply broke down and wept.'

The Navy has apologised for the mistake which caused Jennifer to be sent from Derry Down in Northern Ireland to her home at Polhurst in Sussex today.

Professor Howard said: 'I can understand a mistake being made. What deeply concerned me was that somewhere there was a mother who had just become a widow waiting for a daughter who never arrived.'

Captain Mansett, the CO at RNAS Derry Down, said today, 'It is a most regrettable and unfortunate misunderstanding. The wren whose father had died was also called Howard. There was a mix-up over names and the wrong girl was sent home. The other girl's mother was informed as soon as Professor Howard telephoned us on the arrival of his niece, and her daughter has now been sent on compassionate leave. I appreciate the distress that has occasioned to all concerned, and I shall personally be writing to both families.'

And Nance thought he had had a bad day! It was obviously nothing compared to what the Old Man must be going through. And Jennifer was home in Polhurst – what a mercy he had refused to let Frank take the shoe to the Professor.

Suddenly his blood ran cold as he remembered Frank had said he would be taking the shoe into Brand on Bond Street that very morning. Nance verified the time of his train home, and rang his sister.

CHAPTER TWENTY-ONE

A story at bedtime

Mrs Peggott apologised for the interruption with Jenny who was laughing and crying at the same time as she hugging her uncle.

'Beg pardon, sir, but there was no holding her.'

Margaret stood up tactfully to leave. 'It's been a lovely lunch, Professor–'

'Oh, please,' said Jenny, letting go of the bewildered man before he could open his mouth as she belatedly remembered her manners. 'You mustn't leave on my account. I'm not really crying; it's tears of joy! I was told that my uncle had died and he's alive!' And the whole story came out.

Her three hearers were all appalled. The Professor at once booked a trunk call to the WRNS Chief Officer at Derry Down, the housekeeper clucked over Jenny soothingly, and Margaret waited to take her leave.

On the Professor's return he made a belated introduction between them, and Jenny's eyes widened incredulously.

'Mrs Getty!' she exclaimed. 'Would you be Pen's sister?'

'If you mean Perry Nance, then yes,' agreed Margaret, smiling.

'So you have brought the shoe to Uncle Jay?'

Jenny's question brought an immediate rebuke from her uncle. 'Really, Jennifer,' he said. 'Mrs Getty is my guest.'

Jenny turned to Margaret. 'Mrs Getty, you must have brought the shoe with you. Pen would have asked you to bring it here. He did, didn't he?'

'No, Jennifer,' she replied. 'My husband asked me to bring it to your uncle for a translation of the inscription.'

'So you *do* have it!' she exclaimed, and turned quickly back to her guardian. 'Please, Uncle Jay, it's *my* shoe: I found it. Pen knows it's mine.' She looked back to Margaret as a dreadful thought struck her, 'He hasn't *sold* it to your husband, has he, Mrs Getty?'

'Good heavens, of course not,' But Margaret's laugh was slightly uneasy, as she now realised why her brother had not wanted the shoe to be seen by the Professor.

'Jennifer ...?' Taking her hand, her uncle made her sit down, asking Margaret if she wouldn't mind waiting to hear his niece out. Margaret resumed her seat, and John Howard returned to Jenny. 'Now suppose you begin at the beginning, my dear, and tell us what all this is about, eh?'

'Can I hold the shoe, please?' asked Jenny.

He held out his hand to Margaret. 'Would you mind very much?' he asked quietly. She had no option but to retrieve it from her handbag to give him.

Before Jenny could begin, however, the Professor's trunk call to the WRNS Chief Officer was rung through.

Left to watch Jenny with the shoe safe in her hands once more, Margaret studied the girl's face alight with relief and delight. There was no doubt in her mind where the shoe truly belonged.

When the Professor reappeared, it was with the news that Jenny was not expected to return on the next train back. In the circumstances, and it being their mistake, she was on leave until the weekend.

He patted her hand. 'So now, Jennifer, you have plenty of time to tell us what this is all about.'

Jenny related how she had found the shoe, had met Margaret's brother, been taken out to dinner – taking the shoe with her to show him – and had left it in the lounge. How, going back for it the following day she had seen Pen driving off with it, and been told by her friends that it was one of the *Fairy Shoon of Cladich*.

'… I can even tell you what the Oghamic inscription says,' she said to her uncle 'It says: *Until the day break and the shadows flee,*' and the other shoe says: *Thy feet shall bring my peace*'

The Professor nodded. 'That is a translation, more or less for this one,' he agreed, and looked at Margaret. 'I am very sorry about this, but there does appear to be a genuine question of ownership here. What would you like to do?'

Margaret knew what she'd like to do to her husband. She was feeling inwardly furious. It was a little more difficult imagining how she was going to face her brother.

'Could I make a suggestion?' she asked. They both nodded.

'If Jennifer is in agreement, I would like to take her – and the shoe, of course – back home with me. Then my husband can hear for himself what Jennifer has just told us, and we will then see what Perry has to say for himself when he gets home.'

'That seems fair,' agreed the Professor. 'Just one thing. Jennifer has just had a tiring eighteen-hour long journey to get here. I imagine she must be feeling quite fatigued. Wouldn't that be so, my dear?'

'Oh, I'll be all right now, uncle,' she assured him. 'Now I know *you're* all right and I've got the shoe back, I could go on for ever. But I think I ought to go for a quick wash and change.'

Margaret nodded. 'Of course. I don't have to be back until three for the children … I hope Jennifer can stay for dinner?' she asked the Professor. 'We'll bring her back before it gets late.'

Jenny changed into her best slacks and sweater. She knew Peggsy wouldn't wait to get her uniform spruced up again and looking good, and Jenny was grateful. At the rate she was going, she would never have time to do it herself.

Both her uncle and Peggsy saw her off at the door and in Jenny's fond embrace of them both and theirs of her, Margaret saw the girl's vulnerability and complete lack of sophistication.

*

Jenny chatted away easily enough to Margaret in the car during the journey, telling her how Pen had told her all about his home near Windermere at Newby Bridge and of the sister with three children who lived in Corsham. '… And I never imagined in all the world, I should be meeting you so soon.'

She became shy and awkward though when she saw where Margaret lived. The Getty's house was large and well furnished, surrounded by what seemed to Jenny an endless amount of garden with cedars, large borders of shrubberies, surrounding well-tended lawns, a trellised walk and a tennis court.

Being an only child, and never having been to school, Jenny was also shy when she was introduced to Margaret's children. They were too self possessed for her to know how to relate to them. With their mother present, however, they took their cue from her; Jennifer was their guest and was to be made to feel welcome. So they took her off on a tour of their favourite haunts in the garden.

When Frank got home around five, Jennifer was nowhere to be seen. Margaret followed the sound of voices that led to the children's special den where she could hear Jenny's voice. She was telling a story at which the youngest was shrieking with delight, and the others chanting what was, by then, a well-rehearsed line:

Who cuts the wood
That feeds the fire,
That heats the oven
That bakes the cakes
To keep them from star-va-tion

Margaret crept away then unseen. The story that Jenny had for Frank could wait. She nevertheless had to fill her husband in on why she had brought the girl home. Frank confirmed Jennifer had correctly identified the shoe, and that it was a priceless family heirloom. He then spent the next few hours trying to think up ways of justifying himself to his brother-in-law.

The shoe itself was in the safe in his study. Margaret had managed to persuade Jenny to see the common sense of putting such a valuable object where it wouldn't get lost again, rather than carrying it around in her pocket.

They were just finishing dinner when Nance rang with the time of the train he was catching. He also asked if Frank still had the shoe.

Margaret thought it only right to prepare him for what he would find when he got home.

'It's here. But Perry, I ought to warn you; Jennifer's here, too.'

'I should *have* known,' he answered with edge to his voice. 'Of course she would be: it's the first place she'd make for.'

She stopped him firmly. 'Perry, *I* brought her home.'

'You?' he was plainly astonished. 'I mean, how come? How did you know?'

'Frank asked me to take the shoe to Professor Howard … I know, I know,' she quelled his outrage. 'And you can have it out with him when you get home. For myself, I had no alternative when I heard what the poor girl had to say. And I must say, Perry, it doesn't reflect very well on you.'

'Listen, Maggs, you don't know half the story,' he protested. 'There's a lot more to this than even Jennifer knows. Captain Mansett himself, will bear me out there. So just wait till you've heard *all* the facts before you start accusing me of foul play. Anyway, I've got to go or I shall miss the train. See you later.'

'Bye,' said Margaret, looking thoughtful as she replaced the receiver. She went back to the table.

'I suppose you've told him?' guessed her husband, shooting a glance in Jenny's direction.

'Of course, I couldn't leave it to be a complete shock,' she replied. She turned to Jenny, who had realised the call was from Nance and was looking expectant. 'Perry will be home around eight, Jennifer.'

'That means we won't see him,' wailed Gillian.

'Never mind,' soothed Margaret. 'If you're still awake, I'll let him come up to see you with a goodnight kiss.'

Divining the sudden wistful look on Jenny's face, Margaret smiled at her kindly. 'We'll give you two a chance to talk, too, Jennifer,' she said, and saw William and Millicent exchange looks of surprise before their eyes went to their guest. Their mother could guess they were thinking that this was the real reason Jennifer was there. She was Uncle Perry's new girlfriend!

'Better than some of the others,' Margaret heard William whisper, nudging his sister. Millicent nodded. Her mother knew it was true. None had ever taken the trouble to have fun with them the way Jennifer had, or to meet them at their own level without any hint of condescension.

*

Children being children, they had been quick to pick up on another difference, also. There was something of a mystery connected with their uncle's new girlfriend. It had a lot to do with their father not being in their mother's best books, which also had to do with their having to stay at school for lunch, and the sharpness they had just heard in their mother's voice when she had spoken to their uncle over the phone.

William, who fancied himself as the next Sherlock Holmes, had also overheard his uncle's strange telephone conversation with someone he called Ham about a dangerous American agent who had killed a lady from MI5.

He suggested to his sister after dinner that it all added up to a Most Serious Mystery. William liked to think in capitalised words, having been brought up on AA Milne. He fancied it added weight to his sentences in a largely female household, his father being out so much. He also looked on Millicent as his Dr Watson. Even if she was a girl, she had often displayed an uncanny intuition for the truth, at which he had been astonished on more than one occasion.

She proved it again then when their parents had gone with Jennifer into the study closing the door behind them.

'I know what the cause of the trouble is,' she confided. 'I was with Jennifer when mummy told her the "shoe" would be better off in daddy's safe, than being carried around in her pocket, so it must be valuable. Jennifer didn't want to give it up.'

'It must be a small one then if it could be carried around in her pocket.'

''Tis small,' she confirmed. 'It's made of glass and it's even smaller than a real Cinderella shoe.'

'Wow,' he breathed, then told his sister what he had overheard their uncle saying on the phone the previous day.

Millicent was impressed but reproachful. 'Will, how could you? You know we're not supposed to eavesdrop.'

'Mill, if it's something that's upsetting our household, then I vote it's a Necessity. And this sounds Really Bad.'

There seemed little they could do straight away about solving the mystery but to promise to share and compare notes on anything that was out of the ordinary.

They noted another call for their uncle received by their father from a Lieutenant Hamble who was told that Perry would not be back until after nine. Their father put the phone down with a grumble at their mother that 'the phone bill was going be astronomical at this rate.'

It was an engrossing game, and it wasn't hard either to see Jennifer becoming more nervous as the evening progressed.

The girls wanted her to read them a story at bedtime, and Jenny was glad to have something to do that would take her mind off waiting for Nance. But she was edgy; jumping whenever the phone rang, which it did when their grandmother rang to ask why Perry had not rung her back the previous evening.

William joined the girls in their room, not so much as to be read to, although Jenny read with great expression, as to be supportive. Without saying a word, he felt she was looking to him for protection.

If Jenny had been aware of it, she might have agreed.

When their uncle arrived back, she remained rigidly where she was, but Margaret sent Nance up to say goodnight to his nephew and nieces while she prepared his meal.

The children saw her stiffen defensively when he appeared in the doorway, but if he saw it, their uncle took no notice.

*

Nance was inwardly surprised that instead of their usual rush to assault him, the children stayed where they were, plainly waiting for Jennifer's reaction.

'Hello, Jennifer,' he said with that same easy lightness he always seemed to assume under pressure.

'Hello, Pen,' she returned with apparent cheerfulness. 'Just finishing a story for Gillian and Millicent.'

'You go ahead,' he invited. 'Will and I will listen.' He ruffled the boy's hair as he sat next to him on Gillian's bed, and gave his niece a kiss.

'Me, too,' demanded Millicent, puckering up for a kiss. 'And Jennifer,' she said imperiously. Jenny blushed as he dropped a light kiss on her forehead, before, with all obligations observed, he held up his finger for silence for her to conclude the chapter on Toad's homecoming.

Watchful and listening, Nance found it almost impossible to believe that it had only been five days ago that he had first met this girl, a complete stranger, and here she was in his sister's house, cheerfully and happily integrated with the children. She had changed, too. He had been dreading having to face her at the end of what had already been an immensely difficult day, but the way she had answered him, covering the strain between them with a show of cheerfulness, promised the possibility of some adult understanding when it came to discussing the shoe.

She ended the reading by rounding on the two girls beside her with a growly laugh that sent them squealing beneath the covers.

When Margaret called up that Perry's meal was ready, he banished William to his own room, saw the girls tucked up for the night, allowing Jenny their demanded hug and kiss, then motioned her to precede him down the stairs.

*

Frank had found Nance quite uncommunicative when he had collected him from the station. However, his own conscience being in a slightly worse state than that of his brother-in-law, he apologised for sending Margaret to John Howard with the shoe, and came clean on what Brand had told him concerning it.

'… An absolutely priceless piece, Perry. It's in the safe at home.'

'Then thank God for some good news,' had been the gloomy response, and nothing more said on the subject until Perry had had his meal, in the middle of which his father rang.

He was able to get away with a fairly short conversation, with his dinner going cold, which meant not having to tell him too much of what was going on with him in London.

'But you know what they're like,' he said to Margaret. 'I dread what Dad's going to say if he hears I've been suspended.'

'So what have you told them?' she asked.

'I said I *could* be home at the weekend as I'm over here for an interview at the Admiralty which I can't talk about at the moment – which is true enough.'

'Well, I'd think it will be more a case of *when*, than *if*, Dad finds out. Remember he has friends at the Admiralty and is bound to ask one of them to make a discreet enquiry.'

'Do you have to remind me ...?'

After his meal, and having made up his mind how he was going to deal with the question of the shoe, he joined Frank, Margaret and Jenny in the lounge, announcing it would save a lot of time if he read something to them.

Unfolding *The Evening News*, he went through the article on Mary Little.

Jenny gave a bewildered gasp. 'No!' and went pale. Margaret listened carefully, and Frank expressed bafflement.

'So what's that got to with anything?' he asked when Nance had finished.

'Everything to do with the shoe, precious little to do with the truth,' answered Nance grimly. 'I'm sorry, Jennifer,' he went on, his tone conciliatory in explanation. 'But Captain Mansett asked me to get the shoe verified. Mary Little had rung him and told him of its existence, and he pulled me into see him Sunday morning. There wasn't time to explain to you; I knew you'd find it difficult. So I ran.

'Unfortunately, however, a US Intelligence agent, one Gene Gauss, was also after it and, according to Norman Hamble, was with him disguised as his co-pilot on the flight over here – with the Captain's blessing. The CO had also put Mary on the same plane, so the American agent was following her, thinking she was going to steal the shoe from me at some point or other. He tailed her to her flat where this dreadful accident happened. I couldn't find the shoe when I got home here, so I had to get the car keys from you, Frank, and hare off back to her flat to confront her. I found her almost dead, got the ambulance and went with her to hospital. Yes, I'm the one who gave a false name and address, but I had neither the time nor inclination to be interviewed by the police.

'Hamble had left a message here with Margaret for me to ring him, which I did at six that morning, and found I had picked up the wrong raincoat. The shoe was in mine, which is why I couldn't find it. Simple as that and a mercy, really, or we might never have seen it again.'

'Well, thanks, Perry,' said Frank. 'But why on earth should MI5 *and* American Intelligence be after it, for heaven's sake?'

'I don't understand the technicalities, Frank, but it appears to have a resonating frequency with some secret experiment the Americans were carrying out in Lough Foyle. They had no idea what caused their project to abort, but Gene Gauss was at the site when Jennifer got there and saw her take something from under a fallen tree, so it all started from there.'

'And the Russians? Where do they fit in all this?'

'Benedict Brand,' he said. 'Sorry to be the bearer of bad news, Frank, but Mary didn't know he was a double agent – and *I* certainly didn't – when she asked me to deliver her dying message to him. She thought he was MI5.'

'The old b ...!' Frank exclaimed. 'I remember you saying "a new piece for uncle's setting" when you asked to see him, and thinking you and Margaret were cooking up a birthday present for some relative. Who'd have thought you were engaged in high espionage!'

'It was a password, and I nearly had a fit tonight when I read the evening paper tonight, realised what had happened and that you had said you were taking the shoe to him today.'

'Took it yesterday, Perry,' Frank confessed. '*And* I had to leave it with Adrian for a couple of hours to photograph and find out more about it. I'd just collected it back when

I ran into you. I didn't tell you then, because I wanted to hold on to it a bit longer for the Professor to have a look at today.'

'So what happens now?' asked Margaret, glancing from one to the other of them.

Nance looked at her protégé. 'I think that's really up to Jennifer now,' he said quietly. 'She found it, it is her shoe.'

'I would like to take it back with me,' she said. 'And I'll show it to the Captain.'

'If that's what you want, it's all yours,' said Nance. He personally had had enough of it to last him a lifetime.

'Well, you'd better get it from the safe,' Margaret said to her husband. 'I promised we'd have Jennifer home before it got too late, and it's nearly ten now.'

*

Unknown to the adults, William and Millicent had crept down to the hall, and had had their ears glued on the muffled exchange behind the lounge door.

Satisfied that they now had sufficient information on the mystery to explain all, William pointed his sister back upstairs, and followed as silently as he could until they reached the landing.

'First off,' he whispered, 'not a word of this to Gilly. Second, pretend to be asleep when they come up.'

They heard the lounge door open and their father cross to the study, while their mother, uncle and Jenny went into the hall. Their voices floated clearly up to their listeners.

'You'll run Jennifer home, won't you, Perry?' said their mother and bid the girl goodnight, adding, '… But not goodbye, Jennifer, because now we have got to know you Frank and I – and the children, I know – will be delighted if you would visit us whenever you are on leave.'

Craning around the corner of the stairwell, they saw her embracing the girl warmly, and Jenny hugging her back. Opening the front door their mother smiled at the two leaving, 'Promised you, didn't I, you would have a chance to talk alone?' she reminded Jenny.

Knowing their mother's next step would be upstairs to check on them, William and Millicent melted away with a nod to each other back to their own rooms.

*

But it was a silent drive back to Polhurst for Nance and Jenny, each of them busy with unspoken thoughts, although Jenny had to break the silence to guide him through the village to the cottage.

'Looks pretty; very olde worlde,' he said, peering through the darkness. 'When do you go back to camp?'

'I've got until the weekend now,' she said. 'What about you?'

'It's a day off tomorrow then the Board isn't being convened until Monday. Is there anything you'd like to do tomorrow? Frank says I can use the car; he doesn't need it till Friday. We could take a run to the coast.'

'Really?' she asked, hardly able to believe he meant it.

'Yes, really,' he laughed. 'Or wouldn't you like that?'

'Oh, I'd like it very, very much, Pen. Could we take a picnic, and go swimming as well?'

'Of course,' he said. 'I'll be round at nine for an early start, how's that? It's only twenty miles to Worthing.'

'And I'll bring the picnic,' she said.

He laughed. 'Come here,' he ordered fondly.

It was a long, satisfying kiss that Jenny wished could have lasted for ever, but the housekeeper had heard the car arrive and having judged its occupants had had the right amount of time for their goodnights, was stood framed in the light of the open door of the cottage.

'Uh-oh,' Nance said, 'there's your guardian dragon ready to come to your rescue. Do you think she's going to let you out of her sight tomorrow?'

Jenny giggled. 'Of course she will. It's Uncle Jay who's my guardian, not Peggsy.'

'Well, I know which one I'd rather face,' he said, getting out of the car.

Knowing the drill by now, Jenny waited for him to open the door her side and help her out. She could almost see the look of proud approval in the waiting housekeeper's eyes. Peggsy would be thinking that her escort was a proper young gentleman, and no mistake.

Waiting until she had reached the house, Nance called out, ''Night, Jennifer,' with a wave of his hand and, 'Evening, Mrs Peggott,' before getting back in the car and driving off.

None of them paid any attention to another car that had slowed down as it passed before picking up speed and vanishing into the darkness ahead.

CHAPTER TWENTY-TWO

A swap for two kids

With only one thought in mind, Gene Gauss set about getting his hands on the glass slipper, which meant gathering every bit of information he could on the Gettys in Corsham, and on Professor Howard in Polhurst.

He had already obtained the use of a car via the contact who had given him Mary's address and so, after changing back to his usual nondescript appearance, had his breakfast at an all night cafe in London, and arrived in Corsham around seven on Monday morning,

Posing as a salesman, it was easy enough to find bed and breakfast in the town. It was not so easy to arrange for out-of-hours meals, but a little extra on top of the charge bought the promise of a cold meal and a flask of hot soup to be left in his room when late back.

Some time was spent in careful surveillance of the Getty household. Hamble's arrival in a car that Frank Getty then drove off back the way it had just come with the naval officer still in it was something of a puzzle. Trailing them all the way back to London, however, was useful in view of the meeting he had arranged with Hamble.

He followed Frank the rest of the morning only to find it seemed a normal working day for the man.

It was quick change then back into naval uniform for his appointment with Hamble, which at least established how the shoe had come to be where it had been found.

Knowing what he did about Project Jump, Hamble's story was something that was going to need some deep analysis. If the pilot had thrown the shoe out at the precise moment their missile had been about to materialise, it meant the position of Hamble's aircraft, far from causing him any neurological problems, had simply thrown him ten minutes forward in time. While Nance on the other hand had suffered a loss of memory.

Gene had to get hold of the shoe which he now knew to be in Corsham.

Two hours, and a quick meal later, he was in place to resume his surveillance and see the children walking home just before their father arrived back with Nance.

Tuesday morning, stocking up with packed sandwiches and a flask, he returned to the Gettys. Noting that Margaret drove Frank to the station suggested that Frank was leaving the car with his wife with for the rest of the day. That meant Gene had to keep the house in his sights in order to tail her when and wherever she went in the car.

He watched her send the children off to school, where it seemed they stayed all day. When Margaret left with Nance at lunchtime, it had suggested a mere run to the station, but Gauss was leaving nothing to chance, and his care paid off. Dropping Nance off for his train to London, she continued on alone to Polhurst, coming to rest outside the Professor's cottage.

He drove past, reversed, then parked the car where he could still keep his target in sight, ate his sandwiches, washed them down with the tea, and waited. An hour later he was rewarded with the arrival of the taxi that deposited Jennifer Howard.

It all seemed too odd to be true. He was stuck where he was, however, with no way of knowing what was happening.

Almost half an hour later, Margaret reappeared with Jennifer. From the way the girl took leave of the older people, it appeared she was set to be away for some time, and fair to assume she was being taken back to the Gettys house.

Following at a discreet time and distance, which allowed him to stock up on a scone for tea and a bar of chocolate for afters, he parked in the high street for a change and took a circuitous route back to the house. He could hear the Getty children in the garden long before actually seeing them, and remained in hiding until dark before moving in closer, a plan already forming in his mind.

He saw Frank go out alone and return with Nance. An hour or so later when the pilot came out of the house, he was with the girl, and Gene left to get his car.

Following them, he did a slow run by the cottage to be sure who was where, before driving back to his lodgings in Corsham. It seemed he had made an impact on his landlady because she insisted his having a bowl of hot soup for his supper. It must his native charm, he decided, until she showed him the big story of the day in her part of the world.

'That poor girl sent home thinking her uncle was dead … terrible.'

She simply wanted to talk.

He made appropriate noises, until he caught sight of a few lines of the other story.

Pleading a long day, and thanking her for her thoughtfulness, Gene asked if he could borrow the paper to catch up on the news in bed, mentioning it had been a fine lunch she had done for him that day, and he'd be grateful for similar on the morrow.

In his room he studied the story of Mary's death, which was something of a shock when he remembered everything he had done to get help. He wondered what had gone wrong.

The nameless British officer, of course, had to be Nance, and Gene had to suppose Nance had been hiding under the fire escape, returning to the flat as soon as Gene was gone and before the ambulance arrived. He frowned closely over the Russian agenda, attempting to work through all the implications.

Could Mary have told Nance something and got him to pass it on? If he hadn't been sure whether the Russians had known of the shoe before, such an awful smokescreen told him they certainly knew quite a bit about it now. Yet if Nance still had the shoe, what did the Russians have?

Why, the knowledge of its whereabouts, of course! Using Nance, Mary could have told them … *unless* the unnamed officer was Hamble?

Whatever. If Gene was to succeed in getting the shoe himself it meant the following day wouldn't be too soon for an all out, no-holds-barred effort.

He worked hard on his preparation; checking times, places and distances carefully, and put all the scraps from a now carefully cut up newspaper into his holdall for disposal away from his lodgings before going to bed.

He was up early, and since his plan of action depended on Jenny, she was his target for the day. Again, parking in a different place to avoid any repetition that could cause comment, he was in time to see Nance arrive and Jenny leave the cottage with a beach bag and hamper, which Nance lent a hand with.

Having no intention of trailing them all the way to an obvious destination, Gene, did a quick turnaround to look for a telephone.

A call to the Getty's established Nance was out for the day and unlikely to be back much before tea. He said thanks, and that he would call again later. A step away was the village post office where he made some arrangements.

Back in his lodgings, he retrieved his British naval uniform, returned to Polhurst and presented himself at John Howard's front door.

He was Lieutenant Norman Hamble, he said, a friend of Perry Nance and Jennifer. He was on leave himself, and had read of Jenny's shock the previous night and, being in the area, wondered if he might enquire how she was.

Mrs Peggott immediately invited him in, told her employer, and John Howard welcomed him to stay and have coffee.

He said he was sorry Jennifer was not available And explained that she and Perry had gone to the coast for the day. He was expecting them back around three-thirty that afternoon to drop off Jenny's wet things and the remains of their hamper, before going on to tea with Perry at the Gettys.

Gene acknowledged he had been prepared for Jennifer to be out, and had written a letter. He fished in his pocket, producing an envelope. He asked the man if he would be kind enough to see Jenny got it on her return.

The rest of the time until the afternoon was then his own.

*

It had been a wonderful day at the coast; the drive, the warmth of a sunny day, their swim, the picnic, talk, laughter, and seeing each other in a different light.

When they arrived back Polhurst, it seemed to Jenny that because she'd had a particularly wonderful day, it had been judged by fate to be too good. She must pay, and the dues that lay in wait for her were cold, calculated and chilling.

The envelope she was given on her return contained a sheet of paper with carefully cut-out newsprint words of different sizes stuck onto it:

HoW about a SwAp? THE ShOe and Your absolute sIlenCe in exChaNge for the girls? leave the shoE In an unmArked paPer ParceL aT thE vIllAge POST OFFICE, and meet mE at the scHOOl NO EARLIER THAN 15 mInuteS after the giRls Are duE oUt. NO HARM shall come To them iF you obey tHese INStruCtionS TO THE LETTER. theiR lives are in your hands.

She folded it quickly with trembling fingers before her uncle or Peggsy could see it and looked at her watch; her mind trying to cope with being told that Norman Hamble had left it. It surely had to be a joke, but how tasteless if it were. She had no choice though but to take it seriously.

She would, and could, bear the laughter and inevitable ribbing at her expense if it was a hoax, but she would never be able to live with herself if it wasn't. Her watch said 3:35, Nance was waiting for her in the car.

'Peggsy,' she said, 'I've just been reminded I haven't posted a most important parcel. Have you some brown paper, please? It doesn't need anything big.'

'Will a brown paper bag do, lovie?'

'That'd be fine,' said Jenny, going with the housekeeper to the kitchen, before running upstairs to where she kept the shoe in her wash bag. Wrapping the crystal in the paper with still shaking hands, she ran downstairs and out to Nance in the car.

'Won't be a moment,' she said quickly. 'Just popping down to the post office. Forgot something this morning.'

She left the parcel at the counter where it was received as if expected, and ran back to Nance. 'Can we surprise

Millie and Gillian and meet them from school?' she begged him.

He looked at his watch. 'You'll be lucky,' he said. 'It's quarter to four. They should be nearly home by now.'

'But please, we might still be in time.'

Obviously puzzled by her insistence, he nevertheless humoured her. It could hardly be said the school was out of their way.

To Jenny's relief they found all three children waiting around at the school gate. They came running up when they saw the two getting out of the car.

'What are you lot still doing here?' asked Nance 'Why aren't you at home?'

The girls explained that when they had come out of school, they had seen a man in naval uniform just like Perry's, and had rushed over thinking it was their uncle come to collect them. But it hadn't been.

The man had said his name was Norman Hamble and he wanted to give someone a message. It was a girl, he said, and she was late, and he couldn't wait any longer. He had already been there half an hour and he had to go. He had given them an envelope and asked if they would wait with it until they saw a girl who would come looking for him.

Then William had arrived and stayed with them.

'Uncle Perry, I told Mill and Gilly that Norman Hamble was someone you had been speaking to at the telephone the other night,' said William. 'I told them you could ring the man from home and get him to give you the girl's name and address; then if she was local, we'd deliver the letter to her. But they wouldn't budge. They say this man had said it was terribly important that they waited right here for her; he was so sure she would come, but he had to go.'

To everyone's astonishment, Jenny held out her hand.

'The letter's for me,' she said, her lip trembling. 'I was told the children would be waiting for me here, which is why I said we should meet them.'

Jenny read the note, and then handed it to Nance in silence. Written in normal handwriting, it said:

Good girl! Told you the children would be safe, didn't I? It would have been so easy to have taken them, but I needed the shoe more.

'What's this all about?' asked Nance

She gave him the newspaper note. 'Uncle Jay said Norman Hamble left it. I thought it must be a joke, and how you'd laugh at me if I took it seriously. But I took the shoe to the post office, just in case.'

'If this is a joke,' Perry told her grimly, 'Norman will rue the day he was ever born, and that's a promise! If we hurry, we might just catch him.'

They piled the children in the car but were delayed when reaching the Getty house to find Margaret at the gate looking up and down the road for sign of them.

'Oh, thank God, you've got them. I was beginning to get worried—'

'Listen, Maggs, we're in a hurry,' said Nance. 'Jennifer and I have to get to Polhurst quickly. Tell you all about it when we get back. Kids'll tell you what happened.'

*

At Polhurst, the postmistress confirmed that the parcel had been collected as arranged. When Nance asked for a description of the person who had collected it, she said it was a naval officer – a man shorter than himself, but rather nondescript otherwise – who had been in first thing that morning in civvies to make the arrangement and to say the parcel would be left for him around 3:45. He had called in for it only a moment after it was left.

'At least we know it *wasn't* Ham,' said Nance as they returned to the car.

'No, it was that man Gene Gauss,' said Jenny indignantly, the 'bird watcher/journalist' vividly in her mind. 'I feel such a fool. He knew I would never hang on to the shoe if it put the children in danger. I'm so stupid ... if only I had stopped to think—'

'And if you had, would you have thought of an accomplice the other end to take the children hostage until he had the shoe?' asked Nance.

Jenny had to admit that it wouldn't have occurred to her.

'So you acted the way you did, because you are the person you are and if I hadn't got to know you, I would never have met the girl with whom I'd like to share the rest of my life ... Will you marry me, Jennifer?'

'Oh, Pen, are you sure?' she answered, hardly daring to believe her ears.

'Jennifer, last Saturday evening, I was being sensible and level headed,' he said quietly. 'But things have changed. It's different now ... I know I don't want to lose you. I still don't know where I am career wise, but we shan't starve. If you can put up with that for the moment ...?'

'Pen, I could put up with *anything* if you can,' she assured him. 'I'd love to marry you.'

'Depending on the board tomorrow, and if I can wangle it with the CO, there's a possibility I could take you to meet Mum and Dad this very weekend.'

*

As soon as he could, Nance put a call through to Mansett with a report on what had happened to the shoe, emphasising that it was Jenny's prompt action that had prevented the children's abduction.

'… It's pretty evident that American Intelligence has it now, sir,' he went on. 'And Wren Howard is understandably rather upset about the whole thing. Could I … might I recommend that she be allowed to stay with her family, at least until after the weekend?'

Jenny could not hear the Captain's reply, but Nance grinned and gave her a thumbs-up, silently mouthing the words: 'Back by Tuesday.'

He then rang Hamble. 'Just to let you know I shan't be making the flight back with you tomorrow, Ham,' he said, when connected. 'I've another board to face in the afternoon.' Jenny saw one of his eyebrows lift to what he was being told at the other end of the line, then: 'Thanks, I'll bear it in mind. For the moment, though, I'm still on indefinite leave – all depends on the board's decision, tomorrow. I'll let you know.' Replacing the receiver, he turned to her with a smile. 'Just gets better and better – like it's meant to be. Ham's not returning to Derry 'til Friday when he's been told to pick up a package en route, from Inskip.'

Jenny looked blank. 'Where's that?'

'Naval air base in the Fylde district of Lancashire: HMS *Nightjar*. We get a free lift – if I'm still here after tomorrow, that is. Then it's less than thirty miles from home, as the crow flies.'

CHAPTER TWENTY-THREE

No Way

On Jenny's return home that evening, Nance went in with her to meet her uncle, and after introductions, told the professor that he had asked Jenny to marry him. The pair of them had agreed to say nothing to Perry's own family until he had spoken to her uncle.

John Howard looked taken aback at the news. 'And Jennifer ...?' he said turning to her. 'What did you say?'

'I said, yes, Uncle Jay.'

'And you're absolutely sure about this?'

'Oh yes, absolutely sure, Uncle.'

'Then what can I say but give you both my blessing,' he said beaming over his glasses and holding out his arms to her.

Nance told his sister on his return home 'But I don't want you saying anything about this to Mum or Dad until they've met Jennifer and I've told them,' he said. 'And listen, Maggs. Could you do me a favour tomorrow? Jennifer doesn't know a great deal about clothes, and there's the possibility that I could be taking her to meet Mum and Dad this weekend. Obviously she can't go in uniform –'

'And you want me to suggest she and I go on a shopping spree in Corsham?' his sister finished for him.

'I'd be grateful.'

'Alright. But it depends on Jennifer, you understand. I'm not twisting her arm if she doesn't want to.'

*

But Jenny did want to. Now that she knew she might be meeting his parents, the state of her wardrobe worried her, especially after her experience with Nance in Londonderry, so when Margaret rang the following morning, wondering if she would care to spend the morning doing some girly shopping with her in Corsham, it came as a welcome invitation.

Her uncle agreed. 'You need some nice clothes. I was going to suggest you went on a spree myself. However, if Mrs Getty is kind enough to take you, that's even better. Have the shop charge whatever you buy to my account, and enjoy yourself.'

'Thank you, Uncle,' she cried, hugging him.

*

The outcome of the board interview for Nance that afternoon was inconclusive; with opinion sharply and evenly divided between his reinstatement or discharge on medical grounds. In the end, a decision was taken to reconvene the board on the Wednesday after the weekend to give all those present, time to reconsider their opposing views.

For once, Nance was happy with the way things had gone. It meant his chances were at least fifty/fifty, and he could go home on the morrow, taking Jenny with him.

He rang Hamble who told him to clear it with Stanmore, and he'd be ready for take-off at ten hundred hours the next day. Nance then phoned his parents who were delighted with the unexpected news of his homecoming, and welcomed the prospect of meeting and having his new girlfriend to stay.

He heard his father take the receiver from his mother. 'Your Mother's just told me, Perry. Inskip, eh? I'll pick the pair of you up from the place, myself. It'll be much quicker than the kind of public transport that's available.'

'Okay, Dad, if you say so. I'll look forward to seeing you. But I don't know Ham's eta—'

'Perry, I can find that out for myself, thank you. I'll be there.'

*

Hamble seemed in an amiable mood when he met them on the airfield at Stanmore.

'Over there,' he said, pointing to the only aircraft they could see: the squat grey shape of an Anson sitting on the tarmac in the distance. 'Cold, draughty and noisy, but I love her. How's the shoe?' he asked Nance, as Jenny went ahead.

'A sore subject at the moment,' he was answered in a low voice, with a nod in Jenny's direction. 'The Americans have it. Gene Gauss actually sank as low as to threaten to kidnap my two nieces if she didn't give it to him.'

For a moment, Hamble appeared lost for words, before saying. 'Well, she's well rid, old man. I told you the thing was cursed.'

'Yes, but you still haven't said what made you want to throw it overboard.'

'Okay ...' And Hamble drew a deep breath before going on roughly. 'If you must know, it was my father gave my mother the shoe, then disappeared into thin air leaving her pregnant with me, and unmarried. All my life, I watched her fixate on that damned thing. "It was his promise", she would say. "He promised he would come back, and he *will* come. It's the legend." Well, he never did, and when she died a fortnight ago, I inherited the blasted thing. I knew exactly what I wanted to do with it. I chucked it, first chance I had.'

Nance remembered the ribbing Hamble had received on the quayside the previous Saturday. They knew so little about him, no one had suspected he had been away attending his mother's funeral. 'Ham, I'm sorry,' he said, putting his hand on the other's shoulder. 'We didn't know —'

'And didn't need to,' said Hamble quickly, drawing away and Nance got the impression that Hamble neither needed nor wanted his or anyone else's sympathy. The ferry pilot went on a little bitterly, 'I'd no idea it would cause this much trouble, though – but it's in keeping with its history.'

'Well, if it's any consolation, old man, it's caused me to see Jennifer here in an entirely new light.'

'Then bully for you, Nancy boy,' said Hamble abruptly cheerful again. 'I wish you joy and hope it goes down well with the establishment. You know the rules. It could get her drafted. She looks a nice girl.'

Nance agreed, his sister's influence had achieved a transformation in Jenny's appearance, which was casual but smart. Hamble was right, too, about a possible draft. Nance would need to act quickly if they were to stay together.

*

At Inskip, Lt Cdr. Geoffrey Nance (retired) was as good as his word, he was waiting with his car on the tarmac to take them as soon as they touched down. To Jenny, his short-statured, barrel-like appearance reinforced her impression of boundless energy and a forceful personality who neither hung around nor suffered fools gladly.

When Nance introduced her and she stammered an answer to the simple question of how the journey had gone for them, she sensed a bad start. He turned away without comment, and helped his son and Hamble get their luggage off the Anson and into his car without further ceremony.

'So what's this all about, Perry?' he asked as soon as Jenny was in the back and his son beside him in the passenger seat. 'Even *I* can't get anything out of the Admiralty.'

'It's top secret, Dad. I can't talk about it, but I can tell you that Jennifer was instrumental in saving two of your grandchildren from being as taken as hostages.'

'Good Lord!' His eyes shot up to his rearview mirror to meet Jenny's, whose face suffused with a deep blush.

'And Jennifer can't talk, either,' Nance said quickly.

*

It might have been thirty miles as the crow flies according to Nance, but the journey took a good hour and half before it ended in the driveway of a house that was as large and imposing as any that Jenny had imagined. Where before it had been difficult to imagine how Geoffrey could be Perry's father, it was easy to see how the pilot had inherited his slim build and looks from his mother, Edwina.

She welcomed her son proprietarily, and acknowledged Jenny with a friendly handshake.

'Seems we have a couple of unsung heroes, here, m'dear,' Geoffrey said, and told her their son's news.

Edwina looked surprised, and gave Jenny a second appraisal. 'Thank you, my dear,' she said warmly. 'That sounds very brave of you. Come, I'll show you to your room, where you can have a quick wash and brush-up, then we'll have lunch and you can tell us all about it. You must be hungry after what must be a good ... what four hours getting here? No, leave your holdall where it is,' she added as Jenny made to pick it up. 'Havers will bring it up to your room.'

She continued chatting as she led the way upstairs, with Jenny answering more or less monosyllabically from behind, and feeling aghast at the prospect of having the story of the threatened kidnap dragged out of her.

*

In the event, Nance came to her rescue, and prevented her from having to say anything. He waited, however, until after the late lunch to drop his own bombshell.

'Mum, Dad,' he said. 'I have asked Jennifer to marry me. She has said yes, and her guardian has given us his blessing.'

His mother was the first to break the silence that fell. 'But, Perry, dear, from all that I gather, you've hardly known each other five minutes. Jennifer tells me you met for the first time last Thursday!'

His father said, 'Perry, I'll be frank with you. There *was* something I managed to drag out of the Admiralty. I do now know you have been suspended. I was hoping you would tell me why yourself. But ...' he raised a forbidding hand at his son's quick intake of breath, '... I have respected your being unable to discuss the details. However, even without knowing them, I cannot see that the wisest course of action has to be saddling yourself with new responsibilities before you know where you are in your career.'

Jenny felt her hackles rise at the word 'saddling' but Edwina had risen and was holding out a hand to her.

'Come, Jennifer, we'll retire to the next room for a pot of tea and Geoffrey and Perry can continue their discussion by themselves.'

As they were leaving, Jenny heard Nance saying: 'Dad, the board's re-convening next week. It's fifty-fifty at the moment, but the CO's backing me to the hilt, he knows all the circs. It's practically a moral certainty ...'

*

The rest of the sentence was lost as Edwina quietly shut the door behind them and called to the maid to bring a tray of tea for two into the sitting room; then changed her mind. 'We'll go for a stroll outside in the garden while Blanche is making it,' she said, ushering Jenny ahead of her into the sitting room where she opened a pair of French windows onto a patio with a panoramic view of the gardens that had a broad sweep of a lawn going down to the lakeside. 'I expect you find all this hush-hush business quite exciting,' she went on.

'It has been a bit frightening in places,' Jenny said. 'But I can't talk about it.'

'I realise that, dear. So when did Perry pop the question?'

'It was Wednesday, this week. Just after we had came back from a lovely day by the sea.'

'And have you fixed a date yet?'

'No. Perry said – when we were coming up in the plane – that we could go into Kendal tomorrow and look for an engagement ring.'

Edwina gave a little laugh. 'Oh, my dear, you won't find anything suitable there. I don't know what Perry's thinking about – just like a man. It's all mountain climbing and fell-walking shops. If you want something special, which I imagine you do, you'll need to go somewhere like Woodruff's, and they don't have a branch here.'

Jenny said quickly, 'But it doesn't need to be anything expensive—'

'You mean a brass ring from a curtain rail would do?' Edwina deliberately allowed her tone to be derisive.

Jenny coloured. 'Well, no,' she said hesitantly, then turned it into a defiant, 'but yes, if that was all we could find until we were able to get something better.'

Edwina pursed her lips, raised a cool eyebrow, and changed the subject. 'I gather you and Margaret get on rather well together?'

Jenny's enthusiastic, 'Oh yes. We went shopping together in Corsham yesterday,' won another raised eyebrow from Edwina as Jenny continued blithely: 'We had a great time. She helped me find this,' and she gave a little twirl to show off the neat outfit she was wearing. 'And the children are fun, too …' she paused as if suddenly remembering Edwina's place in their lives, and added uncomfortably: '… Your grandchildren, that is – are.'

Small wonder, thought Edwina. The girl was no more than a child herself, and *quite* unsuitable for the kind of wife her son would need. 'Geoffrey and I thought we would invite a few of Perry's friends around tomorrow evening for his homecoming,' Edwina said. 'We won't get in the way; we'll just leave you young people to get on with it by yourselves. What do you think?'

'Thank you, that sounds really great, Mrs Nance—'

'Jennifer, I have already told you, you may call me Edwina.'

'I'm sorry, Mrs – er – Edwina ...'

*

In the privacy of their bedroom that night, Edwina said. 'Geoffrey, that child cannot be allowed to marry Perry.'

'Couldn't agree with you more, m'dear,' he said, climbing heavily into bed beside her. 'Quite, quite unsuitable.'

'How did you get on with Perry?'

'The boy's as pig-headed as usual and quite adamant he's going to marry the girl. But I'll see he gets seconded somewhere else or even drafted abroad.'

"But Perry's happy where he is. Can't the girl be drafted?'

"She'll know where he is, and could be a nuisance. This way she won't and that'll soon separate them. Perry wants to fly, and it appears his CO is backing him to hilt over re-instatement – which we all want. A word in the right ear for it to be conditional with trial period in a different part of the UK where no one would know what went on where he is, Perry will see sense and put his career first. In the meantime, let the lad enjoy his break …'

CHAPTER TWENTY-FOUR

Conduct prejudicial

Saturday dawned bright and clear. Nance wanted to take Jenny into Kendal, but she hesitated.

'Your mother says we won't find what want there.'

'I suppose she's right, really. We could wait until we get back, and find something in London?'

'Yes – let's do that.'

'So what about today? We could go fishing,'

'I'd like that. I've never been before.'

It proved a happy decision and a happy morning. Nance took them onto the lake in the family's rowing boat; showed her how to thread a rod, bait a hook, and she caught her first fish: a perch.

'Surprise, surprise,' he chuckled. 'That's all there is in this water – apart from eels. They took ninety tons of them out of it last year.'

Her next catch turned out to be an eel, but it felt like a monster fish when her rod bowed in a great arc as she dragged it weaving slowly to and fro up to the surface. It was useless trying to unhook it; it had taken the hook right down into its body.

'All you can do is to cut the line, tie the end to the stern, and hang the thing over the side,' said Nance. 'It'll eventually disgorge the hook and drop off by itself.'

'Ugh, that sounds horrid,' she said, and gladly handed it over for him to deal with it. 'How did you get on with your father yesterday?' she asked shyly, as she waited to have another trace line and hook attached.

'Think I persuaded him … eventually. By the way,' he went on. 'Found out from Ham yesterday, why he threw the shoe in the lough.'

'Oh?' she said, immediately interested, and listened with growing concern to what she then heard. 'Oh, the poor woman,' she said at the end. 'How awful for her.'

'Not too good for Ham, either, by the sound of it. There you are.' He handed her rod back, re-hooked and baited.

'So his father's name must have been Duncan MacTear,' she said.

Nance blinked. 'How do you work that one out?' he asked.

'I thought you knew the legend?'

'Ah,' he said, 'I'd forgotten. Of course,' he went on, 'that American said it belonged to the MacTears of Argyllshire. But where do you get the name Duncan?'

'Don said the legend is that the shoes, or *shoon* as they're known in Scotland, go missing from time to time in search of the man who betrayed Duncan, their first owner, and would do so until "Duncan comes again". So his name *must* have been Duncan, which must have been why he gave it to Norman's mother. A promise that he *would* come back to her. So something awful must have happened to him, and she never knew, learned or got told what it was. After all, you wouldn't give something as precious as that away if you didn't mean to come back for it, would you?'

'Can't fault your reasoning there,' Nance said.

'Wouldn't it be just lovely to tell Norman his father's name, *and* unite him with his family?' she said, her eyes shining.

'Whoa, steady there, Jennifer,' Nance warned. 'I think we'd need to do a lot more research before rushing in like that. Ham's pretty bitter about it.'

'He manages to hide it very well,' she said with surprise. 'He seems so open, cheerful and self-possessed, *and* he sticks up for himself with you lot.'

'What do you mean by that?' he asked.

'I noticed – that time on the quayside last Saturday – Norman was ... well, *different* to you and all your friends. You didn't seem to include him.'

Nance grimaced. 'I never stop learning with you, Jennifer, do I?'

They took the boat back at midday with a good catch of fish, which Edwina gave to the cook to deal with.

'Glad you're back in time, Perry. Your father and I are meeting friends at the local for a drink before lunch. Care to come?'

'Absolutely,' he grinned. 'Give us five minutes to wash and change.'

The pub meeting proved a strange, awkward and disappointing experience for Jenny.

She had to stay with Edwina who joined her female friends and acquaintances in the lounge, which put Jenny out of contact with Nance who was with all the men congregated in another bar. The evening, also, appeared a bit odd.

Jenny thought it was supposed to be a welcoming home party for Nance, but his friends just sat around talking and drinking, not even playing the gramophone.

She decided to show some initiative and liven the evening up with a game. 'Aunt Margaret's dead,' she said to her next door neighbour.

He looked startled. 'Is she? I'm sorry. How did she die?'

'You've got it!' Jenny said excitedly, punching the air and going on: 'She- died blind-in-one-eye-and-her-mouth-all-awry. Now,' she said, keeping her face contorted with the actions, 'you have to pass that on to the next person.'

It had some of them laughing by the time 'Aunt Margaret' had them going with being: 'blind-in-one-eye-her-mouth-all-awry-one-hand-going-like-this-the-other hand-going-like-that-one–foot-going-like this-and-the other foot-going-like-that', but it was evident that it wasn't quite what they were used to. They joined in out of politeness, but one or two eyebrows rose in their host's direction.

The moment the door closed on the last of his guests and they'd all gone, Nance took her to task. 'Jennifer, that was a bit "off" this evening. That sort of thing just isn't *done* —'

'But no one was *doing* any sort of thing,' she said spiritedly. 'There wasn't even any music. I thought it was supposed to be a party for you. Uncle Jay and Peggsy always joined in and enjoyed games whenever there were parties at home.'

'That's as maybe, but it was a bit embarrassing this evening. Sort of thing you can do with Millicent and Gillian, but quite out of context with this evening.' Then he grinned. 'I bet it'll be remembered, though,' he ended with a chuckle. 'I'll never hear the last of it!'

'Hullo, Perry,' said his father coming down the stairs. 'Everyone gone, then? Take it you had a good evening? We heard a lot of to-ing and fro-ing and laughter.'

'Thanks, Dad. It was all right. You could say Jennifer was airing a talent for entertainment.'

*

Sunday meant an early start back to London by train for Jenny as she had to return to duty by Tuesday, and would need to get home and packed, before leaving again straightaway back to London that evening for an overnight train to catch the ferry from Stranraer to Larne at six the following morning. Even then, she faced another long journey by train before she got to RNAS Derry Down by three in the afternoon. Nance, on the other hand, had no need to leave his parents' place until the Wednesday, but went with his father to take Jenny by car to Lancaster for the morning connection to London.

Knowing the difficulties of the journey that Jenny was facing, he put in a call to his sister to help as much as she could with Frank's assistance to get Jenny to and from London in plenty of time.

*

Bea found her busily unpacking her new collection of civvies from her kitbag into her locker to join the little suit already there that Nance had bought.

Bea whistled. 'Hi kiddo, you've got some nice stuff there. I take it you won't be haring over the border in those clothes.'

'Oh, hi Bea! I've not long got back. What's new?'

'*You're* still the latest, kiddo. Caused quite a rumpus here. We were sorry to hear about your namesake, but I'm glad it wasn't your uncle after all. I suppose you've not heard anything more about the shoe?'

Jenny stopped what she was doing and sat on the bed. 'It's a long story, Bea and you'll never believe it. I got the shoe back, got robbed of it a day or so later, but I know who it really belongs to now. *And* I'm getting engaged to Lieutenant Nance, and been to meet his parents who live in a huge house on the side of Lake Windermere.'

Jenny had to laugh at Bea's look of shock and amazement.

'That's quite a mouthful you've just said there, Jen,' she said when she was able to speak. 'Mind if I sit down?'

'Be my guest,' Jenny said, moving up to make room for her.

'Now suppose you go through that little lot again,' Bea said, 'and show me how and where it all fits together.' She looked at the time. 'I'm on dog-watch, so you've got forty minutes to fill in the details. *You* won't be on 'til noon tomorrow,' she added as side comment. 'But I'm on flying tonight.'

'How's Jean?'

'Still off sick. Now come on, spill.'

Jenny told her as much as she could, ending: 'But Bea, don't tell anyone else, yet. It could make it awkward for Perry.'

'Sure. I'll keep schtum. But you said you knew whom the shoe really belongs to. Who's that?'

'I didn't say, because it's a bit awkward when I haven't got the shoe now,' she said, which was as fortunate and legitimate an excuse as any in the light of the advice that Nance had given her for not naming Norman Hamble. 'I could ask Don how to get in touch with the Clan MacTear and tell them the Americans stole it. Perhaps they'd be able to recover it.'

She didn't expect to hear from Nance until if and when he returned to the station, depending on the outcome of the board on Wednesday. When Friday arrived still without contact or news of his whereabouts, she was wondering whether she should somehow try and get hold of his sister, when the duty wren put her head in at the door and called:

'Hi, someone tell Jen, there's a US Navy man at the gate wants to talk to her.'

Jenny blinked. Don Rossini?

It was.

'Look, ma'am,' he said, when she reached him and he handed her a small parcel wrapped in tissue paper. 'I wrapped it up for you. It was too special not to.'

She knew what it was even before he gave it to her.

'The shoe,' she gasped in wonder, separating the snowy white cloud of tissue around the scintillating object. 'It's come back to me,' she breathed. 'Oh, Don, thank you, thank you,' she said, giving him an impulsive hug and a kiss. 'But how did you find it?'

'I didn't, ma'am. It was Gene Gauss. He gave it me to return to you with his sincere apologies for taking it from you. Seems it's one hot potato with your Captain asking our Captain some pretty awkward questions about a piece of very valuable stolen property.'

'Well, we both know exactly where it really belongs,' she said. 'I was going to ask you if you would know whom I should try and contact in Argyllshire.'

'I wouldn't know that, ma'am. It's a long time—'

'But you recognised it when you saw it. Can't you remember *how* you knew?'

But it had been a long time, and the thread too tenuous to hold. 'There are places we could try, though,' he said hopefully. They agreed a time to meet in Londonderry the following week when they were both off duty and the public reference library open.

This time, she decided, she was taking the shoe straight to admin to be put in the safe. When she gave her name to the single wren on duty in order to label the manila envelope that would contain it, the girl looked up.

'That's saved me a job,' she said. 'I was coming to find you, when there was someone else here to man the place. You're to phone the Captain.'

Jenny's eyes widened. 'Heavens …! Which phone do I use?'

'There's that,' said the girl, pointing to the one on her desk, adding sharply, 'Hey!' as Jenny took back the shoe. 'Thought you wanted to put that in the safe?'

'I do. I just need to hang on to it a bit longer,' she said, 'then I'll bring it back.' She was thinking that now that she had it, she might just as well ask if the Captain would like to see it. It was at least something she knew would interest him.

'Wren Howard?' Mansett asked crisply as soon as she was connected.

'Sir.'

'I fully expect the shoe to be returned to you within the next twenty-four hours, m'dear, and I'd like you to let me know when it does. Equally, if it hasn't been returned by this time tomorrow morning, you are to let me know. Understood?'

'I have it already, sir. It's with me now.'

'Good. I'd like to see it if I may?'

'When would you like that, sir?'

'When are you next on duty?'

'Noon, sir.'

'Right, then there's time to bring it round to my office now.'

'Sir.'

*

She had to wait in his outer office a little while until she was told she could go in.

She saluted, and Mansett indicated a chair in front of his desk. 'Sit down,' he said. 'Came as a bit of a surprise, eh?'

'It certainly did, sir,' she said, and unwrapped the shoe to place it in front of him. 'I was going to ask if you would like to see it. And I'd like to return it to its rightful owners: the MacTears of Argyllshire.' She went on as he examined it carefully. 'I don't really know where to start, though. So I thought I'd begin with a look in the public reference library in Londonderry next week.'

'I can do better than that,' he said, looking up. 'I happen to know the Clan Chief of the Macintyre. He should be able to help. Where do you intend keeping this in the interim?'

'In the Wrens' Admin Office safe.'

'Good thinking.'

'Please, sir ...?' she said tentatively.

'What?'

'I'd like to thank you very, very much for getting it returned.'

'It's a pleasure, m'dear. Thank you for letting me see it. It's extremely beautiful.'

Jenny fiddled nervously with her fingers as she plucked up courage for her next question, then asked in a rush: 'Please, sir, do you know what decision the board reached with Lieutenant Nance?'

'I'm glad you asked,' he said unexpectedly. 'Yes, he has been reinstated, and transferred to another squadron.'

'But you don't know where?'

'Do I really need to dot the 'i's and cross the 't's?' he said kindly, as her face fell. 'You know the restraints of service life and the kind of conduct that is prejudicial to good order and discipline. It's unusual to transfer the officer, though, it's usually the rating gets the pier head jump. So you're lucky there. However, I'm sure that if Lieutenant Nance wants you to know his new whereabouts, then you will have to wait to hear from him, himself.'

Of course! thought Jenny. *He'll write.* She just had to be patient and wait for his letter.

*

But Nance never wrote, and the following day brought a letter from her uncle. As soon as she opened it, and read the first few words, she knew, as if she had known in her heart all along since returning from Windermere, that it was all over.

My dearest Jennifer, it breaks my heart to have to write this letter.

This evening I received a call from Lt Cdr Nance. He asked me to inform you that there is no engagement for you to be married to his son. That, as far as he was concerned there was nothing in writing nor any witnessed promise to provide grounds for any legal 'breach of contract'.

I pointed out that I had been asked, and had given you both my blessing, but he insisted there was nothing in writing and certainly no ring.

Jennifer, my dear, I have to ask. Is this the kind of family you really wish to marry into? That of a man controlled by his father? If Perry really loved you, he would make it very plain and not stand for his father's meddling. If, however, it's over then I beg you, my dearest child, to accept it as one of those 'facts of life' that we used to discuss together; the things we each hope for and dream, and plan for are not always the same dreams and hopes of other people that we meet—'

'Jen!'

It was the Duty Wren calling from the doorway. 'Call for you in the office.' Jenny hurried down the hut after her departing figure.

'Did they say who it was?' she asked breathlessly, catching her up.

'It's the Captain again. But I didn't think you'd want *that* shouted to the skies.'

'Thanks.'

*

The Captain had been in touch with his friend the Clan Chief, and had an address for her to write down if she still wanted to make contact.

Jenny was grateful. It was an immediate distraction from her heartbreak and gave her something else to think about.

CHAPTER TWENTY-FIVE

Fools Rush In...

It was a new, more mature Jenny who never read her uncle's letter again; she knew it would only make her cry if she did. She realised she was a dreamer and had been in 'love with love' – a taunt that had been thrown at her more than once in her life. The real thing, she was beginning to suspect, would be far more down to earth and maybe not even recognisable. It was heart-breaking and knife-like to make herself crumple the letter briskly and throw it away, and to turn instead to writing an introductory one to Mr and Mrs Iain MacTear. She gave her age, an outline of her present circumstances, and that she had come into the possession of one of the Shoon of Cladich. She was careful to say no more than that she had found it in woods the other side of the border in the Irish Republic, and had learned its legend from a former native of Argyllshire, now an American. He had recognised it, and she was writing to ask if they were interested in having it returned to their family.

It seemed a necessary question to Jenny. If Norman had thought the shoe was cursed, and her own experience of it hadn't proved a particularly happy one, the family might feel they didn't want it back either.

She also wrote to her uncle begging him not to worry about her; telling him that she had put Perry Nance firmly out of her mind and was concentrating on the shoe.

… Yes, it has been returned to me, she wrote. Captain Mansett had some strong words with the Captain of the USS Chimera, and Gene Gauss gave the shoe to that American Navy man I told you about. Captain Mansett also knows the Clan Chief of the Macintyre, and has given me a name and address to chase. Will let you as soon as possible know how it all goes,.
All my love, Jenny.

She looked at it critically; it seemed bright, cheerful and positive. She hoped it would help to reassure and comfort her uncle that she really was alright and in good spirits.

A few days later brought two letters, one from Margaret in which she said how sorry she was to hear what had happened, and went on:

… They didn't like it when I married Frank instead of the man they wanted me to marry. But to us, Jennifer, you are very dear, and we hope you won't throw us out with the bathwater. None of us chooses our parents – or lack of them in your case. But we have to come to terms with them. You have a wonderful guardian in your uncle and we hope you can find it in your heart to forgive Perry; I know only too well the enormous pressure he would have been under. God forbid we ever inflict the same on ours.
We would be grateful if you could still look on us as your friends. We would be delighted to welcome you whenever you're home and care to call round and see us. The girls would love you to see you, I know.

I understand you made quite an impact on friends and family up there on Windermere! I shall look forward to hearing all about it.

With much love and affection,

Margaret (Maggs) and Frank.

The other letter was from Jessie MacTear, who wrote:

Dear Miss Howard,

It was good of you to write to us, but I have to tell you that my husband, Iain died a wee while back. You write of finding one of our Shoon. I more wish that you had found my grandson with it. We had an only son named Duncan ...

Jenny felt a strange tingle at having her hunch confirmed. The letter went on to tell how he had gone to live in London to study Economics at University College; had found lodgings in Lewisham, and fallen in love with his hosts' daughter, Mary Hamble ...

Jenny paused her reading, again feeling something like an electric shock pass through her. *Norman's mother*!

She read on that Duncan had had a passion for motorbikes, and told his mother how he gave Mary a lift every morning into London where she worked with a firm of solicitors. Then, during their first summer, he had taken her home to meet his parents.

... We're a small farming community here near Loch Awe in Cladich. Old ways die hard; old memories are kept alive and none take kindly to strangers ...

It seemed that his father had refused to accept Mary as his son's proposed wife, saying he would cut his son out of his inheritance if he dared to marry the English girl.

… So I gave Duncan one of the Shoon when he and Mary returned to London. He knew they had come with me as part of my dowry as daughter of the Clan Chief, and were therefore part of his rightful inheritance. He was to take it with my blessing …

But Iain had been furious and ordered Duncan to bring the heirloom back home. Duncan had come – without the shoe – determined to settle the matter between them. There had been a blazing row, and when Duncan left, they never saw him alive again. He was killed in a crash in heavy rain on his way back to Mary. Iain blamed his wife for his son's death.

When, some months later, there had been a letter to addressed to Duncan with a London postmark:

… My husband found me reading it and was very angry. He tore it up and threw it in the fire. I told him he had a grandson. He said he would never acknowledge any grandson of his that had English blood in its veins, and beat me severely for not sending it back unopened. So that poor girl and her babe never knew that Duncan had renounced his father and been killed on his way back to her.

And now, with Iain deceased, all Jessie wanted was to find this grandson. She had written to the last address she had had for Duncan, saying how much she longed to see Mary and her son and make her peace with them before she, Jessie, also passed away. But her letter had remained unanswered.

Jenny knew then exactly what she had to do. She felt it would be pointless attempting to contact Norman Hamble by telephone. She imagined her infamy to be such that she would only have to give her name to be told he was unavailable. She therefore wrote a short note asking if he would take her for a spin on his motorbike that coming Saturday afternoon. Addressing it to Lieutenant N Hamble, c/o the Officers Mess, HMS 'Arctic Tern', RNAS Derry Down, NI, she stamped it first class and asked Bea to post it in Londonderry that day.

'And please ask Abe to tell Don I can't keep the date I made with him for the library, but I'll be in touch later and explain,' she said.

She wrote also to Margaret thanking her for her letter and assuring her that she was not 'throwing them out with the bathwater':

'... I value your friendship, and look forward to the time, when I do find 'Mr Right', that Millicent and Gillian will do me the honour of being my bridesmaids – or Maids of Honour – depending on how old they will be by that time, and William my page-boy or whatever will be suitable for his age by then ...

*

When Saturday came, and Hamble arrived on his bike at the gate, she was ready and waiting, attired for the ride in her new slacks and sweater, and a leather jacket someone had loaned her.

'You look the part,' he said with a grin. 'I've brought along a spare helmet. Where do you want to go?'

'Thanks,' she said, taking it from him. 'Anywhere you like so long as no one recognises us.'

'And then I get to know what all the cloak and dagger stuff's about?' he asked. She nodded, fixing the helmet.

'Fair enough, then,' he said. 'Jump on and we'll go south of 'Derry over the border to Balleybofey. That should be well out of everyone's eyes, ears and hair.'

For Jenny, The ride was long, but exhilarating through the dips and highs of Donegal's still unspoilt and often rugged landscape. No conversation was attempted until they got to Balleybofey, the high street of which struck Jenny as having a great many pink buildings.

Hamble pulled over to stop outside a cafe. 'They do a rare steak and chips here,' he said, taking off gloves and helmet.

'Sounds good to me. But you'll have to eat half my steak, 'cos I can't manage the half-pounders they dish up this side of the border.'

'Sounds like you haven't discovered you can order a quarter steak.'

'Not where I've been in Muff,' she said.

'You can do anything if you know how to,' he said, holding the cafe door for her to precede him.

'I'm learning.'

'What will you drink?'

'Do they do shandy here?' she asked.

'Anything,' he said, beckoning a waiter. After giving their order, he turned back to her. 'Okay, so what's the big secret?'

'Do you mind if we eat first?' she asked, enjoying the easy camaraderie between them that gave her so much confidence. It was that which had given her faith to undertake the challenge of reconciling him with his family ... or what was left of it. She went on: 'And then we'll need to find somewhere quieter and more private to talk than in here.'

'There's the Finn river at the bottom of the road,' he said. It was obvious he was curious, but his body language had become abruptly wary. 'This isn't about finding Nancy boy is, is it?'

'He's the *last* person I want to talk about, thank you, Norman,' she said firmly.

'That's a relief,' he breathed, stretching his shoulders. 'I feel I can enjoy my meal a lot better now.'

And the pair of them did. His keen interest in biking had taken him over a good deal of Ireland, and she learned a lot about his travels, as he did about her interest in books, music and life in Polhurst with her uncle.

'... Which reminds me,' she said. 'Gene Gauss had the nerve to impersonate you, and threaten to kidnap Perry's two nieces to get the shoe off me.'

'Yeah, Nance said something to that effect when I ferried the two of you to Inskip. Did you enjoy your stay on Windermere?'

'You could say it had its moments ... *and* I learnt a lot – like fishing on Lake Windermere. You know what happens when you catch an unwanted eel?'

'No. You tell me.'

'Well, it takes the hook deep, deep down inside it. So you cut the line and hang it over the end of the boat 'til it disgorges itself and drops off – gone.'

'And the lesson?'

'That I know now what it feels like be an undesirable "eel".'

She saw his mouth tighten. 'I'm sorry,' he said stretching out a hand to her, his eyes serious.

Her hand tightened warmly around his as she replied. 'Don't be. I really have *thoroughly* disgorged him. Shall we find that quiet place to talk now?'

*

It was early evening when they found a bench where they could sit and enjoy a view of the river.

'That's Stranorlar, just over the bridge there,' Norman said, pointing 'It's another town completely – nothing to do with this one at all. Just one of those Irish things – odd!' Then, turning back to her: 'Right, I'm all ears – and dead inquisitive.'

'Did you know I've had the shoe returned to me?'

He whistled. 'Now that *is* a surprise!' he said with a grin; inwardly wondering why she was making such a mystery of it. *Perhaps she was afraid how I'd react*, he thought, so added quickly: '*And* congratulations! It appears to have transferred its allegiance from me at last and over to you. I couldn't be more thankful – although I'm sorry, too. It's bound to cause you grief.'

Something about the way she then took a deep breath, letting it out slowly before speaking, alerted him that there was more to come – a lot more it turned out.

'Norman, it isn't the shoe that's brings the grief; it was your paternal grandfather, Iain MacTear. Old ways and habits die hard in out of the way places. Apparently, he grew up with an ingrained hatred of the English, so he hated your mother simply because she was English. Your father died trying to prove his love for her …' And Norman found himself handed a letter …

He had to read it twice before he could begin to cope with the emotions that surged through him. It was the most incredible and confusing experience he had ever known. A whole lifetime turned on its head. All the bitterness of his fatherless childhood; the guilt he had grown up with from his maternal grandparents' refusal to ever speak his father's name – thereby assuring him of some terrible crime. The endless hurt of his mother's betrayal, waiting for the man who never came. The defence he had thrown up against it all; a pro-active cultivation of bonhomie and hail fellow well met that prevented people from getting too close and asking questions. And all because no one had ever told them that his father had died coming back to them.

The letter lanced all the hidden poison that had gathered through the years and broke through in a grief so huge it was uncontainable. His shoulders shook with the emotion it all released and he reached out to the only person who was there who could help him ...

Jenny's arms held him: 'I'm an orphan, too,' she whispered. 'I never knew my father – or my mother.'

He clung to her like a drowning man, burying his head in her neck, and holding her to him and they moulded together.

She wept with him, feeling the paroxysms that shook his body. Although in sympathy, her tears were also those of relief and thankfulness that he had accepted the situation, allowed it to happen and had not pushed her away.

'It's all right, it's all right,' she found herself to keep saying, stroking his head, hugging and soothing him, like a mother comforting a lost boy.

At length he began to calm as the storm of emotion gradually passed to leave him feeling oddly washed and cleansed with relief.

Jenny asked softly: 'Will you be reconciled?'

'I will,' he said, lifting his head to look at her. 'But *you'll* have to come with me to do it.'

'I will,' she returned, then gave a little laugh through her tears, 'There now, Norman! I feel as if I've just become your mother *and* your wife.'

He hugged her fondly 'That's when you say "I do" not "I will",' he said, feeling a rather light-headed humour. 'And, the logical question then is: are *you* prepared to make an honest man of me, Miss Howard?'

'You mean you want me to *marry* you?' she asked in amazement. 'I mean, it's a bit sudden like, isn't it?'

'It's the usual thing to ask when you've fallen in love with someone, isn't it?'

'But I hardly know you —'

'You know more about me than anyone else, I know,' he said with feeling.

'Then, if you *really* want me to, I shan't object,' she said. 'But I'll need to know a bit more about you if I'm to tell Uncle Jay anything. It's only a short time ago that he thought he was giving Perry and me his blessing. So you'll have to be *very* extra convincing.'

Drawing her back to him, he kissed her tenderly. 'Thank you, Jen. I will – I love you! Now let's find a cup of tea somewhere and I'll do my best to fill in the gaps,' he said, helping her to her feet. 'Although there's not a lot to tell …'

*

Walking slowly hand in hand while they looked for a tea shop, Hamble explained how he and his mother had lived with her parents. With their help and encouragement, he had gone to grammar school, thence to a technical college, before passing the entrance exam to the Royal Naval College in Dartmouth, and eventually passing out from RAF Cranwell and RNAS Yeovilton. '... Then I was drafted as a ferry pilot here,' he ended. 'That's all there is. Told you, not a lot to it.'

'I think Uncle Jay will be going on how much you are prepared to defend your choice against your *maternal* grandparents if *they* don't like me …'

'Whether they like you or not, is so beside the point, Jen,' he said gently, stopping suddenly and turning her to face him. '*You* have just given me *everything* I have ever wanted!' he went on, as the growing wonder of his new life dawned on him even more fully. 'You have given me a name, which they wouldn't. You have given me a father – which they couldn't. And you've given me *freedom*. Do you realise that?' he asked earnestly, searching her eyes. 'For the first time in my life I don't feel like a criminal! And I *love* you, Jen. Never mind what anyone else thinks. I want to marry you, so the real question is: is it possible that you could love me enough to marry me? Because I don't think I shall ever be able to let you go.'

*

When they arrived back at camp around nine that evening, Hamble kept the pair of them well back out of sight down the lane. 'I don't mind wagging tongues – I generally give as good as I get – and I want to shout *you* to the whole world: "look here is the girl who's given me the priceless gift of knowing who I am." But it's only those who've had to grow up with a question mark for a father who'd understand what *that* means. I'd just love to hijack the old Anson, and shoot the pair of up to Scotland right now. First chance of a trip, though – and we'll be doing that.'

'But you know *I* can't come with you just like that.'

'No?' he queried with a grin. 'Didn't you know a ship's Captain is licensed for marriages?'

'You mean …?'

'As soon as,' he promised. 'I'll see him first thing Monday morning – duty permitting. Where would you like to go tomorrow?'

'I must write and tell your grandmother I've found you–' she broke off, saying impulsively instead: 'I know, we could write it together. Let's find somewhere we can do that. We can't tell her the whole story, but we can compare notes on what we *can* say.'

'Yep,' he chuckled. 'I lost it – you found it. End of story.' They both laughed.

*

It turned out to be a complete fallacy that a ship's Captain was licensed for marriages.

'… Contrary to popular belief, it just isn't true,' he said, when he had them both before him in his office. 'However, there *is* a great deal I can do to help the pair of you …'

And Captain Mansett was as good as his word. In no time at all, it seemed to Jenny, she and Norman were on compassionate leave to visit his grandparents in London, her uncle in Polgate, including a visit to the Getty family, and arrived in Cladich to meet Jessie MacTear who wept tears of joy when she saw her grandson.

''Tis Duncan! Duncan himself come again!' she cried, drawing him to her with one arm and reaching out the other for Jenny. 'Welcome home the both of you …!'

It was Jessie who made sure their wedding was the event of the year. A truly traditional affair with all their friends and relatives. But as well as a celebration of Norman's homecoming; Jessie had the added joy of seeing her father welcoming his great-grandson into his proper place in the Clan along with his bride.

The Shoon of Cladich had indeed brought Duncan home.

THE END